LIGHTWOOD

LIGHTWOOD

Steph Post

The following is a work of fiction. Names, characters, places, events and incidents are either the product of the author's imagination or used in an entirely fictitious manner. Any resemblance to actual persons, living or dead, is entirely coincidental.

Cover and jacket design by Georgia Morrissey
Interior designed and formatted by E.M. Tippetts Book Designs

ISBN 978-1-943818-30-3
eISBN 978-1-943818-52-5

Library of Congress Control Number: 2016952315

First hardcover edition January 2017 by Polis Books, LLC
1201 Hudson Street, #211S
Hoboken, NJ 07030
www.PolisBooks.com

For Lucy,

In the Stars

CHAPTER 1

THERE WAS NO one to greet Judah Cannon when he got out of Starke, so he just started walking. The sky was gray, the air stagnant, the thick Florida heat already oppressive though it was only early May. Another recently released inmate called out to Judah as he passed through the parking lot.

"Hey, man, you walking or something? You know they got a bus can pick you up, right?"

Judah ignored him.

"You want a ride or something, buddy? My old lady's got the car packed full of brats, but we might be able to squeeze you in the back somewheres."

Judah raised his hand in acknowledgement, but shook his head. He kept his eyes toward the road and breathed a sigh of relief when his boots hit the asphalt shoulder of State Road 16. After three years, he was a free man again and if he wanted to walk all the way to the edge of Bradford County, he was going to do so. He didn't look back and he didn't look both ways for oncoming traffic. He crossed to the right side of the road and headed south.

Judah waited until there was about a mile between himself and the state prison before lighting a cigarette. This had been Judah's first stint at Starke and there was a romantic notion needling him that his first cigarette as a newly released man would somehow be remarkable. He wasn't sure why. During one of the few phone conservations with his older brother Judah had been reassured that getting out of prison was about as sacred as going in. But Judah wasn't so sure. He hadn't acclimated to prison life the way Levi had. He hadn't rolled over, but he hadn't fallen into the rhythm either. He had kept his head down, but his fists raised, and bided his time.

A semi roared past Judah as he was trying to spark his lighter and it took a few flicks for the cigarette to catch. Judah inhaled deeply and tilted his head back to look at the sky. It was the color of burnished steel. The atmosphere was holding its breath, just as Judah was. A hawk circled overhead and a low flying plane hummed in the distance. Judah held the smoke in his lungs and waited.

Nothing. It didn't burn. The world didn't appear clearer, didn't make any more sense. A pickup truck with a bed full of teenagers screamed past him. An empty Coors tallboy landed on the pavement five feet ahead of him accompanied by an insult to his mother. Judah exhaled. The cigarette tasted the same as the last one he had just smoked standing out in the prison yard. As the last one he had smoked before walking into the courthouse for sentencing. The last one he had smoked after his daughter was born. After he had won his first midnight drag race. Lost his virginity. Kissed a girl. Stolen his first pack of cigarettes. It was the same. His brother had been right. Getting out of prison was just another day of getting on with life.

Judah stuffed the lighter back into his pocket and pulled out a crumpled piece of notebook paper. It had been folded and refolded so many times that it was worn soft at the creases. He had taken it with him, telling himself that he didn't care, but knowing that he did. He clenched the cigarette between his lips and opened the letter. It was dated almost a year ago to the day. He squinted at the loopy, girlish handwriting, but didn't let his eyes latch onto the words. He knew them all by heart. *Dear Judah.* And then some bitching about the K-Mart closing up in Colston. Then some more bitching about how her mother had gotten back into bingo at the Elks Lodge, so she couldn't babysit no more. There was no inquiry about Judah's well-being. And then the kicker. She was finished. For real this time. She meant it. There was some guy, a manager at Denny's, who treated her the way she deserved. Gave her everything she wanted. Had even bought Stella some new clothes to wear to preschool. Was thinking about paying for Stella to take gymnastic lessons one day. And, oh yeah, by the way, Stella wasn't his kid after all. She meant that this time, too. So it'd be better for everyone if he just forgot about them. Better for Stella if she didn't have to see him again. She didn't end with an apology or even tell him to have a nice life. The junker he had left her to drive needed a new transmission, so she had decided to sell it to the scrap yard. *Love, Cassie.*

Judah hadn't been surprised about the Denny's man. At least she had waited until he was locked up this time. He wasn't surprised at the part about not being Stella's daddy, though he wasn't exactly sure he believed it either. Every time Cassie had threatened to leave, she had pulled that card and every time she needed money or wanted to get back with him, she had sworn up and down that Stella was his. He supposed it didn't matter anymore. He loved the towheaded little girl, but she probably didn't even remember him. And didn't need to.

He had made himself a deal. If Cassie had been waiting there in that parking lot for him, leaning up against that busted up Oldsmobile, maybe wearing that short blue dress he liked and those white, high heeled sandals, he would have forgiven it all, and he would have gone back to Colston with her. He had played the scene over and over in his head as he lay on his lumpy mattress night after night and stared at the concrete ceiling above him. But if she wasn't waiting for him, well then.

Judah raised the letter until the corner of it brushed the end of his lit cigarette. He inhaled, the cherry flared and the paper began to smoke. He let the letter smolder in his hand and when it began to blacken his fingers he dropped it onto the pavement beside him. Judah kept walking. He didn't look back.

"Nah, man. There ain't no such thing as whales on a moon. Ain't you never been to school or nothing?"

"It ain't like our moon, dumbshit. Were you even watching the show? The guy said Europa. That's near Jupiter. It's one of Jupiter's moons."

"And that's supposed to make a difference? They got whales on Jupiter or something?"

Judah pulled his wallet, Bic lighter and a squashed pack of Marlboro's out of his pockets and tossed them on the bar before sitting down. The legs of the metal barstool scraped against the cement floor as he settled himself and the two men arguing at the other end of the bar looked up.

"Hey, you. What you think?"

Judah rubbed his face and looked around for the bartender.

"About what?"

The man behind the bar, heavy with deep acne scars pitting his pink, waxy skin, nodded to Judah, but didn't make a move to step away from the ratty blonde he was talking to three stools down.

"You think they got whales on Europa?"

Judah wasn't paying attention. Finally, the bartender pulled himself away from the woman and her sob story and asked Judah what he wanted.

"Just a beer. Something on draft."

The bartender grunted and rapped his hairy knuckles on the metal top of the ice bin.

"We got regular beer, light beer, pansy-go-out-and-exercise light beer and pansy-stick-a-slice-of-fruit-on-your-glass beer."

"How about a beer?"

The man grunted again and filled a cloudy pint glass with Budweiser. He set it on the scratched wood in front of Judah and went back to the blonde. Judah eyed the pale amber liquid. Though he'd sampled his share of prison rotgut at Starke, this was going to be his first real beer in three years. After alternately walking and hitching rides for the past six hours, Judah had lost his inclination that things would somehow be memorable now that he was out, but he was still content to be sitting in a dark bar with a cold beer. He took a sip. It tasted as flat and bland as he remembered Budweiser tasting. Judah could live with that.

He gulped half the beer and tried to relax. He put his hands out on the bar in front of him and leaned back in the cracked leather barstool. It had been at least five years since Judah had sat bathed in the gaudy neon light of The Ace in the Hole, but the interior of the bar hadn't changed much. The Hooters girl was from 2011, but the calendar still hung in the same place next to the "Tipping is NOT a city in China" paper sign. The brass tip bucket still hung in the clutches of a stuffed beaver, shot by the owner himself, though one of its glass eyes had fallen out and now lay propped up against the animal's stiff tail. The smeared and oxidized bar mirror, the half-empty cooler of bottled beer, the sour bar mat smell, the pink glow from the oversized Michelob sign: all of it was the same. Even the bartender. The man was new, but the attitude had remained. Judah had been uncertain about coming back to Silas, but now he felt reassured. He took another swallow of beer and lit a cigarette.

"So, hey, you never answered us."

Judah reached for a plastic ashtray and laid his cigarette among the cold ashes. He swiveled around on his stool and looked at the two men to his right. He vaguely recognized both of them. They appeared to be in their early thirties and so Judah reckoned he had probably gone to high school with them. The man sitting closest to Judah had a wandering eye and Judah thought they might have played baseball together. Judah tilted his head slightly.

"Sorry?"

The man with the loose eye pointed up at the dusty television screen hanging in the corner above the bar. Multicolored planets whirled behind closed captioning. Judah glanced at the TV and then back to the men at the bar. He raised his eyebrows and tapped the ash off his cigarette. The second man, with dark hair curling out from underneath his camo netter, smacked the bar in disgust and leaned forward.

"My idiot cousin Pellman here thinks there could be whales on a moon. Mind doing me a favor and telling him that's bullshit so he'll finally shut up? This is why I don't got no cable TV at my house. It's all a bunch of weirdoes flapping their jaws 'bout time travel and how aliens really built the pyramids and shit. What a load."

Pellman shook his head and waved at his cousin like he was a fly. He looked at Judah sideways.

"You ain't look like you from 'round these parts. What do you think?"

Judah glanced back up at the television. A commercial for diabetes testing supplies had come on. An old black woman was holding up her fingers to show that she was tired of pricking them.

"Actually, I am from around here."

Judah ran his hand up and down his glass of beer, cutting through the condensation.

"Oh? I ain't never seen you in here before."

Pellman narrowed his good eye at Judah.

"Well, maybe. I don't know. Anyhow, listen. There's this guy on this science show and he says there's water up on this moon going 'round Jupiter."

Judah interrupted him.

"Why are you watching science shows in a bar?"

Pellman's cousin slapped his palm down again.

"Exactly! That's exactly what I want to know. See, that's why I don't got no cable at my place."

Pellman turned to his cousin.

"Maybe if you did, Erwin, your wife'd finally get some sense and leave your dumb ass."

Pellman and Erwin. Now Judah was certain he had gone to high school with them. Erwin had been an outfielder for the Tigers, and Pellman, on account of his eye and complete inability to catch a moving object, had been the team's Gatorade boy. After getting shoved in the shoulder and spilling his beer, Pellman turned back to Judah.

"Now, just listen. There's this scientist guy and he's saying that there might be water up on this moon going 'round Jupiter."

Judah nodded.

"Uh huh."

"And then the guy said that what with the heat and all, and the way the sun reflected onto the moon or something, and the nutrients in the rocks they thought were up there, and some other stuff, well, he said that if we took a spaceship up to that moon and went under the ice or something like that, and, well, now hold on a minute."

Pellman stopped for a moment, trying to work out the argument in his head. Erwin snickered, but Judah just took a drag of his cigarette and waited.

"Now I remember. He said that if we went under that ice and found some water, there could be life in that water."

Judah finished his beer and looked around for the bartender again.

"Okay."

"So, I was saying that if there's life in that water, there could be more than just little bugs or crawly things. There could be big stuff, too. 'Cause, you know, Jupiter's a big planet. I don't know how big that moon is or nothing, but if Jupiter's big, the moon's gotta be big too, which means big critters in the water."

Erwin shook his head, laughing to himself. The bartender wrenched himself away from the blonde and poured Judah another beer. It slopped onto the bar when he set it down and Judah reached for a handful of cocktail napkins. Pellman was still talking.

"So, the biggest thing I can think of that lives in the water is whales."

Erwin interrupted him.

"What about sharks?"

"Will you just shut up for five minutes? We already been over the shark thing. How many times I gotta tell you? Whales is bigger than sharks."

Erwin snorted.

"Yeah, but not meaner."

Judah pitched the beer-soaked napkins into the trashcan behind the bar. He had to ask.

"How long you guys been sitting here fighting about this?"

Pellman looked up at the television.

"Well, now this show ain't 'bout moons. I think it's 'bout galaxies or something. The show 'bout the moons was the one before that, I think. Or was that the one 'bout asteroids? I can't remember."

Judah looked back and forth between the two cousins. They had obviously been drinking for a while. Pellman drained his bottle of PBR and slammed it down onto the bar.

"You're right. We been talking 'bout this for too long. So, let's settle this once and for all. What you think, newcomer? You think there's whales on Europa?"

Judah stubbed his cigarette out and rested his forearms on the edge of the bar.

"I'm not a newcomer. My name is Judah Cannon and I just got out of prison this morning. To hell with whales on the moon. Let's do some shots."

Sister Tulah Atwell looked up into the sky over Kentsville and could feel its terrible weight crushing down upon her. It was as if someone had thrown a black velvet cloak scattered with diamonds up into the atmosphere, and it was now beginning to fall back down to Earth with the intention of smothering her. She turned away from the heavy darkness and studied the parking lot before her, overflowing with dusty pickup trucks, minivans and cars with a hundred too many miles. Many of the vehicles had parked precariously close to the sodden drainage ditch and were going to have a hard time spinning their wheels to pull out when the service ended sometime in the damp, early morning. Sister Tulah rested her hands on her wide, bulky hips and surveyed the scene without expression. Behind her, through the thin walls of the Last Steps of Deliverance Church of God, the singing was unceasing.

"This little light of mine… I'm gonna let it shine, this little light of mine… I'm gonna let it shine…"

The singers were caught up in the moment, repeating the same verse over and over, accompanied by a piano, tambourine and endless clapping. The revival hadn't officially begun yet and already the congregation was getting worked up. They had been singing hymns for the past forty-five minutes and Sister Tulah was gauging their voices. It was going to be a long night, a long weekend, and she wanted to have some idea of how it was going to go. She snorted and spit in the dirt at her feet.

The back door to the church opened behind her and a thin band of light pierced the darkness. A man's voice, high, wheezy and a little uncertain, edged around the door.

"Is it time?"

Sister Tulah took one last look up at the black, gaping vastness overhead and decided that if she was ready, God must be also. She straightened the lace collar on her long, flower print dress and smoothed back her hair, once dishwater blond, but now a sharp steel gray, making sure that it was pinned in all the right places. She rubbed her pudgy, age-spotted hands together and then licked her lips before pursing them tightly together. Without turning to look over her shoulder at the awaiting sliver of light, Sister Tulah replied.

"It's time."

JUDAH DIDN'T HAVE more than twenty dollars to his name when he left Starke and headed to Silas. As soon as Erwin and Pellman realized who Judah was, however, they announced that they were buying. Judah set down his second shot of whiskey and wiped his mouth with the back of his hand. The two cousins and Judah hadn't been good friends or anything back when Judah still lived in town, but the more he drank, the more Judah enjoyed their company.

"Shit, man. Can't believe you walked here from Starke. Ain't that like twenty miles or something?"

Judah pulled his last cigarette out of the pack and tapped it on the bar.

"Near about. I probably only walked ten of it or so, though. I got picked up by that crazy lady in the minivan I was telling you about."

"Oh yeah, the one who dropped you off at the Wal-Mart in Kentsville and then followed you in and tried to buy you some clothes?"

Judah ran his hand through his hair and coughed. The woman in the beige Taurus, who insisted over and over that Judah call her Trish, had been nice, and Judah didn't want to make fun of her, but her trailing of Judah through the store and then surprising him at the checkout line offering to buy his pair of Wranglers and plaid button-down had been unnerving.

"Yeah."

Pellman shook his head.

"Man, I need to go to jail for a while. Maybe when I get out some broad will want to buy me some new clothes."

Judah lit his cigarette.

"It's not as glamorous as it seems."

It was Friday at The Ace and as the evening wore on, the bar started to fill up. Judah slowly began to recognize more and more of the patrons as they came banging through the front door. The heavy metal door slammed shut after every person who passed through it, and each bang caused Judah to look up into the bar mirror. He kept meeting the eyes of people he knew, but no one seemed to notice him. Judah turned to Pellman.

"Do I look different to you?"

Pellman had been rambling on about the last girl he had spent a bunch of money on, and who then returned the favor by sleeping with Erwin's daddy, and came up short when Judah interrupted him.

"Huh?"

"I look different to you? Than the last time you saw me?"

The liquor was going to Judah's head. Sober, he would never have asked a question like that. But he was starting to feel anxious and out of place. He had returned to Silas because he had no place else to go. He knew that he was lost, though he would never have admitted it, and he knew that Silas was not the swallow that was going to lead him to shore. If anything, the town would drown him, twisting its tentacles around his heart and dragging him down to the depths. Judah would have given anything for the anonymity sheltering him now to last forever. Pellman tilted his head and considered Judah for a moment.

"Hell, man. I don't know. I ain't known it was you when you first sat down. I guess you don't look no different or nothing, though. You just get used to the same people 'round here all the time, you don't think none 'bout people going away and coming back. So, I don't know."

Judah looked straight ahead and stared into the cloudy bar mirror. In the warped reflection he could have been the son of anyone in Silas. But that was only wishful thinking.

"I don't know, either."

Judah stood up and wedged his way through a cloud of stale smoke and sweaty people to the bathroom at the back of the bar. It was locked and he could hear giggling behind the plywood door. He decided not to wait and stepped outside of The Ace into the warm night. A man his age leaning against the side wall of the cinderblock building gave Judah a dirty look as he came around the corner. The chunky teenage girl wearing only half a hot pink shirt and no shoes rolled her eyes and pulled the man's face back to hers. Judah averted his eyes and walked past them to the dirt parking lot behind the bar. He kicked his way through the chunks of rock and tufts of dead grass until he got to the last truck at the end of the crooked row and unzipped his fly. He sort of hoped he was pissing on the front tire of the truck belonging to the man getting with the underage girl, but more likely the white Dodge was owned by a little league coach or an Army vet. Judah was pretty sure he had that kind of luck. It didn't stop him, though. He relieved himself in the faint blue-white glow from the bug zapper hanging from an oak tree branch and scrutinized his reflection in the driver side window.

Judah hadn't spent much time looking at himself in the mirror in prison. Or before that either. He came from a long line of men who carried grease underneath their nails the same way some men sported wristwatches. Men who only changed their undershirts when they were streaked with mud, blood or worse, not just because it was the next day. Men who looked in the mirror only when they shaved and who shaved only when they were trying to get some. Vanity had no part to play.

But for a brief moment, in the watery glare of the fingerprint smeared window, Judah considered himself. He was in need of a haircut, but he still had the same dark, near-black hair that stuck out stiffly in all directions when he wasn't able to tame it with a hat. His brother Levi, not even forty, had developed a strange gray streak through the right side of his hair, but Judah didn't notice anything when he twisted his head. It was hard to tell in the tenebrous light, but he figured his eyes were still the same light gray, surrounded by three layers of crow's feet from spending almost every day outdoors since he was old enough to crawl. Cassie had told him many times that he would be much handsomer with blue eyes, but that was her thing. Whenever they broke up, she always latched onto someone with blond hair, blue eyes and a gold chain. She had always been trying to buy him jewelry, and got upset when he wouldn't wear it. He wondered what type of necklace her new Denny's boyfriend wore.

Judah shook and zipped himself up. As far as he could tell, he looked the same as the last time he had been in Silas, so he wasn't sure why no one recognized him. Maybe Pellman was right; people just got used to seeing the same faces, men wearing the same work shirts, driving the same trucks, drinking the same beers, beating up or hooking up with the same women, in the same bars, where their fathers and their fathers and theirs had done the same. Judah walked back around the building and decided to enjoy the anonymity while he could. As soon as folks found out that another Cannon boy was back in town, he didn't think it would last for long. He swung the heavy steel door open and pushed his way back through the ever-louder crowd to the bar. Pellman was nowhere to be found and his seat had been taken by the last person Judah had expected to see, and the only person in the bar who mattered.

She turned around when she felt his hand grip the back of the barstool and her wide smile stung him in a place he thought he had forgotten about. She ran a hand through her long, tangled hair and rested her elbow on the bar as she regarded him.

"Took you long enough to come back to town."

Judah took a deep breath and realized that he had no idea what to say.

"Hi, Ramey."

CHAPTER 2

THE BARTENDER, WHO in the course of the last four beers and two shots had finally introduced himself and grunted out that his name was Grady, cleared away the remnants of Pellman's eight-hour binger and wiped the square of bar in front of Judah.

"You still drinking the same?"

Judah nodded and eased himself down next to Ramey. He was having trouble looking at her, so he concentrated on the bartender.

"What happened to the guys sitting here?"

Grady capped the plastic ashtray and then slung the ashes from the dirty one into the trash.

"Erwin's wife finally showed up. Good thing you wasn't sitting here when she came in. 'Bout screaming bloody murder to get his ass in the car. Took Pellman, too. They both said to keep your tab open, though, and they'd pay it next time."

Grady set the beer down in front of Judah and crossed his thick arms over his chest.

"Who are you, anyhow? You just get back from the service or something?"

Beside Judah, Ramey lit a cigarette and laughed. Judah kept his eyes on his beer.

"Now, Grady. I always pegged you as a special kinda idiot, but are you really saying you don't know who this is?"

Judah looked up at Grady, knowing what his expression would be. Ramey had a certain way of saying exactly what was on her mind while still making whomever she was insulting fall in love with her. Grady grinned and shrugged his shoulders. So he could smile after all.

"Beats me."

Judah studied the bubbles rising up the side of his pint glass. Out of the corner of his eye he could see Ramey's cigarette pointed at him.

"This here's one of the Cannon boys. I know you ain't been in Silas too long, but you gotta learn these things."

Judah tried to keep a straight face, but he was having trouble. The bartender shook his head.

"There's another one?"

Ramey blew a stream of smoke out of the side of her mouth and nodded before resting her cigarette in the ashtray. Judah felt her hand on his shoulder.

"There is. So why don't you pour us two shots of Jack?"

Immediately, there was a scratched shot glass filled with amber liquid in front of Judah. He had considered sobering up when he had walked outside, but apparently wasn't where this night was headed. He could feel Ramey waiting beside him.

"Pick up your shot, Judah Cannon."

Judah pinched the glass between his fingers. He took a deep breath and raised his shot and his head at the same time. He finally let himself meet her eyes. They were serious. Compassionate, but fierce. How many times had he seen this look in her eyes? He held the shot glass up next to hers and Ramey nodded.

"Now, can we be done with the bullshit?"

"I guess so."

She narrowed her eyes.

"I ain't seen you in near on seven years. I'm gonna need a better answer than that."

Judah touched the edge of his glass to hers and whiskey spilled onto both of their hands. Her eyes wouldn't leave his. Judah knew he was drunk, but he also knew that he meant what he said. And he knew that she did, too.

"Ramey Barrow, walking through that door and seeing you sitting here at this bar is the best thing that's happened to me in seven years. How 'bout that?"

She raised the glass to her lips.

"It'll do."

They slammed the shot glasses down on the bar and Judah knew it was going to be a wild night.

"I WROTE YOU a letter. When you were in jail. I wrote a few, actually."

Ramey slung the last of the beer out of her can and heaved it backwards over the roof of her silver Cutlass. It banged on the already dented hood and rolled down into the long, damp grass. Judah didn't take his eyes off the brilliant stars overhead.

"I know."

"You never wrote back."

The stars appeared to be burning in the darkness.

"No."

Ramey reached into the plastic grocery bag between them to pull out another beer. She tapped the top of the can with a chipped nail, but didn't open it. Judah's face was still turned up toward the sky.

"Want to tell me why?"

Ramey watched Judah's teeth flash in the moonlight as he bit his bottom lip. He lowered his gaze, his eyes moving from studying the stars to contemplating the scars alongside the creases in his callused palms. Judah finally turned to Ramey and exhaled.

"Whew, Ramey. I can't even begin to explain why. Or how. Or what. Or nothing."

She nodded. The headlights from her car illuminated the other side of the field from where they were sitting and in the eerie light her normally reddish-brown hair appeared black.

"You want to talk about it?"

Judah followed the shadow of her jawline with his eyes.

"About prison?"

Ramey nodded again. Every movement she made was so familiar, yet so alien. So comforting, yet so unnerving. Hadn't he sat this far away, inches only, the space of two breaths, from her before? In this same field? Only it had been colder then, a late October night. And the vehicle had been his older brother's truck, borrowed without asking. The light had been dimmer that night, only a sliver of moon fighting its way through the clouds, and he had tried not to focus on the single teardrop that clung to the end of her freckled nose as she confessed in agony that Keith Wilder not asking her to homecoming was a sure sign that no one would ever, ever love her.

"Yeah."

He could have taken off his Mighty Tigers sweatshirt that night and wrapped it around her thin, fifteen-year-old shoulders. He could have told her that she was beautiful, that she was something else, that she broke every guy's heart at Bradford Central High if she so much as smiled at them and that Keith Wilder was a pussy who couldn't get it up unless he was going after a goat. He could have put his arm around her, his best friend in the whole world, and told her all of that and maybe she would have sniffed and thrown her shoulders back and given him that crooked grin he loved so much. Instead, he had handed her the mangled joint he had been trying to roll and asked her to do it for him. She had smaller fingers and could do it faster.

"Not really, no."

She had snatched the twisted paper from his hand and rolled it between her palms, throwing the remnants of dried weed in his face. She had called him an asshole; he had called her a bitch. The next day after school he had brought her a Dr. Pepper swiped from Buddy's as a peace offering and she had punched him in the shoulder. Hard. All of their friends in the dirt lot behind the abandoned liquor store had laughed. Everyone knew that was just how it was with those two.

Ramey tapped the top of the beer can again. Judah looked at her mouth while her eyes searched the darkness before them. Her bottom lip was still full, almost pouting, but there was a sadness lingering at the corners of her mouth that he didn't remember. There was so much he knew, but didn't know, had heard about, but hadn't been there for, had wanted to be a part of, but hadn't dared. Ramey reached over and slid her hand underneath his.

"Well, all right then."

THE SCREEN DOOR of Ramey's apartment rattled open and then she heard the banging. It was delivered from a fist too large and too heavy to belong to Ginny, the girl next door who had no concept that eight o'clock on a Saturday morning was too early to come by trying to borrow cash for a fix. The banging wasn't frantic enough to be Ginny either. Whoever was pounding away at her door was doing it slowly, deliberately, and with no intention of leaving. Ramey pushed her hair out of her eyes, rolled over and slipped out of bed in one fluid motion. She kicked through the scattered clothes strewn across the thin, brown carpet of her bedroom until she located her jeans. The banging continued. She yanked the jeans on while she walked, stumbling as she jerked her heels through each skinny ankle, and closed the bedroom door quietly behind her. She lifted a dirty T-shirt from the orange love seat when she went through the living room and pulled it over her head. Ramey slammed her shin into the sharp corner of the coffee table as she tried to walk and dress at the same time, and she gave up trying to be quiet.

"Damnit!"

Judah was probably already awake anyway.

"Just give me a minute before you break my damn door down!"

Ramey leaned one hand against the wood paneled wall and made sure her shirt was pulled all the way down before opening the door. She raked her hair back into a ponytail, but realized she had nothing to tie it with, so she let it fall from her hands. When she squinted through the peephole she was not surprised to see a distorted figure somewhat resembling the man still in her bed. Ramey rolled her eyes and slid the metal chain over before turning the deadbolt and opening the door.

Levi had drawn his fist back to hit the door once more and almost punched Ramey in the face before catching himself. She crossed her arms in front of her chest and narrowed her eyes. Levi braced himself with one arm against the doorjamb and tried to lean into the apartment. He barely gave Ramey a second glance.

"Is he here?"

He tried to push past her, but Ramey didn't budge.

"Who?"

Levi stepped back now and regarded Ramey, as if remembering finally that it was her front door he had almost knocked a hole through.

"You know who. Judah."

Ramey shrugged.

"Haven't seen him."

"Bullshit."

Levi tried to look over Ramey's shoulder to see into the apartment, but Ramey shifted and blocked his view again.

"I thought Judah was in prison."

Levi glared at Ramey. He was bigger than her, bigger than Judah, though they shared the same squared jaw and squinting eyes. Levi was bulky and boxy, heavy on his feet but quick with his thick, meaty hands. He was quick to anger, too, but only when someone had directly insulted him. He ignored innuendos, but had never walked away from an outright challenge in his life. Levi was a good person to have on the winning team and a dangerous person to have if the odds turned in the wrong direction. Ramey had known Levi her entire life and had long ago stopped being impressed. Levi huffed.

"He got out."

"So you come to my door hunting him? I ain't laid eyes on Judah in years."

Levi frowned at her. He was stubborn, but not stupid. He stepped closer and looked down at her.

"If you see him, you tell him Sherwood needs to talk to him. Now."

Ramey returned the look.

"If I see him."

"Girl, you better be listening to me."

Ramey didn't blink.

"I said, if I see him."

She shut the door and twisted the deadbolt. Ramey ran her hand through her hair, snagging her fingers. She expected Judah to be out of bed when she swung open the bedroom door and wasn't surprised to see him fumbling with the buttons on his shirt. She stood in the doorway and clenched her jaw as she watched him zip up his jeans.

"You heard?"

Judah sat down on the edge of the disheveled bed and laced his boots. He didn't look at her.

"Yeah."

"Don't go."

Judah paused when he set his foot back on the ground and looked up at Ramey. The tone of her voice told him that she knew he was going to leave no matter what she said, but underneath that resignation was a veiled entreaty. He stood up and shook out the cuffs of his jeans.

"I need to get this over with."

She jammed her hands into her back pockets and rocked on the heels of her bare feet.

"You been home less than a day."

Judah felt in his pockets for his wallet and grabbed his cigarettes and lighter off the bureau underneath the window. The intense morning light was glowing through the translucent plastic blinds. Judah brusquely rubbed his face and didn't bother with his hair. He turned back to Ramey and set his hands on her shoulders. She raised her head to look at him and he kissed her quickly.

"And in that less than a day, I went from being completely alone, almost not existing, to finding my best friend waiting for me, to finally having the courage to open my eyes and see who and what my best friend really was."

Ramey continued to look at him with ambivalence. She didn't take her hands out of her pockets and she swayed slightly when he pulled her to him and touched his forehead to hers.

"And is. I meant every word I said last night, Ramey. Every word. And I mean it still. Okay?"

She nodded, but he was already letting her go. He walked past her and she waited for the sound of the front door to open and close. She stood underneath the humming ceiling fan in the steadily warming room and imagined she could still smell him, could still feel his presence beside her. But she knew she was alone.

Sister Tulah looked up from her biscuits slathered in gravy to find her nephew standing in the open doorway, watching her. Waiting for her to acknowledge his presence would probably be a more accurate description, though. No one watched Sister Tulah. They glared at her, cowered before her, spun their eyes in wild fear at the heavy thud of her footsteps approaching, but they did not watch her. She was the watcher, and Bradford County and its inhabitants stood by silently and waited for her verdict.

Sister Tulah picked up a thin paper napkin and shredded it between her greasy fingers. Then she picked up another, folded it and pressed it slowly to her mouth. She performed the action over and over until she was satisfied that Brother Felton's bad knees were beginning to ache and his wide, doughy legs were trembling. Tulah pulled the ragged paper away from her face to reveal thin pink lips, much too small for the breadth of her face. She clutched the sticky napkin in both hands and finally spoke.

"Yes?"

Brother Felton leaned on the doorjamb to help support himself and eyed the spread before his aunt. Two Styrofoam takeout containers from Jimmy Boy's were popped open on the cluttered desk in front of her. One contained the half-eaten carcass of a fried chicken breast, along with a puddle of stewed okra and tomatoes and a deformed mound of crusty macaroni and cheese. The other box corralled what was left of three biscuits drowning in thick, gray gravy. He was about to start slobbering where he stood, but it was easier to look at the food than at his aunt. Even though the overhead fluorescent tubes in the tiny office were dim, bathing the cramped space with the same flat, aseptic light normally found in used car dealerships, Tulah's eyes were terrifying. Colorless, nearly translucent, save for pinpoint pupils as black and dead as a shark's, Sister Tulah's eyes could reach inside a man's chest and twist his soul, all without ever blinking.

Felton watched a fat black fly circle the food and then land on the back of

Sister Tulah's hand. She didn't flinch.

"Well, it's just that it's been five hours now."

Sister Tulah picked up the plastic fork she had dropped into the gravy and poked around the swamp of biscuit mush, the fly still clinging to her hand. She located the piece she wanted and began to carve into it.

"And?"

Brother Felton tugged on the sweaty waistband of his maroon suit pants. He wished he could loosen his belt another notch, but it was already straining at the last hole.

"Well, it's starting to really heat up in there."

"When the devil begins to leach his way out of men's hearts, the air surrounding the men must surely bear the consequences."

Felton licked his dry lips and yanked a stained white handkerchief out of his pocket. He wiped his high forehead and then patted down the fringe of dark brown hair crowning the back of his skull. He blew his nose on the handkerchief and wadded it back up in his pocket.

"Yes, that's surely true."

"Then why are you bothering me?"

Sister Tulah reached for the thirty-two ounce Styrofoam cup of sweet tea on the edge of the desk. She slurped through the straw and fixed her pale eyes on him. He cleared his throat and tried again.

"They were saying in the newspaper this morning that this was going to be the hottest day of the year so far."

"Do you think God reads the newspaper?"

Brother Felton averted his gaze and glanced out of the small, square window that looked out onto the dirt parking lot. The Buicks and Fords glittered in the beating sun and he wondered what the temperature was in the shade.

"I don't know. I know better than to presume what God does."

Silence filled the room like hot air expanding inside a balloon. Sister Tulah picked up the remains of the chicken breast, but then dropped it back down in the container with disgust. She leaned her great bulk back in the squeaking office chair and rested her forearms on the desk in front of her.

"What exactly is it you want, Brother Felton?"

Felton would have taken a step forward, but he needed to keep his hand on the doorframe to hold himself up.

"As I said, the doors have been locked for five hours now. Two of the boys have relieved themselves in the corner and Sister Nessie fainted. She's eight months pregnant, you know. It's probably not good for her to still be in there. I mean, with a baby on the way and all."

Sister Tulah spread her thick fingers over the scattered piles of grease-spotted paperwork.

"Bleach and an afternoon nap. What else?"

Felton swallowed; his tongue was beginning to swell up inside his mouth.

"No one has been filled with the Holy Spirit since ten thirty. Everyone seems to be in the same state since you left. Except now I can't even get them to sing. I think that maybe the Spirit has moved on for the day."

Brother Felton was beginning to feel dizzy, so he spoke faster.

"It has been a blessed day, Sister Tulah. Brother Mark finally repented and atoned for attacking his wife at the Easter picnic and Sister Sipsy has repented and atoned again for watching those late-night cable television shows. The collection has been bountiful today. Perhaps it is time to let everyone have a break."

Tulah eyed her sniveling nephew, but did not speak.

"Or maybe, if you believe there is still more good work to be done, we could bring out the box fans? Perhaps the Spirit will fill the congregation again once they have cooled off some."

Sister Tulah lifted her heavy arm from the desk and flicked the fly from the stringy dregs of okra. In the other container, the gravy was beginning to coagulate. Tulah looked at her food and frowned.

"Has everyone repented?"

Felton stood up straighter and wheezed.

"Not everyone, but most."

"Has Brother Jacob repented for the treacherous lies he dared to utter against this church?"

"Not yet. Though perhaps if he had another week to think on his sins. Another week to come to his senses and revel in the Lord's blessed light and the gift of his forgiveness. He might even be persuaded to submit a larger reparation to the church."

Sister Tulah seemed to consider this for a moment as she closed and fastened the lids on the takeout boxes, but then shook her head.

"No."

"No?"

A line of sweat ran down the side of Felton's face, but he didn't bother taking his handkerchief out again.

"No. Today is the day of his salvation. It must happen today or it will never happen. Brother Jacob must admit his guilt. When he is ready to do so, come get me so that I may guide him in deciding just how much his sin has cost him. He must demonstrate to the church that God is merciful enough to forgive all trespasses as long as they are sincere."

Sister Tulah waved her hand in dismissal.

"Until then, the fans stay in the storage room and the doors remain locked. You know what to do, Brother Felton. So do it."

"Yes, Sister Tulah."

Felton backed out of the room and disappeared down the hallway. Sister Tulah grunted and slid open the metal desk drawer at her side. She pulled out a bag of cheesy puffs and ripped it open. She could wait all day if she needed to.

CHAPTER 3

JUDAH HADN'T EXPECTED the town of Silas to change since the last time he had visited his family, and it hadn't. It hadn't changed since the last time he'd lived there, since high school, since kindergarten, since he'd been born. The graffiti spray-painted on the sides of buildings had become more intricate and there were now five stoplights instead of two cutting across the lazy expanse of Central Street, but like many other small, purposeless rural towns, Silas had ceased evolving back in the late 1960s. Instead of developing, it had curled its tail up inside its shell and let the moss grow and the cracks form. Silas was the type of town that would only be useful when the zombie apocalypse hit and the survivors needed an abandoned Save-A-Lot to loot and empty store fronts to hide in. And a Mr. Omelet, of course.

Judah pushed open the glass front door and was relieved to find the diner mostly empty. By ten there would be standing room only at the front of the restaurant and six to a booth in the back. Right now, though, the freckled teenager behind the hostess stand was bored and didn't bother looking up from her pink, rhinestone-studded cellphone.

"How many?"

Judah ignored her and scanned the narrow restaurant. The bar facing the open kitchen was empty save for an old woman carefully guiding a shaking spoonful of grits to her mouth. A young couple with a listless baby in a highchair sat at one of the square tables running down the length of the room. He couldn't see the occupants of the vinyl booths in the dim light at the back of the diner, but he noticed the trail of smoke rising from one of them. There was no smoking in restaurants in Florida any longer. Judah figured it had to be him.

"I'm meeting someone here. I'll just go on back."

The girl shrugged and set her phone down long enough to hand him a sticky plastic menu and a roll of silverware. Judah slowly walked to the back of the restaurant and slid into the seat across from his father.

"You wanted to see me?"

Sherwood grinned.

"You got here sooner than I thought you would. Don't tell me that Barrow girl turned you out already."

Judah tossed the menu and silverware down and ran his hands through his hair. He eyed the white ceramic mug of coffee on the table.

"Well, I was hoping to get this over with as soon as possible."

Sherwood stubbed his cigarette out in the runny yellow goo from a plate of fried eggs over easy.

"That's not very hospitable."

Judah rested his forearms on the hard edge of the table and leaned forward.

"What do you want, Sherwood?"

"Welcome home, son."

Sherwood laughed and Judah knew this was going to take a while. He leaned out into the aisle and waved at an older waitress meandering her way with a pot of coffee. Satisfied that at least some sort of relief was on its way, Judah turned back around to his father.

Sherwood Cannon was a big man, in every sense of the word. He had a good three inches on Judah and at least an extra hundred pounds. His hands were wide, his forearms thick and his chest broad beneath the sandbag of weight that had wrapped itself around him at the onset of late middle age. His hair was colorless and limp, but he still wore it long, tied back in a thin, stringy tail that hung between the mounds of his shoulders. A matching scraggly mustache hid yellowed and broken teeth, but his eyes were the best distraction from his lack of oral hygiene. They were piercing blue and set oddly deep for a face so large. Red, burst capillaries clustered on Sherwood's bulbous nose and sunburned cheeks, and, though he couldn't see it from the angle he was sitting, Judah knew there was long, thin scar running past Sherwood's left ear, from the edge of his jaw up to his now receding hairline.

The waitress slopped an oily cup of coffee down in front of Judah and didn't wait to see if he wanted to order. Judah was reminded that there were two types of people in Silas: those that wanted members of the Cannon family in their establishments and those that didn't. This waitress obviously fell into the latter camp. Judah hoped another girl would come by who felt differently. He could feel his stomach starting to chew on itself and was hoping for some toast and eggs.

Judah took a sip of the burned coffee and felt a layer of skin rip from his tongue as he swallowed the scalding liquid. He didn't make a face. Judah liked the intense feeling of a small burn; it woke him up and cleared his head. He continued to drink, rolling the coffee around in his mouth each time before slowly swallowing, while he waited for his father to say something else. Sherwood had his eyes on the other side of the diner, fixed to the back end of a waitress built like a Mack truck. Judah knew this game. Sherwood had been the last one to say something, welcoming Judah home, and now he would wait, and make Judah as uncomfortable as possible, until his comment was acknowledged. Another of the tiny power struggles Sherwood engaged in throughout the day, almost as if by compulsion. The stubbornness of Sherwood was staggering. Judah had once sat next to him in a Ford cab for five hours without saying a word as they played out the classic struggle of father and son in a silent rage. Right now, Judah had no intention of spending more than twenty necessary minutes with Sherwood. He had things to do. He wasn't exactly sure what they were, but they were there. He had a life to rebuild.

"So, nice job picking me up from Starke. Real nice homecoming, you know, walking and hitching rides from soccer moms all the way here."

Sherwood slowly dragged his eyes away from the waitress.

"Well, shit happens. I had things going on yesterday."

Judah reached into his pocket and pulled out his pack of cigarettes as he rolled his eyes.

"Why am I not surprised?"

Sherwood grunted and shrugged his shoulders.

"Ain't all about you, boy. Besides, what happened to Cassie?"

Judah held the box between his thumb and forefinger and shook it. Sounded like only one left.

"I told you a while back over the phone, me and her are through."

"She mean it this time?"

"I guess so. I mean it, at any rate."

Their waitress stalked past the table and Sherwood grabbed the hem of her denim skirt. She turned around, but her face remained expressionless. Sherwood gestured at the remains of his own breakfast and then raised his eyebrows in the direction of his son. Judah fumbled for the plastic menu on the table in front of him, but the waitress just nodded and rolled her eyes before continuing down the aisle. Judah hoped that meant she was putting in an order. Maybe bringing out more coffee as well. Though the way Sherwood leered at every female body with an apron and "Hi, My Name Is" button, Judah wondered if he would ever be able to get a meal sitting across from him. It seemed as if every step he took in Silas, every motion he made, every hour that went by, reminded him of why he had left in the first place. Except, maybe, waking up next to Ramey.

Sherwood leaned back against the sticky vinyl booth and spread his hands wide on the table, satisfied.

"Good. Never liked that skirt in the first place. Always walking around with a look on her mug like she smelled trash. 'Course, maybe that's 'cause she was spending all that time with you."

Sherwood smirked, but Judah didn't respond to the joke. He flipped open the top of the cigarette pack. Yep, only one left.

"Still woulda been nice if someone had been there to give me a ride."

Judah could hear the hollowness in his voice even as he said it. He didn't know why he felt the need to bring this up. Sherwood couldn't care less, and, frankly, Judah hadn't been expecting anyone in his family to be there when he got out. He probably would have been furious if they had. He had wanted to walk out of prison a free man, and that meant free from Sherwood as well. But then why had he come back to Silas? Judah didn't know. He didn't know anything. Except that he wanted some eggs. And a warm up on his coffee. And for his lighter to catch a spark.

"Oh, quit your damn bellyaching. It ain't like it's the first time you got outta jail. What, you want us to throw you a party or something? Invite Houdini the Clown so he can make some balloon animals for you?"

Judah ignored that last part and reached across the table for Sherwood's Zippo.

"Jail, no. Prison, after being in for three years, yes."

Sherwood slammed his wide palm down on the table, rattling the silverware on his empty plate.

"At some point, Judah, you gotta get your panties out of a wad and get over it. We all take our turn in the barrel. Levi did time twice before you. But you stood up, you took it like a man, and now you need to move on and get over it like a man. That's what the Cannons do. And so that's what you're gonna do."

Judah grunted and lit his cigarette. He blew a stream of smoke out of the side of his mouth and thought about it. Did he take it like a man? What did that even mean? If it meant keeping his mouth shut in front of the judge when she asked him who else had been involved in the stupid smash and grab, well, then yeah, Judah guessed he took it like man. He was the one who had gotten caught in the police headlights, he was the one who got thrown in the back of the cruiser. So he'd clenched his teeth, stood tall and refused to point the finger at anyone but himself. And he had wished to God that he'd never answered his phone that night and thought that working with his family again would be a good idea.

The play had been simple enough, tantalizingly simple, and difficult to pass up. Especially since Cassie and Stella were living back at his place once again and he knew he needed the cash to keep them there. The pharmacy they planned to rob was in Colston, which made Judah uncomfortable, but it was exactly the reason, Levi had explained over the phone, that Judah had to drive. Not only could he outrun any cop once he got going, he would know the best routes to take, the best way to navigate the back roads if needed and so on. The first part was true, the rest bullshit, but like Sherwood, Levi always felt the need to try to manipulate the situation even when there was no need for it.

A clerk at the My Family Pharmacy on the corner of 5th and Wheeler, who owed Sherwood a loan debt, had come up with the plan. He agreed to make sure that the security cameras were switched off, the alarm system down and the back door unlocked in exchange for being cleared with the Cannon family. All Sherwood and Levi needed to do was stroll right in after closing and clear the shelves of bottles that would fetch three thousand dollars a pop on the street. The whole score could top a hundred thousand easy and the clerk wasn't even taking a cut. Judah didn't have to get out of the car, just drive Sherwood and

Levi there, be on the lookout from the front seat of the Oldsmobile, and then drive away with enough dough to keep Cassie happy for a little while longer.

It had been a sure thing, the type of robbery his family excelled at: using intimidation to coerce dumb people into helping them make an easy score. There seemed to be almost no risk or danger involved. Unfortunately, as also happened often with the Cannon family, luck was not dancing with them that night and the police had rolled up right after Levi and Sherwood had dropped a bag of pills in the backseat of Judah's car and run back into the store for a last look around. Judah had managed to lay on the horn before being dragged out of the driver seat, and so Sherwood and Levi were able to take off through the woods behind the pharmacy without getting caught. That left a tight-lipped Judah with a car load of stolen prescription drugs. His only saving grace was that he hadn't actually entered the store or touched any of the bottles. He was only the getaway driver after all, and so the most the judge had been able to pin on him was grand larceny and obstruction of justice.

A plate of bacon, toast and eggs slapped down in front of Judah, but the waitress stalked off before Judah could ask for more coffee. He started to call after her, but decided it wasn't worth it. He didn't plan on spending any more time at the Mr. Omelet than he had to. He began to shovel runny eggs into his mouth, sopping up the yellow goo with soggy toast, and hoped that Sherwood would hurry up and get to the point.

"Guess you finally come to terms with the fact that the kid ain't yours."

Judah felt a quick stab in his chest, but tried to ward it off by chewing faster. He answered with his mouth full.

"Cassie says she ain't."

Sherwood laughed and blew his nose into a paper napkin.

"Hell, son. We all coulda told you that just from laying eyes on the girl."

Judah reached for the salt without taking his eyes off his food.

"Shut up."

Sherwood crumpled the napkin and tossed it onto the pile of cigarette butts accumulating on the dirty plate in front of him.

"I ain't trying to rile you up. I ain't. But we all knew that woman you wasted so much time on couldn't keep her legs closed to save her life and that whole situation she had you spun up in was just a piece of work. I'm glad you wised up and decided to come home."

Judah gnawed on a piece of limp bacon.

"I'm not sure there was any decision involved. I just didn't have no place else to go."

Judah heard a phone vibrating and Sherwood began patting around in his pockets.

"Well, you're here now and I hope you're ready to be back in the game."

Judah swallowed the last of his breakfast and eyed his father.

"I'm not sure about that either."

But Sherwood held up a finger to silence Judah as he flipped open his phone and answered it. He didn't say hello, didn't say anything, only grunted and nodded to himself. Judah wiped his mouth with the palm of his hand and drained the last of the cold coffee. He shoved the plate to the center of the table and made to slide out of the booth. Sherwood caught his wrist and flipped the cellphone shut before Judah could stand up.

"Sit down, boy."

He bristled and tried to wrench his wrist away, but Sherwood wasn't letting go.

"Now you listen to me, son. You think you're so tough now? You think you're so big and bad 'cause you survived a couple of years in the pen? Bullshit."

Sherwood released Judah and banged his fist down on the table again. Judah raised his chin defiantly.

"I don't think nothing. I just want to go my own way and live my own life."

Sherwood burst out laughing.

"What life? What've you got? You got no money, you got no job, and in case you forgot, you're a felon now. Jobs are scarce enough 'round here as it is and now you got a record. Who the hell is gonna hire you, huh?"

Judah lowered his eyes.

"I can manage."

"And where you gonna live? You gonna keep crashing with Leroy's girl? Maybe sponge off her for a while?"

Judah balled his hands into fists on the edge of the table, but kept his eyes down.

"You leave her outta this."

Sherwood laughed again, enjoying himself.

"And let me tell you, I know women and I don't think that one's looking for a man to support."

Judah looked up and met his father's eyes.

"I said to leave her outta this."

"Even if she did let your sorry ass stay with her, what've you got to offer? No job, no money, no skills, no way to make a future. In short, you got nothing. Without family, you got nothing. But with family, you got everything. You best remember that, son."

The grin on Sherwood's face had been swept away by a dangerous scowl. Judah knew what that look meant and knew he was slowly being backed into a familiar corner. His face was burning, from fury and from shame, but he couldn't think of a rebuttal to his father's assertions. They hit too close to the mark to be argued with. Sherwood reached for a manila envelope on the booth seat beside him and slapped it on the table. Judah eyed it like a snake.

"What's that?"

The booth shook as Sherwood heaved himself up and stood in the aisle next to the table, brushing toast crumbs from the front of his shirt.

"Phone, keys, cash. The car's with Benji."

Sherwood peeled a twenty dollar bill from the money clip in his back pocket and tossed it onto the pile of shredded napkin and crushed cigarettes.

"Keep that phone on you. I'll call you when I need you. And don't go getting no crazy ideas about not answering."

Sherwood gripped Judah's shoulder as he passed by him. Judah remained sitting in the booth alone, staring at the envelope, until the waitress finally came and cleared away the table.

SISTER TULAH COCKED one of her round hips out so that she could lean against the waist-high marquee outside the church. The black plastic letters were warped and peeling, but the message was straight and clear:

Last Steps of Deliverance Church of God

Pastor Tulah Atwell

"Stir the Fire!"

After the final soul saving, Tulah had retreated to the office to carefully re-pin her hair. She had made sure the lapels of her lacy collar were straight and even before walking out the back door and coming around the church to assume her place by the marquee. The blazing sunlight had finally abated, but some light still leaked its way out through the heavy, building cloud cover and the heat had become smothering. She rested her hand on the top of the marquee and nodded to Felton, waiting by the church doors.

Brother Felton, bovine and complacent now that the service was over, yanked the heavy double doors open and took his place at the head of the line. He led the procession slowly, so the followers wouldn't get the idea to bolt to their cars. One man gave the minivan keys to his daughter and pointed across the parking lot, but his wife quickly snatched them away. No matter how hot, how tired, how hungry, how desperate for air conditioning and a bathroom, the day wasn't really over until one had said goodbye and thanked the preacher.

That was how things were done, and everybody knew there were no exceptions at the Last Steps of Deliverance. Brother Felton took his place beside Sister Tulah and clasped his hands in front of him. The line moved slowly.

"Thank you for coming, Brother Henry."

Sister Tulah shook hands.

"Thank you for letting God into your heart today, Sister Regina. And for allowing His mercy to open your eyes to the light and guide you in your contribution. Bless you."

Sister Tulah made a point of touching and addressing every member of her congregation as they filed past her. A few stopped to exchange words with her, to remark on God's glorious gifts or the power of the Holy Spirit, but most merely murmured an exhausted word of gratitude and slipped past her as quickly as they could. Brother Jacob and his wife kept their faces down and their eyes on the cement walkway as they hurried past, but Sister Tulah's hand found Jacob's wrist and held him fast. He had no choice but to stop.

"Brother Jacob."

The man stood before her, his red-rimmed eyes still cast down at his scuffed, steel toed work boots. Tulah did not let go.

"Brother Jacob, look at me."

The man raised his balding head and looked into Sister Tulah's eyes. His hands were trembling.

"Brother Jacob, I wanted to thank you for finally seeing the light of God and letting Jesus into your heart. I look around and I see the sweat, I see the tears drying on the small faces of the little children and I know that it was worth every merciful moment that it took to help you discover the error of your ways and open yourself to the true mission of God and His church."

Jacob parted his cracked lips and began to mumble.

"My heart has always been with God..."

Sister Tulah gripped him tighter.

"Now, Brother Jacob. If you want to start with those false declarations again, we can go back inside."

She raised her voice and a few of the escaping families jerked their heads around.

"We might need to go back inside the house of the Lord right now and revisit what I had previously believed to be your moment of grace. Perhaps I was mistaken. Perhaps I have been deceived. Is this the case, Brother Jacob?"

"No, Sister Tulah."

The receding families gratefully turned back toward the parking lot.

"Very good, Brother Jacob. I will send one of the elders over to Landy Park to collect your donation this afternoon."

Jacob nodded.

"Yes, Sister Tulah."

"Have a blessed day, Brother Jacob. And you, Sister Diane."

They both bowed their heads and quickly walked away. The rest of the followers trickled past and Sister Tulah made sure to lay her hand on every member. When the walkway had cleared and only a few cars remained in the lot, Sister Tulah finally turned to her nephew and pursed her lips.

"You seem out of sorts this afternoon, Felton."

Brother Felton pulled his twisted handkerchief out of his pocket and snapped it back and forth between his hands.

"It's the heat."

Tulah pushed herself away from the marquee and began to walk back to the church. Felton followed at her side.

"You've been saying that all day."

"Did I mention what the paper said about the heat index? Highest so far this year, or something like that."

Tulah was silent, slowly putting one foot in front of the other.

"And, you've got to admit, it was a long one today. Who would have thought it would have taken that long for everyone to find salvation? That Brother Jacob, whew, he really held out until the end. I mean, he must have some real troubles weighing on his mind for him to keep his heart so stubbornly closed like that."

Sister Tulah nodded.

"I wonder if he is the only member of our flock who has such troubles weighing on his mind."

Sister Tulah stopped at the open doors of the church and looked into the stifling darkness of its interior. The smell of dried sweat and urine was overpowering. Felton waited on the steps beneath her while she reached for and pulled the heavy wooden doors closed. When she finally turned back around, her pale pink mouth was drawn in an ugly line. She stayed standing above him.

"I am not so worried about the troubles of the congregation right now as I am worried about the troubles of my own blood."

Felton looked up.

"Pardon?"

"Is there something you would like to share with me, Brother Felton?"

CHAPTER 4

JUDAH PRESSED THE sweating can of Budweiser to his forehead and listened to the rattle of Ramey's refrigerator. Since Judah had deposited a twelve-pack on its bottom shelf, the fridge now contained just slightly more than nothing. He sat at the cramped table wedged into the tiny kitchen and watched the afternoon light slowly change from day to dusk through the square window over the kitchen sink. The window faced west and as Judah sat at the table and nursed his beers, the room became filled with a ghostly orange light that reflected off the dark wood cabinets and peeling linoleum floor. It was a lonely place and even though there was evidence that Ramey lived there—a photograph of her and her sister on the refrigerator, a free calendar from the Humane Society pinned open to the month before, cardboard salt and pepper shakers on the counter—a transitory feel pervaded the place. It didn't feel like a home. And, Judah supposed, it wasn't meant to be one. In a way, Ramey was even more lost than he was.

He had been in prison only three months when he heard the news of the wreck down in Silas. A red Jeep doing sixty in the rain along Blind Pass had flipped, rolled and smashed into a telephone pole, killing the driver instantly. Judah had heard the story from an inmate whose wife had known the passenger in the Jeep and kept harping on the fact that the girl had been pregnant and lost the baby and wasn't that just the worst thing in the world anybody could imagine? The inmate had rolled his eyes when he related the story and Judah had agreed that there were a lot worse things in the world than never being born. He hadn't thought too much of the story until a week later when he received a newspaper clipping in the mail from his Aunt Imogene, Sherwood's sister. It retold the story of the crash in all its dramatic and gory detail, and also the tragic tale of the young, unmarried couple who had been in love and expecting their first child. There was no note to accompany the clipping, but his aunt had circled the last paragraph of the article several times in red pen. It assured the reader that though the woman had lost the child, her own life had been spared. There were two photographs set into the article. One of them was Ramey's senior picture from high school.

Judah stood up and retrieved another can of beer from the refrigerator. It wasn't very cold and he pressed his hand to the side of the fridge to feel the tepid temperature. Maybe there was a reason it was empty. He leaned over the sink and cracked the beer, watching a feral cat stalk its way across the overgrown lot next door. Its bony shoulders hunched up through its matted gray coat with every step and its scabby tail flickered up though the weeds. Judah drained the beer and pitched the can into the sink. He slumped down at the table and picked up the prepaid cellphone Sherwood had given him. He flipped it open and closed a few times and then set it back down next to the Bronco key. Judah picked up the key and smiled to himself as he twisted it back and forth between his fingers.

"Goddamn Benji."

He tossed the key on the table and rubbed his face with the palms of his hands and then raked his fingers back through his hair. He was still as uncertain about where to go from here as he had been when Sherwood left him at the Mr. Omelet.

Judah had walked across town from the diner to Cannon Salvage on the outskirts of Silas, just at the point where the speed limit changed from thirty to fifty-five. Though he and his brothers had grown up outside the town limits, they had still wreaked plenty of havoc on Central Avenue whenever they could hitch a ride. Judah had walked past the drugstore they had shoplifted Icy Pops from every summer and the 7-Eleven that had been the staging ground for many a parking lot fight. The owner of the convenience store had been standing outside the glass front doors, smoking a cigarette as Judah cut between the gas pumps, and scowled at him. It had been more than a decade since Judah had duked it out with anyone in the glow from the orange street light on the corner, but Mr. Winston still remembered him. And most likely still remembered the twelve-person brawl Judah had started his senior year of high school with the sore losers of the homecoming game. The owner had eyeballed Judah and then shaken his head in disgust. The Cannon boys, no matter how old or how much time had passed since they had ground an adversary's face into the broken asphalt, were still bad news. Judah hadn't been able to keep the grin to himself as he lifted his arm in a wave.

When he had approached the salvage yard, the place had appeared to be closed. The double bay doors of the garage were pulled down and the dirt lot in front of the office trailer was empty except for four used cars lined up with prices spray-painted across their windshields. The sign out front announced to any possible buyer that as long as he was an American and could pay cash, any car was his for a steal. Judah eyed the cars, each dripping rust and missing something—an antenna, door handle, front tire, back window—and wondered which one the key in his pocket would unlock. He walked past the line of cars and climbed the rickety steps up to the trailer. The door rattled when he pounded against the thin, painted metal, but there was no answer. He hopped down from the steps and had been about to peer into the garage windows when he heard a familiar voice calling from across the street.

“Hey there, brother! They finally let you outta the can?”

Judah had turned around to see Benji walking straight across the road, not bothering to look out for traffic, carrying a Styrofoam takeout box from Sarden’s Barbeque up the street. Judah had shaded his eyes against the sun and grinned as he waited for him to cross. When he made it to the lot, Benji tossed the takeout box onto the hood of one of the parked cars and enveloped Judah in a hug. They pounded each other’s backs a few times and then Judah took a step back to look at his younger, and favorite, brother.

Benji was the baby of the Cannon family, and even at twenty-five still looked it. Whereas Levi had the bullish looks of Sherwood and Judah was a darker, strained version of Levi, Benji had inherited his soft features all from their mother. His sandy blond hair flopped in his eyes and curled up at the back of his neck. His eyes sparkled a pale blue and showed no trace of Levi’s unpredictable anger or Judah’s brooding and doubt. He was generally happy-go-lucky and was the only Cannon family member who got free drinks in a bar because he was liked, not because he was feared. It was exactly this likeability, accompanied by his inability to keep his mouth shut to anyone, especially whatever girl he was entertaining that week, which led Sherwood and Levi not to trust him. Benji was always willing to help out with whatever odd job Sherwood might need done, but he was usually passed over. The rest of the Cannon family and crew was forever exasperated by Benji’s flippancy and carelessness, but Judah didn’t mind. His younger brother had always been able to make him smile, and in Judah’s world that counted for something.

Benji picked up his box of barbeque and dug the office keys out of his jumper pocket.

“Come on inside. I’m sweating like a whore in church out here. I heard ‘em saying on the radio this morning that it were gonna be the hottest day of the year so far. Record high by this afternoon. I just got me one of them window units going, don't work for shit, but it's better than nothing."

Judah had laughed at Benji's ability to curse and grin at the same time and followed his brother into the cramped office. The flimsy floor creaked beneath their boots and the air conditioner buzzed and dripped from the window, but it was cooler than outside and Judah was glad to take a load off for a moment. Benji stashed his food in a little mini fridge underneath the desk and then leaned back in the rolling chair. He pulled a pack of cigarettes out of a drawer and tossed it to Judah.

"You here 'bout a car?"

Judah lit a cigarette and slid the pack back across the desk.

"Yeah, I guess so. Shit, Benji, I don't even know."

Benji tossed his lighter up in the air and caught it. He tossed it again and rocked backwards in the chair.

"What're you talking about? You staying in Silas? When Levi called me up saying you needed a car, I figured you was planning on hanging 'round for a spell."

Judah blew out a stream of smoke.

"Yeah, I am. I mean, I guess I am. Me and Cassie are through. Don't see no point in going back up to Colston."

"Then what's the problem? You're talking like somebody already rained on your parade and I don't think you even been in town long enough to have one."

Judah had wanted to say something to Benji, something about his trepidation toward being back around his family, but knew that he wouldn't understand. Benji didn't have to worry about what Sherwood was going to ask him to do next, because Sherwood would never ask him in the first place. Judah loved Benji, and wanted to confide in him, but knew it was better to keep his thoughts to himself. He crushed his cigarette out in the plastic ashtray on the corner of the desk and tried to force the feeling of dread away.

"You're right. And I'm sure I'll be around for a while. Don't got no place else to go anyhow."

"You planning on staying shacked up over at Ramey's?"

Judah looked at his brother, wide-eyed.

"How in the hell does everybody know about…"

Benji interrupted him and laughed.

"You're back in Silas, brother. This town ain't big enough to keep no secrets. Everybody knows everything 'bout everybody, usually 'fore it even happens."

"I knew there was a reason I moved away."

"Oh, come on. Don't get sour 'bout it. 'Sides, Ramey's a helluva girl. Surprised it took you guys this long to get together."

Judah ignored Benji's smirk and pulled the key out of his pocket.

"So, what does this get me? I'm hoping for the Datsun with the crack across the windshield."

Judah tossed it into Benji's lap and Benji picked up the key and laughed.

"Man, not one of them cars out front will last you more'n a week. You'd be better off riding a bicycle with one wheel."

Judah smiled.

"Well, that makes more sense now. I was starting to worry that the Cannons were getting into the legit car dealing business when I saw that sign out front. I was afraid I'd walk up in here and see you wearing a suit, playing solitaire on a computer or some shit."

Benji stretched his neck to look out the office window at the sad row of cars.

"That'd be the day. Nah, just trying to make the place look a little more respectable, that's all."

Judah raised his eyebrows.

"You're kidding, right?"

Benji turned back to Judah with a sheepish grin on his face.

"And there might be this one girl I'm going after. She's kinda outta my league, so I'm trying to make an impression."

"Well, I think that heap of cars out front will definitely make an impression."

"You think so?"

Judah kept his face straight.

"Sure. But not the kind you're going for."

Benji laughed and stood up with the key in hand.

"Well, guess I'll just have to resort to my winning personality. Come on, this is for the Bronco I got out back. Help me change the spark plugs and she'll run like a charm."

It had been nice to kick around the salvage yard with his brother for a few hours, drinking beers and getting grease under his nails again. He hadn't wanted to leave once they were finished with the Bronco, but when a redhead pulled up in a midnight blue Trans Am and batted her eyes at Benji, he had felt it was best to be on his way.

Judah glanced at the clock display on the stove. Five thirty. He had no idea what time Ramey was going to be home, or if she even wanted him to be there when she returned. He hoped she did. She had said something last night about a key under the broken terra cotta flower pot by the front door if he needed a place to stay while he figured things out. Well, he guessed that was exactly what he was trying to do, so this was as good as any a place to do so.

Judah had his hand on the refrigerator handle when the inevitable happened. The cellphone on the kitchen table vibrated. He turned around and looked at it. It buzzed and vibrated again. Judah kept his grip on the door handle and watched it vibrate a third time. He grit his teeth and snapped it up on the fourth.

"What?"

Sherwood breathed hard into the phone.

"You gonna take all day to answer the phone?"

“I was busy.”

“Yeah, well, get un-busy.”

Judah heard the sound of a key clicking in the apartment door lock.

“Why, what’s going on?”

He turned and watched Ramey come in the front door carrying a paper grocery bag. She kicked the door closed and smiled in his direction. As soon as their eyes met, however, her face fell.

“I gotta tell you everything? Where are you? You shacked up over at that broad’s house?”

Judah turned away from Ramey as she came into the kitchen and set the grocery bag down on the counter.

“Is that really necessary?”

“Hell, I known Ramey since she was running ‘round our front yard yanking the heads off Barbie dolls. I can call her whatever I want.”

Ramey crossed her arms in front of her chest and leaned back against the counter. Judah raised his eyebrows at her, but she wasn’t buying it. He walked out of the kitchen into the living room.

“Yeah, I’m at her place.”

“Good, you’re not too far, then. We’ll pick you up in about five minutes.”

Judah sat down on the arm of the love seat and poked at a run in the orange, corded upholstery.

“Who’s we? And what are you picking me up for? I thought I said…”

Sherwood snorted in disgust and cut him off. He could picture exactly the way his father’s mouth twisted in response to Judah’s protest.

“You got your head up your ass or something? I ain’t got time to explain it now. Just be outside waiting.”

Sherwood hung up, but it took Judah a moment to do the same. He was turning the phone over and over in his hand when Ramey came into the living room, arms still crossed, and leaned on the doorjamb. He kept his eyes on the phone in his hand, knowing that she was waiting for him to say something, but having nothing to say. Finally, she broke the silence.

"Sherwood?"

Judah nodded and tossed the cellphone onto the coffee table. His mouth was set in a hard line, but he still didn't look up at her.

"I'm guessing he's not calling to invite you to Sunday dinner."

"Nope."

Ramey blew a stray length of hair out of her face and cocked her head.

"You're not even back in town forty-eight hours and he's already asking you to do a job with him, ain't he?"

Judah banged the bottom of the love seat a few times with the heel of his boot and finally raised his eyes up to meet hers. He started to explain himself, to come up with an excuse as he had so many times before with Cassie, with other girls. The familiar, *"Honey, it's not like that,"* or, *"You don't know what you're talking about,"* was on the tip of his tongue, but he could tell from the look in Ramey's eyes that bullshitting would get him nowhere.

"Yep."

"Are you going to?"

Her tone was biting. She wasn't nagging him; she was demanding to know where he stood. She needed him to know more than she needed to know herself, and Judah recognized this. He knew what his heart wanted, but he also knew that Sherwood was right. Judah squeezed his eyes shut and swallowed the suffocating tightness in his throat. Sherwood was always right.

"I am."

THEY RODE TOGETHER in silence. Levi had clicked the radio on in the beat-up Chevy Suburban and twisted the dial until he found his favorite radio station, WDNT, out of Alachua, but Sherwood had switched it off as soon as the bass vibrated the speakers. Levi had protested for a moment, but Sherwood had told him to just shut up and keep driving, he needed some peace and quiet to think. Judah, sitting alone in the backseat of the truck, had said nothing. In a sick but comforting way, it was like old times again: Sherwood and Levi sitting up front, knowing the plan but fighting over trivial issues, and Judah riding in back, staring out at the passing trees in the glow from the headlights, just going along for the ride. This scene had played itself out in the same way at least a dozen times since Judah had first been invited to come along, back when he was still in high school.

That first ride had taken him to the trailer of a meth junkie and cock fight bookie who owed Sherwood some money. Judah had been told to wait in the car, he remembered it was a red Buick with mauve upholstery across the long bench seat, and he had listened. When Sherwood and Levi returned from the singlewide, his father was carrying a folded envelope and his brother was sporting a set of bleeding knuckles. They had laughed when they got in the front seat and Levi had reached over and grabbed Judah's shoulder, shaking him and then slapping him on the back. His hand had left a smear of blood on the edge of Judah's T-shirt collar. Before Sherwood had put the car in gear, he had opened the envelope and peeled two bills from the wad of cash. He had tossed them into Judah's lap and when asked what they were for, Sherwood had grinned and told him that it was just for going along for the ride. Judah had spent the two hundred dollars on a four-barrel Holley carb for the 1964 Chevelle he and Benji were rebuilding in the backyard and had waited, with anticipation and with dread, to be asked to go along again.

Sometimes the jobs were like the first one, collecting a debt or strong-arming someone who didn't see eye to eye with the Cannon family's prerogatives. Sometimes it was outright stealing, sometimes it was about drugs, other times just money, or a scheme that had gone wrong, or a lie, or a betrayal. Sometimes Judah was only the getaway driver, sometimes he was standing up next to his brother, a tire iron, a length of chain or a 12 gauge gripped in his hands as he let Sherwood do the talking and Levi initiate the violence. Judah usually just stood there, trying to look tough, trying to feel nothing, and hoping that he wouldn't be called on to act. So far, he had only fired shots into tires, and once up into the rafters of a tractor shed and once out into the night. Never at a person.

"So, little brother, what'd you think of your stint in the big house?"

Levi, unable to take the silence any longer, dragged Judah away from his wandering thoughts and anchored him back in the present. Judah turned away from the window and looked at his brother through the settling darkness in the truck. Judah could see half of his brother's face reflected in the sickly green glow from the dash.

"Well, it sucked. What'd you think? Nice of you to come visit everyone once in a while."

Judah couldn't hold back his sarcasm, but Levi just shrugged his thick shoulders and kept his eyes on the road.

"Hey, man, that's just the way it goes. Trust me, it's easier when you can just focus on doing the time. When I was in there the first go-round, Susan was pregnant with Carl and she wouldn't stop coming by to show me shit. Ultrasounds and test results and all kinda doctor paperwork that I couldn't read nothing of no how. Every time I'd get to where I was in a groove they'd haul me up and I'd have to sit and talk with her and hear 'bout her morning sickness or her headaches or God knows what else that I don't want to know about."

"Sounds rough."

"Seriously, man, when I went back in that second time I told her that if she started showing up with little league pictures or wanting to talk 'bout her mama or God forbid those damn breeding Chihuahuas, I was gonna leave her ass. I told her flat out, and I meant it. And let me tell you, brother, that second time 'round was a helluva lot easier. Weren't even half bad at times."

Judah cracked the window and searched his pockets for his cigarettes.

"Probably helped that you were only in there for a year that time, too. How's Susan doing anyway?"

He didn't really care, but he guessed it was what he was supposed to ask after not seeing his brother for three years. He pulled a crooked cigarette out of the pack and straightened it between his fingers.

"She's nuts like always. But let me tell you, she ain't got nothing on this piece of tail Carol over in…"

Sherwood banged his fist on the passenger side of the dashboard and cut Levi off before he could finish.

"For the love of God, son, will you just shut your damn flapping trap?"

Levi gripped the steering wheel tighter but closed his mouth and kept his eyes on the road. Sherwood shifted around in his seat so that he could see Judah as well as Levi. Judah concentrated on lighting his cigarette.

"Now if you two are finished doing your hair and nails, catching up on old times, we need to go over the plan again. We'll be there in less than half an hour and I don't want no stupid mistakes on this one."

Judah blew a stream of smoke out of his nose and looked back out the window.

"You never told me the plan in the first place. I don't even know what the deal is."

Judah knew Sherwood was staring hard at him, but he wouldn't return the look. He kept his eyes on the trees, starkly illuminated by the truck's passing headlights.

"The deal, son, is probably the biggest score we've ever pulled in our lives, so I hope you're gonna be ready."

Judah still didn't look at his father.

"I'm ready. Now what is it?"

Sherwood explained the situation. Last Wednesday, a man had come to the salvage yard looking for the Cannons.

"Idiot-looking fella too. Like maybe his pants were on too tight, squeezing his balls or something. Had a girly, wheezy voice. Complete sucker."

At first, Sherwood had told the man to get lost, but he kept on about needing them to do a job for him. Sherwood had been suspicious, but decided to hear the man out. He seemed too pathetic to be lying or setting Sherwood up, so Sherwood had called Levi into the garage to listen to the man's offer.

"Still not exactly sure how a chump like that ended up with that kinda information, but hell, to each their own."

The man had told Sherwood about an outlaw motorcycle club up in the central part of Bradford County, a little ways outside of Kentsville. They called themselves the Scorpions, and Sherwood had vaguely heard something about them. They were a small outfit that had only ever shown up on the radar for dealing a little meth, banging up a few bars and busting a few skulls.

"My friend Alvers, up at the VFW, had a cousin whose son tried to make it with one of the Scorpions' old ladies and they came to his house and bashed his face in with a ball peen hammer. Still, they ain't no Mongols or Hell's Angels, that's for sure."

The man sitting awkwardly on the folding chair in the Cannon's garage had said that he had the details about a big deal the Scorpions were going to pull off. They had gotten together enough dough to buy a shipment of cocaine from a source down in Miami and were going to run it up to a contact in Brunswick, Georgia where they could sell it for near triple what they paid for it. The bikers were looking to make a hefty profit, just for making a trip up and down the length of the state.

"'Bout this point I was gonna kick this sorry guy's ass outta my shop. The last thing I'm looking to do is buy coke from a pack of road rats. I already got that area covered. But then this little peckerwood pulls out the kicker."

The man knew exactly when the Scorpions would be in route from Brunswick back to their clubhouse, and that they would have a hundred and fifty thousand dollars riding in their saddlebags. He wanted Sherwood to rob the bikers and was willing to give them twenty percent of the haul for doing the job. Sherwood and Levi had left the man alone in the garage and gone out into the bright sunshine of the gravel lot to confer. Levi made a couple of phone calls and it turned out that someone had heard about a biker gang doing a coke run down to the Everglades, but that they weren't bringing any product back to sell.

"I went back inside and shook that man's gross, sweaty hand. I think he was 'bout to piss himself the whole time he was sitting there. Probably thought we was gonna pop him or something. What a clown. But I told him we'd do it. Easy money all around, I said."

Judah had been listening while Sherwood gave him the details and though he was still wary of him, and still bitter about the last time he had agreed to work with his family, he could feel the familiar rush building up inside him. It wasn't about the money, it wasn't even about the excitement. It was about being a Cannon. Judah finally nodded and flicked his cigarette out the window.

"All right then. That's the deal, so what's the plan?"

Sherwood pulled out his cellphone and dialed a number.

"The plan is simple. We go pick ourselves up a farm truck."

CHAPTER 5

THE DRIVING RAIN slid down the windshield in heavy waves and obscured Judah's view of the road ahead. The interior of the parked Suburban was stuffy, the air filled with the acrid smell of stale smoke and greasy hamburger takeout bags. Levi had cracked the passenger window to let in some air, but the rain was erratic, blowing sideways, and he had to roll it back up. A thin blanket of condensation smeared the inside of the windshield, but Judah made no move to wipe it away. He sat calmly in the driver seat with his palms resting on the thighs of his jeans and waited.

He had sat like this once before, inside a stuffy truck, breathing stale air and staring into the cloud of vapor pressing against the glass. Only his hands had not been open, resting calmly, they had been clenched into fists, his nails digging into his palms, and it had not been Levi, restlessly scrolling through his cellphone in the passenger seat, but Ramey, with her legs drawn up to her chest, her chin resting on her knees, staring at him with those unblinking hazel eyes. He had been sixteen, with a bloody lip and a bruised fist of pride squeezing his heart. He hated the world, everything in it, and especially his father.

They hadn't spoken much. He had spun out of his family's driveway in a blind rage, adolescent tears burning behind his eyes, with the intention of driving to the ends of the earth and never looking back. He had slowed only a few miles down the highway when Ramey's slight form had emerged on the shoulder through the rain. He never asked her where she was walking to or from, but had stopped the truck long enough for her to get in. He had been afraid that she would ask what had happened. Why his lip was bleeding, where he was going, what he was going to do. But she didn't. She had sat silently in the seat next to him, watching the trees and fallow fields passing by through the window. It had been winter and the rain muted everything around them into smudges of pine green, oak gray and sandy dirt brown. It had been cold and Ramey had pulled her wrists up into the man's flannel she was wearing against the weather.

She had finally suggested that they drive out to the boat landing. When they pulled up at the deserted clearing alongside the Sampson River, Judah had turned off the truck and they had sat together listening to the steady rhythm of the rain on the wide, rusted metal roof. She had reached out and taken his hand and it had made all the difference that day.

Judah and Levi waited for hours. He had his hands crossed on the steering wheel and his forehead resting on the back of his hands when they finally heard the sound. It started out as a dull whine in the distance, but by the time Judah raised his head and began wiping away the film from the windshield it had become a distinct, grinding roar. They leaned forward, peering through the thin veil of trees separating the dirt clearing they were parked in from the main highway. Suddenly, daggers of light broke through the darkness and they watched as the motorcycles, four Harleys, screamed past them in the rain. Levi nodded to Judah and snapped open his phone to make the call. Judah started the engine and slowly crept out onto the highway, keeping the truck's headlights off. Judah waited until the red taillights of the motorcycles disappeared around the curve ahead and then turned to his brother.

"Ready?"

Levi grinned at Judah and pulled the black ski mask down over his face. He snatched the .45 from the floorboard and snapped the slide back. Even in the darkened truck, Judah could see the gleam in Levi's eyes.

"Floor it."

"We need to talk about the world!"

Sister Tulah slammed her worn leather Bible down on the wooden pulpit between a Mason jar half full of strychnine and a squeeze bottle of olive oil. The clear liquid sloshed in the jar as the pulpit shook from the force. Sister Tulah did not notice. She picked the Bible back up and walked to the edge of the slightly raised stage. Her long, navy blue dress came to her ankles, exposing white Reeboks and athletic socks, and the plywood platform creaked as she prowled across it. It was raining outside the Last Steps of Deliverance Church of God, but the real storm was just beginning to rage inside. It was four hours into the second night of the weekend-long revival and the Holy Ghost had already come down once. The congregation was galvanized; a charged current seemed to run along the empty rows of backless wooden benches. Everyone was on their feet. They had been clapping and swaying, singing along to the piano player and drummer in the back corner, until Sister Tulah had let her Bible fly out of her hands. The singing had stopped and the movement had ceased. The piano player, a teenage girl with blond hair down to her waist and a bad case of acne, stood up, but the drummer continued, providing a primitive, rhythmic accompaniment to Sister Tulah's diatribe.

Sister Tulah looked out over the crowd and focused her eyes on the painting of Jesus on the cross hanging over the heavy wooden doors. A hand lettered banner tacked below the painting proclaimed *He Is Always Watching*

You—a reminder and a threat to the congregation when they exited. Another sign, posted between two windows, the thick glass painted over to keep out prying eyes, made sure everyone knew that *This World Is Not Your Home*. Sister Tulah waited until she knew the electricity in the room had finally been routed directly to her before she repeated herself.

"We need to talk about the world."

Sister Tulah lowered her voice as she crept along the edge of the stage, making and holding eye contact with her followers standing in the first row.

"Anybody remember what John said about the world?"

At the mention of the disciple's name, a Hallelujah was thrown up from the back of the room. Sister Tulah tapped the back of her closed Bible.

"John said, '*Love not the world, neither the things that are in the world.*' Remember that? He said, '*If any man love the world, the love of the Father is not in him.*'"

Several unintelligible shouts rose up from the crowd. A middle-aged woman put her palm up into the air and nodded her head. Sister Tulah took a few steps backward and looked down at the Bible in her hands for a moment.

"Did you hear that right?"

She gripped the Bible in one hand and raised it over her head. Her voice was growing louder, filling the room and commanding the attention of everyone in it. No one could keep their eyes from her, not even to look upwards to God.

"He didn't say that you could love the world and receive the love of God at the same time."

Sister Tulah slammed the Bible back down on the pulpit and left it there as she stalked across the stage.

"There's nothing in there about being able to have your cake and eat it, too."

Another chorus echoed back to her, but Sister Tulah dispensed with the dramatic pauses. She charged ahead now, hurling her words toward the eager, desperate listeners.

"So, the way I see it, brothers and sisters, the way I see it tonight is that you've got a choice. And it's not an easy one. You may be standing there, right now, and you're thinking to yourself, no way, Preacher, it's not a hard choice. I'm standing here in the house of the Lord on a Saturday night. I've given myself over to God. I'm safe from those burning flames of Hell. I'm safe from the fiery pit. When the Latter Rain comes, I know I'm going to be standing on Christ's side of the line. Well, let me tell you something, brothers and sisters, and you'd better listen good. You are wrong!"

The congregation erupted with another bout of Hallelujahs as they stamped their feet and clapped their hands. Sister Tulah paused to lick her lips.

"Now, I know you've been sitting in this church these past two days. I know you've been singing and sweating and calling out to God and some of you have been filled with the Holy Ghost and some of you have not."

Sister Tulah raised her hand to her heaving chest and shook her head.

"I don't know how many of you have been out in the world, though. I don't know how many of you are backslidden. But God does!"

Sister Tulah came up to the edge of the stage and jabbed her finger into the air. The congregation was quivering before her and many of them had tears in their eyes already. A rail thin old man standing out in the aisle had two rivulets of tears streaming down his cheeks. He didn't wipe them away.

"I can tell you that! God knows which ones of you have been to the movie theater and let yourself be decayed by the demonic filth they show on those screens."

She lurched across the stage, pointing out into the crowd.

"God knows which of you girls have given yourself over to vanity by wearing lipstick and reading fashion magazines and assuming the role of the harlot. He knows which of you men have let the devil's poison pass your lips to pollute your bodies and endanger your families. He knows when you associate with adulterers and fornicators and those who are the sons and daughters of

Babylon. He knows!"

A low susurration was circulating through the church now, responding to Sister Tulah's every word. Two women in the front row fell to their knees and held their heads in their hands while they rocked back and forth on their heels. Sister Tulah turned her back to the congregation for a moment, gathering her breath, and then whirled around, cracking her arm out like a whip.

"And when the devil comes! When Satan comes knocking for your soul and his demons are fighting amongst themselves over who has the privilege of ripping you apart and dragging you down into that fiery lake, into that never-ending torment filled with searing flames and burning brimstone and misery for all eternity, God is going to know what you've done."

A haunting, high-pitched wail came from the back of church, and several men fell to their knees and threw their hands up toward the rafters.

"And He's going to know if you've listened to false prophets or if your heart is pure. He's going to know if you've given in to sinful cravings of lust and pride. God is going to know and He's going to have to make a call on you."

Sister Tulah walked back behind the pulpit and gripped the edge of it, leaning over her Bible and letting a note of pity creep along the edge of her booming voice.

"God is either going to tell Satan and his legions of demons to go ahead and take your soul and drag you down to the agony of the burning pit for all time, or He's going to keep you for Himself and let you be with Him in His everlasting glory."

She picked up the Bible and held it over her head, her voice growing louder and louder to compete with the roar building up from the church members before her. An old woman had fallen down at the end of the aisle, her frail body twitching against the rough floorboards and her skeletal hands clawing upwards into the air. Her eyes were glazed and her mouth was open and twisting, uttering nonsensical sounds. Her pale green dress had been flung up above her bony kneecaps and another woman quickly covered her shaking legs with a white sheet.

"So what is it going to be, brothers and sisters? What is it going to be, saints?"

Sister Tulah came once more the edge of the platform and stared out at the faces twisting in agony and ecstasy before her. She shook the Bible over her head with one hand and made a fist with the other.

"What are you going to choose? Do you want to live in the world or do you want to live with God?"

A fathomless scream pierced the air, followed by a strangled babble. The stage vibrated as Sister Tulah stamped her foot.

"For as it says in the good book, '*Ye cannot drink the cup of the Lord and the cup of the devil.*' And remember, '*The rod of the wicked shall not rest upon the lot of the righteous; lest the righteous put forth their hands to iniquity.*'"

The rhythm of the drums had intensified and now the church was continually filled with short, raw barking laughter and long, low wails. A teenage boy banged the back of his head on the wooden bench behind him as he went down, but no one noticed. Sister Tulah raised her voice against the raucous din a final time, sweat beading on her forehead and upper lip as she shouted out the remainder of her sermon.

"I know where my hands are going, brothers and sisters! They are going up to God! They are going up to Jesus! They are reaching out for the Holy Spirit! Amen, amen, amen!"

Sister Tulah seized the plastic bottle of olive oil from the pulpit. She squeezed it onto a white square of cloth and then stepped down from the platform, ready to anoint her following.

CHAPTER 6

THE DRIVING RAIN felt like a dusting of needles against his face and his curly orange hair was plastered uncomfortably against his high forehead, but Jack O' Lantern Austin was feeling pretty good. With the Scorpions' colors flying all the way, he had successfully pulled off one of the biggest scores in the motorcycle club's history and it had gone off without a hitch. In the span of a little over forty-eight hours and eleven hundred miles, he had turned fifty thousand dollars into three times that much and was now on his way to restoring the Scorpions' sullied reputation and reestablishing the outlaw club as a force to be reckoned with.

Jack O' Lantern gripped the slick handlebars of his Harley with his wide, scarred hands and lowered his chin down against his collarbone, trying to keep the rain from stinging the raw skin of his neck and dripping down inside his weathered leather vest with the Scorpions' logo and top and bottom rockers sewn onto the back. He had been wearing his cut for almost twenty years now and wasn't concerned about the state of the leather, but rather the red rash developing below his armpits. It had been a fantastic run, but they hadn't stopped for anything except to periodically chow on burgers and snort a bump in truck stop bathrooms, so he was ready to get back to the clubhouse, peel off his stinking, wet clothes and sleep for three days straight. After he hid the money that was bulging inside his Harley's saddlebags, of course.

He looked back over his shoulder into Slim Jim's, Legs' and Tiny's headlights as they rounded the last curve on County Road 225 before the final long straightaway. He couldn't see their faces, but he was sure Slim Jim was riding with his mouth open, despite the rain, because he couldn't breathe through his broken nose, and that Legs' long, ratty ponytail was streaming out behind him like a windsock. Jack O' Lantern's crew was small, but he was proud of them. He twisted his head back around just in time to slam on the brakes and grind his bike to a screeching, sliding halt on the slick asphalt. The other Scorpions pulled their motorcycles up behind him. Jack sat on his bike in the middle of the road and revved the throttle.

A white farm truck was broken down in the middle of the road lengthwise, blocking it completely. The motorcycles' headlights reflected on the pale, rusted body and long, extended bed that appeared to be empty behind the wooden rails. The hood was popped up and a man was standing out in the pouring rain with his head and upper body underneath it. Jack O' Lantern couldn't see the man's face and didn't care to. He sat on his bike in the middle of the road and revved the engine again. The man beneath the hood didn't look up or make any indication that he had heard the approaching motorcycles. Jack revved his engine once more and then started yelling through the rain.

"Hey! Asshole! Move it! What is this, a Jiffy Lube out in the middle of the road? Come on!"

The man didn't straighten up. From his bent back and slow movements, Jack O' Lantern could tell that he was old. The man's tan colored windbreaker and white sneakers gave him away as well. Slim Jim wheeled his bike up next to Jack's and wiped the rain out of his eyes. They watched the old man's silhouette in their headlights. He didn't seem to be moving too quickly.

Slim Jim shielded his eyes and squinted.

"The hell, Jack? What, is this dude, like, ninety years old or something? You think he got a hearing problem?"

Slim Jim stood up off his seat and cupped his hands around his mouth.

"Hey! Old timer! Move your damn truck off the road! What are you, deaf or something?"

The old man still didn't acknowledge them. It looked like he was unscrewing the cap off of something and Jack O' Lantern shook his head.

"He can't be deaf and blind if he's out here driving. He's gotta see our lights."

Jack O' Lantern knocked the kickstand down and lifted his leg over the seat of his bike. Slim Jim watched him.

"What're you doing? Gonna see if he's got engine trouble or something? We gotta get back to the clubhouse, man. You forget how much cash we got riding on these bikes?"

Jack O' Lantern signaled behind him for Legs and Tiny to get off their motorcycles. He glared at Slim Jim and grimaced through the rain. It was starting to come down even harder.

"You want to try and go 'round? I'm not mucking up my bike trying to go through that ditch. That truck can sink in it for all I care. Come on, let's push it. I'll grab the old man and make sure he don't put up too much of a fuss."

Jack O' Lantern was soaked and exhausted, but he was always in the mood to bully someone, even if that someone was an old man stranded out on the road in the middle of the night. He waited until Slim Jim slid off his bike and then they spread out and started toward the truck in a staggered line. He was almost close enough to see the old man's face peer out at him from under the hood when he heard the growl of an engine behind him. Jack whipped around and was immediately blinded by the high beams of an oncoming vehicle.

The truck screamed down the highway, racing full speed straight toward them, and only squealing to a halt at the last second. Before the vehicle could even come to a full standstill in the middle of the road, a barrel-chested man leaped from the passenger side with a .45 in his hand and a black ski mask over his face. Jack O' Lantern immediately reached for the gun he always kept in the waistband of his jeans, underneath his cut, but he stopped short when he heard the old man behind him bark out an order to freeze. Jack O' Lantern closed his eyes and clenched his jaw in anger, but slowly raised his hands above his shoulders. He knew it in an instant: they had been played.

Another man, skinnier and also wearing a ski mask, jumped down from the driver side of the truck with a 12 gauge and the two men stood side by side, silhouetted in the dazzling headlights. Jack O' Lantern glanced over at his crew. None of them had managed to pull a weapon in time and they all stood as he was, hands in the air like a pack of school boys caught with their pants down. Jack waited to see which one of the three armed men was in charge. The driver of the truck, now blocking in their motorcycles, seemed to hang back slightly in the shadows, and the heavier man was clearly the muscle. As Jack O' Lantern figured, it was the man who had set them up in the first place who spoke.

"Get on the shoulder of the road."

Jack O' Lantern turned around slowly and faced the man he had mistaken for a stranded farmer. Now that the man's head was out from underneath the hood of the truck, he could see that he was also wearing a ski mask and had a Magnum .357 pointed at Jack's gut. Jack O' Lantern blinked the water out of his eyes and tried to size up the situation. In the shadows, he could make out the man's hands and saw that he was, in fact, dealing with someone older. He stayed where he was.

"You the deaf one now? I said to get on the shoulder of the road. Now move."

Jack O' Lantern knew that Slim Jim, Legs and Tiny were watching him to see how he was going to respond. He was used to bar fights and parking lot brawls. He'd had a gun shoved in his face at a stoplight a few times, but this was different. This had been planned, down to the timing and the exact location on the road. He realized that the men must have known what the Scorpions were transporting in the saddlebags of their bikes and how much was on the line, but he decided that there was no way he was going to part with a hundred and fifty thousand dollars without bloodshed. Especially when all he was facing was an old man and two idiots who probably hadn't shot anything much bigger than a lame buck from a tree stand. Jack O' Lantern was trying to think of the best way to catch them off guard when the man in front of him jerked his head slightly to the right. A second later, he heard the shot and Tiny went down, screaming and clutching his leg. The man's eyes hadn't left Jack's face.

"Well, I guess that one can stay where he is. You three should probably do what I told you to do in the first place. Or we can shoot out everybody's legs. Or brains. Hate to waste the ammo, bullets being so expensive these days, but it's a sacrifice I think we can make."

Jack O' Lantern nodded slowly and backed toward the muddy shoulder of the road. Slim Jim and Legs lined up next to him, their faces pale, livid with anger at the situation. Slim Jim cut his eyes sideways at him, but Jack kept his eyes locked with the man who still stood in front of the farm truck. He could hear Tiny whimpering on the slick pavement. The man who had shot him came forward and pointed his .45 at Slim Jim. The skinnier man had lowered his shotgun and began snapping open each saddlebag hanging from the sides of the Harleys. Jack O' Lantern had divided the money between the bikes in case one of them had wrecked or gotten pulled over. He was hoping that once the man took the cash from one of the motorcycles he would assume that it was the payload and leave the other bikes. No such luck. He checked each one and collected every last crumpled paper bag filled with hundred dollar bills. When he had completely cleaned them out, the man circled around the truck and jumped into the driver seat. Jack O' Lantern exhaled.

"So you got the money. You gonna kill us or what?"

Slim Jim hissed next to him, but Jack O' Lantern ignored him. He knew that if these men were planning on killing them they probably wouldn't have worn masks. And they most likely would have done it already. The old man tilted his head, questioning the other two masked men.

"Do you think we should?"

Jack O' Lantern returned the man's stare, but a strangling sound came from Tiny and he couldn't help himself.

"No. Mister, no. You don't gotta kill us. You don't gotta do nothing. You can just let us go."

Jack O' Lantern cringed. If he'd had his gun out, he probably would have shot Tiny first and the man from the farm truck second. The man didn't respond to Tiny, though, and climbed up into the passenger side of the truck. He shook his head as he pulled himself in and the man with the .45 got in behind him. The doors slammed shut and the truck backed up and then peeled out the way it had come. Legs rushed over to Tiny, still quivering with his blasted leg pulled up to his chest, and Slim Jim walked dejectedly over to his bike. Jack O' Lantern couldn't move. He let his gaze fall down to the wet, black asphalt at his feet and then finally shut his eyes against the rain. He had just lost the biggest score of his life in less than five minutes.

The sound of the key scratching against the lock and the deadbolt clicking over caused Ramey's eyes to snap open and her temples to pound. She slid her arm out from underneath the sheet and groped beneath the bed, trying to make as little noise and movement as possible. Her fingers connected with the cool, burnished metal and she slowly sat up, raising the Smith and Wesson 9mm in front of her. She had left the kitchen stove light on and by shifting her weight and leaning over to the right she had a clear view all the way through her narrow apartment to the front door. It swung open quietly and she heard a scuffling of boots on the rag doormat and then the man entering her apartment raised his head. Ramey exhaled as the fear fled from her body.

"Jesus Christ."

Judah saw the light glinting off the gun and immediately put his hand out to calm her, as he would a dog barring its teeth.

"Whoa, whoa, Ramey. It's me. It's Judah. It's okay."

Judah gently closed the door behind him and locked the deadbolt. When he turned back around he was relieved to see that Ramey had let the gun sink to her lap. She exhaled again and shook her head, her tousled hair framing her face. She put the gun back in its place beneath the bed and then slid down to the edge of the mattress, her feet dangling to the floor. Judah came into the bedroom and kneeled down in front of her. He rested his palms on her thighs and she ran her hand through his hair.

"You're soaked."

"It's raining. Has been for a while."

Judah raised his hand and cupped Ramey's cheek in his palm. She leaned into him and listened. Now that her heart was no longer racing, she could hear the steady drumming of raindrops against the metal air conditioning unit outside the bedroom window. It was a lulling sound, comforting and safe, and Ramey closed her eyes for a moment and heard only the rain, felt only Judah's rough palm against the side of her face. A strange feeling of serenity crept over her. It was as if for one perfect moment, a frozen instant in time, everything was as it should be.

Judah pushed a lock of Ramey's hair behind her ear and she opened her eyes to meet his. He was staring at her intently.

"I've just done something."

Judah paused and looked past her, over her shoulder into the darkness of the room, and then began again.

"I've just done something that could change things for us."

Ramey narrowed her eyes.

"Us?"

Judah met her eyes again. Ramey wasn't sure exactly what was behind them, but she knew that she was witnessing a side of Judah that only she would ever know about.

"Us."

Ramey bit her bottom lip and nodded once. She knew that she was on the edge of a cliff and that she was terrified. That below her was an ocean with drowning waves, and above her, a pitiless sky. But she knew, too, that if she let herself go, the wind just might carry her and she might even discover that she had wings not of lead, but of light. She nodded again and let herself fall.

"Want to tell me about it?"

Judah shook his head.

"Tomorrow."

"Okay."

Ramey reached out and began to unbutton Judah's wet shirt. He stood up and shrugged out of it while she lay back down in the darkness. She felt the bed sink with his weight and then his arms wrapped around her, enveloping her, his body pressed against hers and his head in her hair. She listened to his breathing slow, and to the rain outside the window, and then she closed her eyes and slept.

Felton held his hands in his lap and looked out into the empty parking lot. The rain was scuttling in brisk waves across the deserted expanse and the few street lights reflected down onto the sheet of water glazing the glistening asphalt. The K-Mart sign on the front of the building was lit, but the M blinked on and off with a staccato fury and Felton stared intently at the letter, focusing all of his attention on this blatant inadequacy affronting the otherwise harmonious night. The discord bothered him, but he couldn't look away.

"*And the Lord said unto him, Go through the midst of the city.*"

The preacher's voice crackled through the static, but Felton's Buick radio only picked up a few AM stations. Tulah would be mad if she found out he was listening to a Baptist radio broadcast, but he couldn't bear the silence. He wasn't listening to the words anyway, just the lull and cadence that was so familiar to him.

"*Through the midst of Jerusalem, and set a mark upon the foreheads of the men that sigh and cry for all the abominations that are done in the midst thereof.*"

Felton kept his eyes on the blinking letter, but reached across the dash and turned the radio volume down. He felt around in the center console for his cellphone. He kept his eyes on the K-Mart sign and redialed the number. No answer. Felton shifted in his seat and looked at the digital clock above the radio. The eerie green numbers glowed 12:43. He pursed his lips and dropped the phone back in the console and then rested his hands in his lap. He was starting to get nervous. Very nervous.

It had all started with the snake. It was an Eastern Indigo snake, and Felton had glimpsed it a few times underneath the azalea bushes that ran alongside the church. Five days ago, he had seen a flickering movement in the tall weeds beneath the bushes and had decided to go after it.

Felton loved reptiles. Turtles were his favorite, especially Red Bellies, but he appreciated snakes and lizards, too. He had collected and taken care of reptiles his entire life, ever since he had come home with a mangy gray kitten when he was seven years old. A family down the road had given it to him and he had brought it home in a brown paper grocery bag. When his aunt found out where he had gotten the wretched creature from she had smacked him across the face and forbidden him to ever again touch the filth handed out by sinners. She had made him promise not to speak to anyone who was not a member of the church and then she filled up the bathtub and made him put the kitten back in the paper bag. Her long, sharp nails had cut into Felton's hands as she covered them with her own and forced him to hold the bag under the water. The tears had streamed down Felton's face, but he hadn't made a sound. His mother had died the month before and he was beginning to figure out what his new life was going to be like.

After the incident with the kitten, Felton had begun collecting reptiles. Tulah abhorred them and so as long as Felton kept them out of the house, the animals were safe. He trapped turtles in the drainage ditch and unearthed snakes beneath rocks and tree roots on the edge of the thirty-acre property Sister Tulah's house shared with the church. The Last Steps of Deliverance Church of God followed many of the signs laid out in the book of Mark, but Tulah refused to allow snake handling in her service. For this, Felton was grateful. He wanted to keep his animals to himself.

When he was a child, he had kept the snakes and lizards in wooden crates inside his lean-to clubhouse made from squares of plywood and a plastic tarp. He didn't have to worry about anyone messing with them because he was the only member of the club. He kept the turtles in a rusted bucket outside of the lean-to and they were his favorite. He named each one after an angel from the Bible. They often died soon after he captured them, and when they did, Felton buried them in a special cemetery he made on the bank of the ditch. Their deaths never affected him as the kitten's had, but he felt a terrible ache of loneliness when he had to stare down into the empty tin pail.

Eventually, when Felton was in his twenties, he began to receive a stipend from Sister Tulah for running errands and cleaning the church and he was able to save up and buy a used camper from another church member. He set it up at the very edge of the property, far away and out of sight of the house he still shared with his aunt. He bought special terrariums and heat lamps and ran them from a generator. Inside the camper, every animal had a cage, and every cage had a specific place on the long shelves he had built into the gutted space. He spoke to the reptiles while he fed them and told them about his day: who had been filled with the Holy Ghost and hit their head on a bench going down and what flavor of pudding he had eaten at Golden Corral. All of the turtles were still named after angels.

So when the black snake had crossed his path and slithered underneath the church, Felton had to go after it. The squat, narrow building was raised up on brick supports and there was a dark, cool crawlspace running all the way beneath the floor of the church. It wasn't the first time Felton had chased a snake through the crawlspace, so he didn't hesitate. He pried away a loose piece of plastic siding and lay down on his belly to pull himself through.

Once he was through the hole, Felton had been able to raise himself up on all fours and crawl through the dirt in the dimly lit space. Streaks of light came through the cracks between the siding and the bricks, but mostly he made his way by feeling and sifting through the loose dirt and chunks of gravel and rock. Finally, his hand brushed up against what he was looking for. There was a snake nest in the far corner, and as his eyes adjusted to the dusky light, he could see that there were at least three black snakes coiled inside the hollow. They slowly slid under and over one another and didn't seem to be disturbed by Felton's presence. He studied the snakes, trying to decide which one he wanted to take, when he heard the floorboards over his head creak and a slight dusting of dirt and grime fell through the cobwebs above his head and into his eyes. Felton froze.

"Huh. You'd better be certain it's a sure thing. I know that we've done business before, Mr. Austin, and it was profitable for both of us, but that's quite a lot of money you're asking for."

Felton had cocked his head and looked up at the rotting wood supports above his head. He couldn't see anything through the boards, but he could hear the weight shifting over his head and he could hear Sister Tulah clearly. He had never been underneath the church when there was someone in it. He thought about the space in the siding he had crawled through and the direction he had gone in and realized that he must be directly underneath Tulah's office in the back of the church. He was pretty sure she would have no way of knowing that she was standing right over him, but he held his breath anyway.

"Of course I can get you fifty thousand. Who do you think I am? I'll have someone meet you in the same place as before. But this is not a long term investment, you understand?"

Even though it was cool underneath the church, the closeness of the air had caused Felton to sweat. He had wiped his forehead on the sleeve of his shirt, but didn't dare turn around and leave. His head began to buzz as he became aware of what he was overhearing. This could be his chance.

"Let me just get it straight. You take my money down to Miami, buy your stuff, take it up to Georgia, sell it for triple what you paid for, and then bring me back seventy-five."

Felton had heard a thud and a squeaking and knew Tulah had just sat down in her office chair. From the sound, he could tell that she was swiveling in the chair as she listened to the other side of the conversation. One of the black snakes had left the nest and slithered over Felton's hand on its way through the dirt. Felton had been too intent on what was happening above him to care about the snake.

"Just let me tell you something, Mr. Austin. So we're clear. This deal of yours had better be, as you say, a sure thing, because I hope you have some idea of what would happen if it isn't."

Felton's mind had been racing even as he kept his body stone still. Though he had never met him, he knew who Mr. Austin was. He knew many things about his aunt and her affairs, but only in bits and pieces. He had seen glimpses of bank statements, legal documents with large numbers and checks with strange signatures. He had once found a cereal box stuffed with rolls of hundred dollar bills and, on another occasion, a manila envelope filled with awkward and naked photographs of a county commissioner and a woman who most certainly wasn't his wife. Mostly, he had overheard snippets of coded conversation before Tulah became aware of his presence and slammed the door in his face. This time was different.

"All right, fine. But if you're coming back from Brunswick on Saturday night, then I want my money delivered Sunday. I'm holding a revival this weekend and it ends Sunday at noon. You will call me then and I'll have someone come and pick it up. Do not contact me otherwise."

Felton had waited, but there had been only silence and then the sound of Sister Tulah heaving herself up out of her chair and leaving the office. A slow grin had crept across Felton's face and he had begun to formulate a plan.

Felton twisted the radio volume knob again. The preacher's breathless voice had been replaced by a choir, their voices sounding as if calling up from the bottom of a well as they clapped and sang the chorus for *Give Me That Old Time Religion*. It was one of Felton's favorites and he tapped his shoe against the worn floor mat of the Buick. He nodded his head along to the music for a few beats, but he couldn't drive the growing anxiety from his mind. He looked down at his pudgy, pale hands and squeezed his eyes shut. He willed the cellphone in the console next to him to ring. There was only the sound of faraway clapping and voices lifted up to God. And the rain. Always the rain.

The doubt and shame began to creep over Felton like a sickness. He knew nothing of the man he had hired to rob Jack Austin and his motorcycle club, aside from the near infamous reputation that was whispered across Bradford County. To Felton, his plan had seemed so simple, so foolproof. So easy. Now he knew why. He had entered a world he knew nothing about, and Sherwood Cannon had seen him coming from a mile away.

The clock on the dash glowed 1:59 and blinked to 2:00 as Felton stared at it. He picked up the cellphone and dialed. Each ring seemed to stretch out longer and longer and Felton felt his eyes burn. He again focused on the winking neon letter in the K-Mart sign to keep the tears from spilling over the edges of his eyelids. He blinked and blinked to keep his weakness at bay. No answer. Felton gently set the cellphone down on the seat beside him and scanned the parking lot through the rain. It was empty. They were not coming. He had utterly and completely failed and he knew that there were going to be consequences. He put the Buick in gear and slowly crept across the glittering asphalt, into the night.

CHAPTER 7

JUDAH SHADED HIS eyes against the afternoon sun and watched the plume of dust trailing behind the silver Cutlass headed his way. Though the low lying field had been nearly flooded the night before by the downpour, the late morning sun was quickly burning away any moisture left clinging to the tall whips of cogon grass and the narrow dirt road skirting the edge of the field was already baking in the heat. Judah's eyes followed the path of the Cutlass as it turned onto the track surrounding the field. It slowed into park a few yards from Judah's Bronco and the purring engine was quickly silenced. The driver side door opened and Ramey stood up from the seat, flashing Judah a grin as she hooked her arms over the window frame.

"Thought I might find you here."

Judah kicked one leg up behind him and leaned on the dusty back bumper of the Bronco. The edge of a smile crept across his lips.

"You're good like that."

Ramey slammed the car door behind her and walked over to lean next to Judah. He nudged her shoulder.

"You always were."

"I brought you a cup of coffee from Buddy's, but I'm pretty sure it's gone cold by now."

Judah glanced at Ramey. She was wearing sunglasses against the glare, but he could still see her eyes through the lenses. He looked back at the abandoned field in front of them.

"Thanks."

They were at the edge of the same field, very nearly at the same spot they had been only two nights ago when Ramey had found him at The Ace. The field seemed smaller in the daylight, and the screaming cicadas buried underneath the unruly grass lent the atmosphere a wild air. Less majestic, but no less familiar. A kestrel swooped down out of the pine trees surrounding three sides of the field and crashed into the grass, sending up a spray of tiny winged creatures. The bird rose in discontent, its claws empty.

"You like working at your brother-in-law's place?"

Judah turned to look at her. He loved the way the sunlight caught some of the red strands in her hair and made them glow. When she tilted her head a certain way, she almost had a halo about her face. He thought about reaching out and touching her hair, but didn't. Ramey shrugged her shoulders.

"Not especially. If I have to hear one more time from some old geezer in a fishing hat about how I shoulda scrubbed the grill before making his daily grilled cheese, I swear, I'm gonna lose my mind."

Ramey straightened up and pulled a pack of cigarettes from the back pocket of her jeans.

"But I started working there to pay back Aubrey and Cade for taking care of me when I got out of the hospital, after, you know..."

Ramey flicked her lighter and lit the cigarette clenched between her lips. Judah had noticed that she tensed in some way every time she mentioned the accident. Her shoulders rose up or her fingers curled or her chin jutted out as she tightened her jaw. They were small movements, but Judah understood what they were holding back.

"And then I guess I just got kinda stuck. Bills to pay and life to live and so on."

She laughed bitterly and exhaled a stream of smoke as she leaned back against the Bronco. She was wearing a black tank top and her bare arm brushed against his. She braced herself against the bumper and he laid his hand over hers. It was warm. He looked down at their entwined hands as he spoke.

"What would you want to do?"

"You mean anything?"

"Sure. Let's say you came home and checked that Powerball ticket on your refrigerator door and found out you'd won."

Ramey took another drag on her cigarette and then passed it over to him with her free hand. He took it from her fingers without glancing up.

"How much?"

"Nothing crazy. Say, fifty grand. What would you do with fifty grand?"

Judah looked up at her out of the corner of his eye. She cocked her head to the side and considered his question.

"Quit working at Buddy's, that's for damn sure. Cade could hire a halfwit teenager to do what I do there. Don't think it would put them out none."

Judah nodded.

"What else?"

"I'd move out of that rat hole apartment I've been stuck in for the past two years. I hate living in town. Feels like I can't breathe half the time. I'd get a mortgage on a house, nothing fancy, but with a front porch and a real yard. Maybe something out near Spinner Creek. You remember how we all used to drive out to the creek? And there was that stretch of road with the trees all hanging over with moss? Benji used to say it looked haunted? Something out there maybe. Then I'd go back to work as a nurse like before. I really miss that, you know? And just build my life back up from there. I'd have a foundation to start over on."

She kicked the heel of her boot in the dirt and turned to smile at him.

"Why, you got some premonition about the winning lottery numbers?"

Judah passed the cigarette back to Ramey and let go of her hand. He stood up and walked a few feet away, jamming both of his hands in his pockets and hunching up his shoulders.

"Ramey? Do you remember the time we lit that fire in the woods out back of your daddy's place? When we were kids?"

They had been ten, maybe eleven. Judah couldn't remember exactly and it didn't matter. It was the night that mattered. In his mind, he knew every detail. The bright glow rising up from the center of the tin drum, reflecting up into the surrounding dark pines and onto the face of Ramey, next to him as always, her eyes fearful and wide. The sound of popping wood and the smell of burnt pine needles and the smear of brittle flakes of rust that broke off against Ramey's bare arms when she reached down inside the barrel to light the fire. The heat from the flames, but also from the hot tears he could no longer fight back. And the gun, his father's revolver, heavy in the limp hand dangling at his side.

"I remember. That was the night your mama died."

The night Judah's mother had finally succumbed to the disease that had seized her body and destroyed her mind. The night his father had abandoned himself to the wild grief that had been eating him alive as he had helplessly watched Rebecca sink deeper and deeper into the arms of an enemy he couldn't raise his fists to. The night Judah showed up at Ramey's back door, bloody from Sherwood's rage, terrified of the vastness of a world without his mother to protect him and filled with the bitter resolve to take matters into his own hands. She had opened the back screen door, raising her finger to her lips so that he would not wake her younger sister. Her own father, Leroy, was out searching for Sherwood, his best friend, after news of Rebecca's death had spread. Ramey had been waiting for Judah, knowing he would need her and knowing that he would come, but she had not expected him to be covered in dried blood and carrying a pistol in one hand and a tube sock of bullets in the other.

She had taken the sock from him and together they had walked through the woods until they reached the clearing where they had dragged the barrel. They had been filling it for weeks with fallen tree branches and chunks of two-by-fours, planning on making a fire on Halloween night. Judah watched dumbly as Ramey disappeared into the pines and returned with an armload of what she called lightwood. Lightwood. Only Ramey would call it that. Only she listened to the stories of old women shelling peas on front porches and found their anachronistic vernacular poetic. Ramey lit the kindling and blew down into the barrel, sending sparks up into her face and hair. They stood in front of the fire together, still not having spoken about the death or the beating. Or the gun. Ramey had not tried to take it from him. Finally, Judah handed her the revolver.

"You gotta do it."

Ramey took the pistol from him, holding it awkwardly out in front of her like a snake. She still had the sock full of bullets.

"No."

Judah clenched his fists at his sides, his sinewy arms rigid and his narrow back ramrod straight. He wouldn't look at her. He focused on the flames.

"You have to. We said we would. If it ever got so bad."

Ramey's voice was hollow.

"That was just talk. We didn't mean it. You didn't mean it for real."

"Yes, I did. My mama's dead. My daddy's got the devil inside him. He said so himself. He told me he'd kill me anyway if he ever had to look at me again."

Judah looked at Ramey, his eyes flat and dark. The tears were gone, only empty resolve left in their place.

"You have to do it."

Ramey began to cry.

"I can't."

He took the gun from her trembling hand and cracked open the chamber.

"It's empty. You gotta load it. Get those bullets out."

Ramey lifted the sock and emptied the slim bullets into the palm of her hand. Her eyes were shining as she looked down at the metal casings sparkling in the light of the fire.

"I can't."

Judah's mouth was set into a grim line.

"Fine. I'll do it."

He had reached for the bullets, but Ramey closed her fist tightly around them. Judah dropped the gun to grab her wrist and pry her fingers open, but she wrenched free from him. She pulled her arm back and then hurled the handful of bullets as far as she could into the trees. Judah screamed and started to run into the woods, but Ramey tackled him. He was bigger than her, and stronger, but the fight had gone out of him when the bullets had disappeared into the darkness, and he had let her wrap her arms around him and drag him down to the ground. She held him while he sobbed and held him as he grieved and held him as he slipped into the twilight that follows childhood. She had held him until the fire burned low and the blue glow of approaching dawn began to tinge the sky above them and he felt that he could maybe handle being alive again. They had never spoken of that night.

"You saved my life at that fire."

He turned around. She pushed her sunglasses up onto her head and met his eyes.

"Maybe."

They stood in silence for a moment, staring at one another. The air around them had turned serious, but finally Judah smiled. Ramey smiled back in relief.

"But what does that gotta do with fifty thousand dollars?"

"Nothing. Everything. I don't know. But I told you last night that I could make things change for us and I meant it. We can get that house you're talking about. We can build up a life. If that's what you want, I want it, too."

Ramey opened her eyes wide.

"That job last night? Are you serious? Fifty thousand?"

Judah nodded.

"What do you think? You with me on this?"

Ramey stared at him for a moment longer and then squealed. She ran up to Judah and jumped on him, wrapping her legs around him. He staggered backwards, but caught himself and held her. She grasped his shoulders and leaned her forehead down so that it was touching his.

"I'm with you. But it ain't 'cause of the money."

Judah smiled, and for the first moment in a long time felt like he was doing something right.

"No?"

Ramey sighed.

"No. I was with you all along."

CHAPTER 8

"How was the revival?"

Jack O' Lantern's face had carried the trace of a smirk as he watched Sister Tulah enter the sanctuary through the back door by the stage, but as she came closer, her pale eyes locked on his, unwavering with every heavy step she took, the nonchalant sneer had fallen from his lips and he became more and more uncomfortable. He had thought to catch her off guard and therefore begin with the upper hand, but his plan didn't appear to be working. Tulah walked around the stage and stopped a few feet away from him, crossing her arms in front of her chest.

"What are you doing here, Mr. Austin?"

Jack O' Lantern shifted his weight on the hard, backless bench. Tulah's eyes scanned him up and down like he was a piece of meat being held up for her inspection in the deli section of the grocery store. She pursed her lips, waiting. Jack broke away from her gaze and looked around the church. He waved his hand at the crosses and hand-lettered signs painted with Bible verses and tried to keep his voice casual.

"You know, my great-aunt Mona, she was a real Bible thumper, too. Took me once to a camp meeting out on the Santa Fe River 'fore she died. I remember they tried to baptize me or something in the water, but I couldn't swim none and just about clawed out the preacher's eyes trying not to drown. Never really went in for religion after that."

Sister Tulah's expression didn't change. Her mouth was set in a firm line and her colorless eyes remained trained on Jack's face. She didn't blink.

"I don't care about your great-aunt Mona. What are you doing here?"

Jack O' Lantern stood up from the bench and walked to the far wall of the church, putting some distance between Sister Tulah and himself. When he turned back around to face her, he saw that she hadn't moved. Jack sighed and tugged at the bottom of his leather vest.

"I need to talk to you about our arrangement."

"You are supposed to be delivering the money this afternoon. What is there to talk about?"

Jack O' Lantern turned and ran a finger down the church wall. It came away covered in a layer of grime. He wiped it off on his jeans, but kept his back to Tulah. He didn't want to see her face.

"Yeah, well, that meeting ain't exactly gonna happen."

"Mr. Austin. I would advise you to turn around, stop stalling and tell me what you need to tell me so that you can get out of my church."

Jack O' Lantern turned around and coughed.

"We got robbed on the way back from Brunswick last night. Everything worked out like I said it would, we made the cash, made enough to give you exactly what I said we would, but we got setup. They were waiting for us, and knew we had the money. They took everything."

Sister Tulah's expression didn't change.

"So. What you are saying is that you don't have my money."

Jack O' Lantern rubbed the back of his head violently. Her lack of response was exasperating, and her composure made him nervous. Very nervous.

"I'm saying I don't got your money right now. But I'll get it for you. Whoever did this, it was an old guy and two others, they gotta be someone who knew. They were right there on the road, at the exact time we was coming through. It's gotta be someone who knew about the deal."

"I see."

The inside of the church had become ridiculously hot. Jack O' Lantern shrugged his shoulders and tugged at the leather sticking to his back.

"What I'm trying to tell you is that I'll get you your money back. I'm gonna root out whoever robbed us and then I'm gonna ride around with his head on a pike."

Sister Tulah's eyes narrowed and she pursed her lips again.

"No. What you're trying to tell me is that you don't have my money."

Jack O' Lantern held his hands out in front of him. Sister Tulah hadn't moved, but he felt like she was getting closer. Her eyes still hadn't left his face and her presence seemed to be growing somehow, filling up the space between them. Jack O' Lantern wished he had left the doors of the church open when he came in. He needed some air.

"I'm telling you that I don't got your money right now. Just give me a little time. A week, even. And I'll take care of it. I just need you to be patient."

He suddenly realized that telling Sister Tulah to be patient was the wrong thing to say. On his ride up to the church, as he was going over in his head what he was going to say to her, Sister Tulah had not seemed such a formidable force. He had heard rumors, whisperings, of what happened to folks who stepped in the crosshairs of Sister Tulah's wrath, but, after all, she was just a crazy old preacher lady, thumping her Bible and rolling in the aisles. Slim Jim had told him an unbelievable story about someone who had spoken out against her at a town council meeting. Apparently, he had woken up the next morning with a nest of rattlers at the foot of his bed. Like something out of a movie. Slim Jim had seemed pretty convinced the story was true, but he had never actually met Sister Tulah. Jack O' Lantern was well aware of Sister Tulah's malevolent and intimidating reputation, but in his mind she remained the fat woman he had met ten years before at a Klan cookout. She had certainly ruled the roost over her impotent husband and short bus nephew, but she wasn't exactly what Jack O' Lantern would have called a dangerous threat.

Now, standing in the dark, stifling church, with only the septic air hanging between himself and those nefarious, colorless eyes and heavy jowls and crossed arms, he realized that he had miscalculated. He watched her small mouth twitch as if she were running her tongue over her teeth and he knew that he was in the presence of someone capable of filling a man's bed with snakes and having no remorse about it.

Jack O' Lantern squirmed.

"I mean, what I meant was…"

Sister Tulah held up a hand and silenced him. Jack glanced toward the church doors, but knew that he wasn't going anywhere unless she let him. He bit his tongue and lowered his chin, trying to appear respectful. Sister Tulah cleared her throat.

"Did you know that my grandmother, my mother's mother, was fortunate enough to hear Benjamin Irwin preach?"

Jack O' Lantern cocked his head slightly.

"Um, who?"

Sister Tulah uncrossed her arms and ran her hands down the sides of her dress as if trying to smooth out unseen wrinkles in the immaculately starched and pressed fabric.

"He was run out of the church for some trumped-up scandal back in nineteen hundred, but he was one of the original saints, spreading the message of charismatic religion. He really knew how to preach on the blood and fire of Jesus and the Holy Ghost. My grandmother said that watching him was one of the most inspiring moments of her life."

Jack O' Lantern nodded cautiously.

"Okay."

"Some people disagreed with his ideas. Thought they were a little too radical, a little too much."

Sister Tulah took another step toward him.

"You need to understand. We don't believe in any of that willy-nilly stuff your Baptist aunt played around with. Pouring water over folks' heads and calling it a day. We believe in the truth: a person needs to be baptized three times to really become one with God. You get saved, you get sanctified, and then you receive the signs of the Holy Spirit. We call this being baptized by fire."

Jack O' Lantern glanced around the church, trying to focus on anything but the pale eyes boring down on him. He was doing his best to stay calm.

"Uh-huh."

"Irwin took it a little bit further. He said it didn't have to stop at fire. Why limit yourself when there was more to be had? He preached that after fire, you could be baptized by dynamite, then lyddite and then oxidite. He was a sort of chemist as well as being a preacher, you see. Most other preachers didn't see any use for baptisms beyond fire, so his ideas never really took hold."

"Oh."

Sister Tulah crossed her arms in front of her chest again. She stared at Jack O' Lantern until he was forced to return her gaze. The space between them seemed to shrink rapidly. Jack O' Lantern was six feet, two hundred and fifty pounds, but he felt himself cowering against the wall of vertigo assailing him. The room seemed to grow even darker and suddenly it felt as if all the air had been sucked into the corners and he was standing inside of a vacuum, struggling to breath. Sister Tulah was monstrous.

"I always thought he had an interesting way of looking at things, though. People sometimes think there's nothing more powerful than fire, but there is always something. And there is more than one way to baptize a man, let me tell you."

She took a final step toward him. They were now standing less than three feet apart, and Jack O' Lantern's head was buzzing. He had the vague sense that he was choking, but that his throat was paralyzed and he could do nothing about it. He stared into the clear depths of her eyes, but it was like trying to elicit compassion from a stone. Her voice became very quiet.

"Mr. Austin, I have no responsibility over your immortal soul. Only God can judge you, can save you, can decide where you're going to end up when you leave this wretched earth. But I do have the power to baptize you. Let's consider this moment right now your salvation. Your sanctification. Your baptism by water. If I don't receive my money before the evening service Wednesday night, you will experience baptism by fire. And after that, well, there is always dynamite. Do you understand?"

Jack O' Lantern nodded furiously. He thought he was going to pass out and was beginning to see black and white splotches in front of his eyes, when he heard a scuffing sound and felt fresh air break over him like a wave. He turned to look at the sudden, blinding light and saw Sister Tulah's nephew standing in the open church doors. Jack O' Lantern didn't wait to hear if Sister Tulah was finished; he bolted and stumbled out into the sunlight.

FELTON PUT THE spotless black Lincoln Navigator into reverse and braced his arm against the back of the passenger headrest so that he could back out of the church parking lot. He was used to driving his ten-year-old Buick, but Sister Tulah would never ride in any vehicle but her own. She bought a brand new Lincoln every year in the fall, as soon as the new models arrived on the car lot. Felton didn't know what half of the buttons on the dash were for, but it didn't matter because he wasn't allowed to touch them anyway. Sister Tulah didn't have a problem driving herself around, but if Felton was with her, he knew automatically that he would be behind the wheel. Driving with Tulah made him anxious: she watched him like a hawk and berated him for driving too fast, too slow or not flipping on his turn signal at the precise moment, but he never argued. He knew he didn't have a choice.

He eased the car into gear when he reached the road and headed east toward downtown Kentsville. He tried to look at Sister Tulah in the passenger seat out of the corner of his eye, but she was staring straight ahead, her neck stiff, and her hands folded in the trough of her wide lap. Felton knew it was coming, he just didn't know when.

"So, Golden Corral?"

She didn't answer him. There weren't many cars on the road at this time on a Sunday afternoon and Felton kept turning his head to look at his aunt. He gripped the steering wheel firmly with both hands, however. It was sweltering inside the Lincoln, and Felton wished Tulah would turn on the air conditioner. His hands were sweating against the shiny gray leather.

"You know, I heard Brother Graham say that this new buffet over by the senior center just opened up. He said they have real good fried chicken and you can pick whatever piece you want out of the pan. Plenty of dark meat pieces, like I know you like."

Her voice suddenly filled the car like a crack of thunder.

"I'm only going to ask once more. Is there something you want to tell me?"

Felton twisted his hands up and down the sides of the steering wheel. He stared at the rear window of the minivan that had pulled out in front of him. A *Life is Good* sticker beamed at him from the bottom corner of the glass.

"No."

Sister Tulah rubbed her hands together.

"Fine. Let me put this a different way. You have something you want to tell me."

Felton shook his head fiercely, like a child refusing to eat his vegetables. He had quickly given up on trying to play dumb. He knew it wouldn't work. Sister Tulah released her hands and laid the left one on Felton's thigh. She began to dig her nails in, all the while continuing to stare straight ahead.

"And if I were you, I would do so. Now."

Felton slammed on the brakes and swerved the Navigator into a strip mall parking lot. He slammed the gearshift into park in front of a nail salon and covered his face with his hands. His words came out muffled.

"How did you know?"

Tulah grunted in disgust.

"Because I know everything."

"I did it for you. For the church and for you."

Sister Tulah removed her hand from Felton's leg and shifted slightly in her seat so that she could look at him. Felton let go of his face and banged his palms against the steering wheel.

"I thought, I mean, if it had worked, I would have been able to give you three times the money you lent them in the first place, and then you would have seen…"

"Stop."

Felton breathed deeply, sucking in air and wheezing it back out. He couldn't look at her, though he knew she was staring at him with disgust. Tulah's voice was calm, but biting. Her words came out weighted and measured.

"You did not think. It did not work. The Lord has seen fit to curse me with an imbecile as my only surviving relative. But that is an issue between God and myself that one day will be sorted out."

Felton laid his sweating forehead against the steering wheel and rolled his head back and forth.

"I'm sorry, Sister Tulah. I'm sorry, I'm sorry, I'm so sorry."

Tulah sighed.

"Yes, you are. But we will deal with that later. Right now, I need a name."

Felton raised his head.

"A name?"

"A name."

JACK O' LANTERN killed the engine and heaved his leg over the seat of his motorcycle. He stared at the shiny red gas tank of his bike, painted with flames and swirling skulls and burning from the late afternoon sun. Jack loved this motorcycle. He had custom designed it and built most of it himself from the ground up. It was only one in a long line of bikes he had owned since he was sixteen, but he was proud of it. Jack O' Lantern studied the paint job to avoid walking inside the clubhouse. They would all be waiting to hear how his meeting with Tulah had gone. He was sure that Slim Jim had already hyped the guys up on stories of the atrocious and absurd things she had done to people who pissed her off, and even if he yelled at them to shut up as soon as he walked in the door, he knew they wouldn't leave him alone. Some were scared, some angry, and all were chomping at the bit for revenge.

He knew that Legs, who didn't hold stake in Slim Jim's stories, had already been whispering to some of the others about going up to Kentsville themselves and trying to intimidate Sister Tulah into backing off. On his way up to see her, he had thought that maybe that strategy wasn't half bad. That was before encountering her in the church, and seeing what he had seen, and feeling what he had felt. Jack O' Lantern had never been a religious man; he thought God was for losers who couldn't take responsibility for their own problems and actions. He believed that churchgoers were fools and preachers either deluded morons or scam artists. Now, he wasn't so sure. He had never come up against the likes of Sister Tulah, and though he thought her whole baptism speech was bullshit, it still made him anxious.

He heard the door of the clubhouse slam and looked up to see Slim Jim standing on the cement stoop, waiting. Jack O' Lantern sighed and was heading across the gravel lot when his cellphone vibrated inside his jeans pocket. He pulled it out as he walked, but froze as soon as he saw the text message appear on the screen. It was from an unknown number and contained only two words, but Jack O' Lantern knew what it meant. He stood at the bottom of the steps and interrupted Slim Jim before he could start asking questions.

"What do you know about Sherwood Cannon?"

CHAPTER 9

THE OPENING RIFF to *Life is a Highway* blasted from the internet jukebox and Benji twisted around on his barstool and raised his Coors Lite bottle over his head.

"Yeah, buddy!"

Benji shouted to a swaying man in a red baseball cap leaning against the jukebox for support. The man squinted across the bar's tiny dance floor and then gave Benji an awkward thumbs-up. Benji swiveled back around on the vinyl barstool and took another swig of his beer. He glanced over the top of the bottle at the woman sitting all the way down at the other end of the bar. It seemed like she had been eyeing him ever since she came in the door an hour ago. He winked at her and she smiled back shyly before quickly looking away at the television set above the bar. Benji took advantage of the fact that the barstools between them had momentarily cleared and gave her a good once-over.

The woman was older than Benji, maybe thirty-five to his twenty-five, but still had it going on. Her processed blond hair was pulled back in a high ponytail and she had dangling silver earrings that curved down the length of her face. She was wearing a low cut leopard print tank top that was barely keeping her contained and a short, black pleather skirt. Benji leaned back from the bar slightly to get a better angle and watched the skirt ride up higher as she crossed one leg over the other on the barstool. Her black ankle boots matched the skirt and made her long legs appear even longer. Benji grinned to himself as he sat up straighter and sipped his beer. Good music, pretty girls: it was a perfect Monday night.

Most nights at Limey's were perfect nights for Benji. There weren't too many bars to choose from in Silas, but still he thought that Limey's was pretty near the best place on Earth to drink a cold beer, swap some stories with the boys and decide which girl to go home with. He had been drinking at Limey's since he was sixteen and loved the fact that he was the only Cannon who ever spent time in the joint. Judah and Levi had always been regulars at The Ace, but Benji couldn't understand why. The place was always filled with old timers wanting to sing along to Hank Williams on the jukebox and guys with too many kids at home looking to get smashed and beat the tar out of each other with pool cues. Every time he had ever been to The Ace in the Hole with his older brothers, he saw somebody wind up with blood on his shirt. It just didn't make sense to him. Levi and Judah told him that Limey's was for pussies, but at least he didn't have to worry about being smashed over the head with a pint glass on his way to take a leak. Sherwood, too, had his own place; he almost never left the VFW for a drink, preferring to surround himself with war veterans who had grown up with him and knew what he was capable of. They figured it was better to go along with Sherwood's wild stories and buy him drinks than question anything he said. Benji thought it was funny that a family so well-known and so close knit never drank together in the same bar, but he thought it was just as well. At Limey's, he wasn't Benjamin Cannon, he was just good old Benji.

And the girls loved him. Of course, they loved him everywhere, but at

Limey's, he knew he wouldn't have to work too hard, and that was part of its appeal. Benji leaned over the bar and tossed his empty beer bottle into the plastic trashcan next to the sink. Rooter, the same bartender who had served Benji his first drink on a barstool, waited until a commercial interrupted the re-run of *Survivor* he was watching and opened another bottle for Benji. Rooter rested his thick, hairy forearms on the sticky bar mat and surveyed the room.

"Starting to quiet down a little, ain't it?"

Benji swiveled on the barstool again and looked around. The shiny wooden dance floor was nearly empty. Two girls, both of whom Benji had gone to high school with, were dancing with each other in front of the flashing jukebox. Benji knew they weren't sisters, but they might as well have been. Both wore cut-off jean shorts, tight white T-shirts and had tortured brown hair that hung to their shoulders in overworked curls. The only difference between them was that one was chunkier than the other, and though Benji couldn't for the life of him remember their names, he knew that the one with the belly roll of fat peeking out from the bottom of her shirt was much more fun in the sack. A few beers ago, Benji had his eye on taking her home, but she had wandered off at some point and Benji had forgotten about her. From the way she and her friend were sloppily clinging to one another as they swayed to the music, he figured they were both likely to puke in his truck before he could get either one back to his trailer. The skinnier one saw him looking and tried to raise her hand to wave at him, but her wrist fell limply across the other girl's back. Benji mentally crossed them both off the list.

In a corner of the bar, backlit by too many neon beer and liquor signs, a game of foosball, guys against girls, was winding down. Neither of the girls twisting the plastic handles and laughing were bad looking, but Benji had gone to school and played football with both of their boyfriends and wouldn't make a play for them with the guys present. The tall blonde in the see-through shirt had been with his buddy Joey for the past three years and so she was pretty much off-limits anyway, though Benji had some pretty vivid memories of this one thing she could do. He knew that the other girl had been hooked up with Joey's cousin for a few months, but he still considered her available when she was alone. The girl, Benji thought her name was Marissa or Melissa, something like that, had gone home with him a few weeks ago, but she must not have been that exciting because he couldn't remember anything about her except that she liked to talk about some reality housewife show. A lot. Marissa/Melissa definitely fit into the end-of-the-night desperate category. And with her boyfriend in tow, she was a no-go anyway. There were rules after all.

Benji turned all the way around on the stool. At the other end of the bar, away from the TV, the McCaulghy brothers were arguing about baseball stats in front of two empty shot glasses. He finally turned back to Rooter, who had been following Benji's eyes and knew his thought process as if it was his own.

"Slim pickings this late, huh?"

Benji smiled and nodded. Rooter picked up a gray rag and started scrubbing down the bar.

"You getting off your game or something? There were at least five honeys in here earlier who couldn't stop making eyes at you. You been spending too much time drinking and not enough time listening to those girls prattle on. You're gonna lose your edge."

Benji pushed his blond hair out of his eyes and took another sip of beer.

"Never."

"I bet you're still holding out for that Ellie girl. She's something else, ain't she?"

Rooter raised his eyebrows, but Benji just looked down at the polished bar.

"Yeah, she's okay."

"Okay? I seen how you look at her whenever she comes in here. And I seen how you look the next day. You may not want to admit it, but I think maybe you got a thing for her. Like an L-O-V-E thing for her."

Benji grinned to himself.

"Shut up."

Rooter laughed and started wiping out the ashtrays stacked on the bar mat.

"We might just be nearing the end of Benji the Bachelor. What do you say to that? I know Levi and Judah are ahead of me in line, but I'd like to put my name in the hat for being best man, considering the two of you met in my bar after all."

Benji smiled to himself again, but then raised his head and nodded to his left.

"Who's the girl in the leopard print been sitting down at the end of the bar all this time?"

Rooter looked over and frowned.

"Don't know. I never seen her in here before."

"I've never seen her in town before."

Rooter snapped out the rag and then folded it on the bar.

"When I asked her, she said she was supposed to be meeting somebody here tonight, but from the looks of it, they ain't never showed up. That's a waste, if you ask me. Who would stand up something that looks like that?"

Benji stood up and passed his empty bottle to Rooter.

"I think I'll have my next one down there."

Rooter opened the beer cooler and pulled out another bottle.

"Don't you think she's a little old for you, sonny?"

Benji grinned and swiped the bottle out of Rooter's hand.

"Don't you think she's a little young for you, old man? 'Sides, don't you have grandkids at home to take care of, or something?"

Rooter glared at Benji.

"Asshole."

Benji laughed and smacked his palm down. He took his beer and moved down to the end of the bar. He slid onto the barstool next to the blonde and waited for her to turn away from the television show she was engrossed in. When she finally looked at him, he flashed her his biggest smile and turned on the charm.

"I hope you don't mind, darlin', but I couldn't help but notice you sitting here alone, and I was just wondering if you'd like me to beat up the prick that could've left you all by yourself."

The woman laughed and touched Benji's arm. Up close, he could see that her makeup was caked on a little too thick and her lipstick was just a little too bright. Still, if he kept his eyes mostly on her body, and not on her face, she was a real knockout. For a brief, lucid moment he had the feeling that he wouldn't like what he saw when he woke up in the morning, but then the beers kicked back in and the feeling dissipated.

"No, that's okay. Though I appreciate the thought. I ain't used to being stood up, so I'm sorry if I look a little pouty."

She pursed her sticky pink lips together and fluttered her spidery eyelashes at Benji. He laughed back.

"You don't look pouty. You look gorgeous. My name's Benji. You ain't from Silas, are you?"

She touched his arm again and this time let her fingers rest there. Her long nails sparkled under the neon lights.

"No. I'm Shelia. It's really nice to meet you."

"The same."

The woman's eyes drifted back up to the television and Benji's eyes drifted down to her cleavage. They sat awkwardly in silence for a moment until Rooter came down to check on them.

"Can I get you two anything else?"

Shelia seemed to be aware that both men were fixated on the deep neckline of her tank top, but didn't appear to mind. She laughed again and Benji thought it sounded like the bell on a convenience store door tinkling. It was almost a child's laugh. She turned to Benji and raised her thinly plucked eyebrows.

"Want to do a shot?"

Benji smiled and inched a little closer. Her hand was still on his arm.

"Sure."

Benji looked at Rooter, waiting expectantly.

"Um, how 'bout an Alabama Slammer? You like those, Shelia?"

She thought about it a moment.

"How 'bout something stronger? I wouldn't mind getting a good buzz on. Maybe we can salvage the night after all."

Benji lifted his free arm and smacked his hand on the bar.

"Tequila it is, then! Lime, salt, give us the works, Rooter."

Rooter set two large shot glasses on the bar in front of them and filled them to the brim. He placed two dried out limes on a cocktail napkin between them and then hunted around for the white plastic salt shaker. He left them alone and walked away, shaking his head. Shelia picked up her glass and held it out to Benji.

"Here's to new friends."

Benji clinked his glass against hers.

"To new friends!"

They downed the shots and slid the empty glasses to the edge of the bar. Shelia pushed the limes and saltshaker away and leaned her chin on her hand. She was deliberately pushing her breasts out toward Benji, and he certainly didn't mind the view. She took Benji's hand and laced her fingers with his.

"So, Benji, huh? Is that short for Benjamin?"

She lazily stroked the back of his hand. Benji was still feeling the rush in his head from the tequila. He tried to count how many beers he had consumed before the shot, but gave up trying.

"Yep. No one but my mama ever called me that, though. Everybody always just calls me Benji. My mama died when I was six years old."

Just as he knew they would, the girl's lips turned down and her eyes opened wider. She edged a little closer to him.

"I'm so sorry. That must be awful to have grown up without a mama."

Benji looked away from her and nodded.

"It was pretty rough."

She gripped his hand tighter.

"That's just heartbreaking."

He nodded again.

"I know."

He looked at her out of the side of his eyes. He could see the edge of one of her black lace bra cups peeping out of the top of her shirt. She must have followed his eyes because she let go of his hand and adjusted herself slightly, as if out of modesty. Benji watched her tug on her bra and got even more excited. She had obviously taken the bait and was playing the game with him. She put her hand back on his.

"So, Benji. The only Benji I ever heard of 'round these parts is one of the Cannon brothers."

Benji stiffened. It was going so well with this girl. The last thing he wanted was for her to start talking all about how she had once dated Levi or had a crush on Judah. Or, God forbid, had slept with one of them. It didn't happen often. Thankfully, Levi was married and only hooked up with stray tail from out of town, and Judah had been in prison and before that, wrapped up with that gold digger in Colston. But when it did, it was the biggest turn-off Benji could think of. He loved his brothers, just about worshipped Judah, but there was no way he was going to share a girl with one. He frowned and answered cautiously.

"Yeah, my last name is Cannon."

The girl shrugged and picked up the watered down drink in front of her. She bit the little red straw between her teeth.

"One of my girlfriends mentioned that there was this crazy Cannon family down in Silas. I ain't never heard of them before. You don't look crazy to me."

Benji breathed an inward sigh of relief. He could go back to putting the moves on her now. He reached out and touched her waist.

"Well, not in no bar no how."

She laughed and set her drink down.

"So, you saying you're crazy someplace else?"

Benji looked around Limey's again. The two dancing girls and the foosball players had left. Only the brothers remained, though it looked like their argument had ended. Rooter was standing in front of them, while the younger brother looked down into his wallet like he was viewing alien terrain. Benji turned back to Shelia and saw that her drink was empty.

"What do you say to getting outta here and maybe I can show you that crazy side a little?"

Shelia covered her mouth with her hand and laughed again. She almost looked as if she were blushing. For a moment, Benji thought he might have moved too soon, but then she sat up straight and cocked her head at him.

"Okay, Benji Cannon, why not? I wouldn't mind having a little fun. You got a place 'round here? I'm staying at my aunt's house right now, and we'd better not go back there. She likes it kinda quiet."

Benji pulled two twenties out of his wallet and dropped them on the bar. He slid his arm around Shelia as she stood up and he put his lips to her ear.

"Don't worry, baby. I'll take good care of you."

Benji waved to Rooter as they walked out of the bar and laughed to himself as the bartender rolled his eyes. He grabbed Shelia's hand and steadied her as her wobbly boot heels sunk into the gravel parking lot. They walked around to the passenger side of his truck and he unlocked the door for her. Now that he was on his feet, the world was starting to spin slightly and he looked out around the parking lot to fix his gaze. His eyes fell on two Harleys parked near the back of the lot.

"Say, those are some pretty sweet bikes."

He opened the door for her.

"You ain't usually see many Harleys 'round here."

Shelia paused before stepping onto the running board.

"You know anything about motorcycles?"

Benji put his hand on her waist and grinned.

"Sure, honey. That's what I do. Work on cars and bikes. I don't got no Harley or nothing, but I know how to fix 'em. Can make one like purr like a newborn kitten."

He was waiting for her to step up into the truck, but she had an excited look on her face. He ran his hand up and down the side of her hip while she held onto the truck door. She reached up and put her hand on his shoulder.

"That's so hot, baby."

He dropped his hand lower to her thigh.

"You think so? Why, you got a thing for motorcycles? That kinda engine turn you on or something?"

She nodded, but didn't answer. She slid around closer to him and leaned back against the side of the truck. In the bright moonlight, Benji could only focus on the tops of her breasts, heaving against her shirt as she reached for him. She put her arms around his neck and pulled him close against her body. He felt her lips against his neck and he closed his eyes. Then he felt a sharp crack against the base of his skull and a zing of pain shoot through his head and neck. The world went black.

CHAPTER 10

THE FIRST THING Judah saw when he opened his eyes on Tuesday morning was a cascade of unruly, dark auburn hair falling down a long, naked back. When Ramey shifted slightly to sip from the cup of coffee clasped between her hands, the tracks of scars arcing along her left hip came into view. Judah opened his eyes wider and swallowed.

The first thing Jack O' Lantern saw was the dingy red and white Scorpions' logo, sewn onto the cut of a man face-down on the pool table in the clubhouse. He gripped the corduroy arm of the recliner he had fallen asleep in, leaned over and vomited tequila onto the floor. He'd get one of the prospects to clean it up later.

The first thing Felton saw was the dark, beady eye of a canebrake rattler staring back at him through a wall of glass. The snake's eye was unblinking, but it shifted its coils and its forked tongue flicked in and out of its mouth as Felton watched. From the other side of the camper, his collection of mice was squeaking frantically inside their cardboard box. Felton wondered if the snake was hungry.

The first thing Sister Tulah saw was the dark mahogany cross she had mounted on the opposite wall of her bedroom. It had hung in Tulah's room when she was a girl and her mother had told her that it was the only thing protecting her from being snatched away by Satan in the night. Sister Tulah kept the cross hanging in her bedroom now to remind herself of how foolish she had been. She didn't need a stick of wood to keep her safe. God would always be on her side. Satan, too.

Benji didn't see anything.

By the time Sherwood made it out to the crossroads of County Road 225 and Old Line, Rooter was waiting for him alone. Sherwood pulled his truck over into the high weeds on the road's shoulder and cut the engine. Rooter was leaning against the hood of his car, arms crossed in front of his chest, a deep V creasing the leathery skin of his forehead. Sherwood eyed the bartender through the smeared windshield of his truck. Seemingly overnight, love bug season had begun and the remains of smashed insect bodies were streaked across the front of every moving vehicle in the county. Sherwood sighed and slowly opened the truck door and descended from the high seat. He lumbered across the deserted road with the tips of his fingers wedged into his pockets and waited until he was standing in front of Rooter to speak.

"Bingo already take him to the ER?"

Rooter nodded, keeping his eyes on the warming asphalt in front of him. Now that there was no glass or distance between them, the two men wouldn't look at each other.

"Left 'bout twenty minutes ago. Soon as I got here."

Sherwood looked at the single track of burned rubber on the road. It was fresh and ran for about three feet.

"How was he? When you got here?"

Rooter shrugged his shoulders, but the motion was stiff and tense.

"Alive. Unconscious, but breathing."

"What else?"

Rooter ducked his chin down and tried to keep his voice steady.

"Sherwood, man. I don't know what you've gone and done, but…"

Sherwood banged his fist down on the hood of the car.

"I said, what else?"

Rooter cleared his throat and pointed to an area of matted weeds in the ditch alongside the road.

"That's where my son found him this morning on his way to work. Bingo said he saw the burnout and thought maybe somebody had run their bike off the road. Stopped to check it out. He found Benji lying there in the ditch."

Sherwood wouldn't look at the place where Rooter was pointing. He kept his eyes on the reflecting metal of the car hood.

"And?"

Rooter walked away from Sherwood and stood at the edge of the ditch. He poked the toe of his boot into the soft earth.

"It was pretty bad, Sherwood."

"He beat up?"

"Yeah, but not by fists. Road rash all the way down his body. Everywhere. I almost didn't recognize his face. Had a rope tied 'round him."

"Jesus."

Sherwood raised his hands to his face, but then quickly dropped them and bunched them into fists at his sides. He turned and stared at the ditch. Rooter slowly shook his head in disbelief.

"Somebody dragged him. Don't know how far. I seen this done before, but not 'round here. And not from behind no motorcycle. Look at that tire burn. Had to be a bike."

Sherwood's face was expressionless.

"Yeah."

Rooter kicked at the ground.

"Sherwood, man, it's Benji. Boy doesn't even know how to have enemies. It don't make no sense."

Sherwood kept his eyes on the ditch. His mouth was drawn into a hard line and his eyes were glassy.

"He at your bar last night?"

"Sure. Left around one, right 'fore we closed. He was making time with some blonde at the bar and they left together. He was fine. Weren't nobody messing with him. It just don't make no sense."

Sherwood jerked his head up and scowled at Rooter.

"Some blonde? Who?"

Rooter shook his head.

"I didn't know her. Said she wasn't from 'round here when I asked. You think she had something to do with this?"

"Maybe."

"Like some jealous boyfriend? One of them things? Christ, man. I mean, really? I can see some guy knocking Benji around if he caught him going at his old lady, but this?"

Sherwood stepped away from the ditch.

"Only thing I can think of."

Sherwood pulled his keys out of his pocket and started walking back to his truck. Rooter followed at his side.

"You heading over to the hospital?"

Sherwood nodded.

"Want me to ask around? See if I can find something on that girl?"

Sherwood opened his truck door and rested one foot on the running board.

"Not yet. Let's just keep this quiet for a bit, okay?"

Rooter frowned.

"You're not gonna call the sheriff?"

Sherwood hauled himself up into the truck and jammed the keys into the ignition.

"Like I said, let's just keep this quiet for a minute."

Rooter grabbed the truck door before Sherwood could close it.

"I swear to God, Sherwood. If this happened to Benji 'cause of something you did, something he's got no part of..."

"What? You're gonna do what?"

Rooter grit his teeth, but said nothing.

"Exactly. Now get your hand off my door before I break your fingers. And keep your damn mouth shut."

Rooter let go of the door and backed away. His eyes were full of loathing, but he stayed silent. Sherwood slammed the truck door shut and cranked the engine. He took his cellphone out and dialed a number while he watched Rooter walk slowly back to his car. Levi picked up on the third ring.

THE HEADQUARTERS OF the Scorpions Motorcycle Club was a termite-infested duplex that had been gutted down the middle, outfitted with a couple of security cameras and surrounded by a warped chain link fence. Jack O' Lantern's uncle, Oren, had won the property in a lucky hand of poker and set the place up as the club's base back in 1972. Not much had changed about it since, except that the pit bull guard dogs had been replaced by a second-rate alarm system and Oren Austin, the former club leader, was dead in the ground in the Kentsville Public Cemetery after being dragged a quarter of a mile by a semi-truck on Interstate 95. Jack had sewn the president patch on his cut the morning of his uncle's funeral and done his best to fill his idol's shoes. He had kept the club's initial goals of being an on-the-fringe outlaw club, but replaced the tool shed full of weed with a singlewide meth lab way back in the woods off Highway 18. Jack

O' Lantern loved his club more than his family and was willing to do just about anything to protect the men he had surrounded himself with. He had thought the coke run down to Miami would solve a lot of the Scorpions' debt problems, but instead it had opened a can of worms that Jack O' Lantern didn't even begin to know how to close. The rest of the club thought he had it all under control, but Jack knew they were only hiding their heads in the sand.

Jack O' Lantern dug the toe of his boot into the baked ashes of the fire pit he had constructed in one corner of the gravel lot. After drinking a quart of tomato juice that he found in the club's refrigerator, he had stumbled outside, puked a stream of red vomit onto the tire of one of the prospect's bikes and collapsed into a canvas lawn chair next to the pit. It had been too hot the last month to have any kind of fire, and the remains of the charred wood had been beaten down by the rain until they were only smudged lumps of charcoal. Jack rested his forehead on the palm of his hand and stared into the black mess.

He had encouraged the guys to get lit after Slim Jim, Legs and Shelia had returned from Silas with the news that the deed had been done. Jack O' Lantern had decided they should celebrate, hoping that no one would dwell on the fact that all they had done so far to get their money back was drag an innocent man almost to his death. He had seen the look in Slim Jim's eyes over a shot of tequila, not of remorse, but of uncertainty. The Cannon boy was a message, but hardly a solution. They had lit a match and thrown it into the haystack, hoping to drive the Cannons out into the open, but they could just as easily be setting their own field on fire. Jack adjusted himself in the chair and pulled his cellphone out. It was just after noon. He was sure that someone would have found the kid by now. He needed his men up and ready, primed for retaliation, out on the road and on their phones, checking for smoke signals. Instead, even he was having trouble standing up for more than five minutes at a time. This was not a good sign.

He heard the clubhouse door slam and turned around, hoping Slim Jim had managed to peel himself off the pool table and was ready to get to work. He needed him to head down to Silas and scout around, see what the news on the street was. But it wasn't Slim Jim walking unsteadily across the gravel lot toward him. It was Shelia, trying to smooth her disheveled hair and twist her miniskirt the right way around. Jack O' Lantern mumbled under his breath.

"Christ."

Shelia walked up and stood awkwardly next to him, waiting for him to say something. He didn't raise his head to look up at her. She tapped her foot impatiently and then huffed and plopped down in the lawn chair next to him. With his head still down, Jack O' Lantern watched her pull a pack of Capris out of her bag. She put a slim cigarette between her lips and continued to dig around in her purse.

"Hey, Jack, you got a light?"

He kept his head down.

"No."

"Come on, I know you do. Oh wait, I got it."

She pulled a hot pink lighter from the bag and lit her cigarette. Jack O' Lantern smelled the smoke as Shelia exhaled and immediately began craving a cigarette, but there was no way he was going to ask for one of those pussy sticks. They sat together in uncomfortable silence until Jack realized she was not going to go away on her own. He finally grunted, raised his head and stretched his back out. She was sitting with her legs crossed, skirt hiked up too high, staring at him. Jack O' Lantern rubbed his face with his callused hands and then smacked the tops of his thighs.

"What do you want, Shelia?"

"Good morning to you, too."

She twisted her lips in a sour expression and Jack O' Lantern had the urge to slap her. She wasn't his old lady, but she'd still give him just as much grief as if she was. At this moment, he could not bear to hear her shrill voice screeching at him. It was easier to just placate her and hustle her out of there.

"I'm serious, Shelia. I ain't got time for this. What're you after?"

Shelia uncrossed her legs and took another drag from her cigarette.

"I know what you did to that boy last night."

"You don't know shit."

Shelia pulled at the hem of her skirt. She looked over at Jack O' Lantern and then through the chain link fence beyond. The long, sandy driveway was glaring in the noon sun.

"I was there. I know what you did to him."

"You don't know nothing, girl."

Shelia continued to look off down the drive.

"I don't know what he did to you, but he seemed like a real nice guy. Just a sweet kid. I can't imagine what he coulda done to deserve that."

Jack O' Lantern suddenly reached over to Shelia, grabbed her leg and jerked her closer. With his other hand he reached behind her head and yanked a handful of hair so that she was forced to look straight up at him. Her eyes were wide with fear and the tendons in her neck bulged out from the way he was holding her. She had dropped her cigarette.

"I ain't gonna say it again. You don't know nothing. Do you understand?"

Shelia couldn't nod her head, but she whispered. Her lips were trembling.

"Yes."

"Good."

Jack O' Lantern released her and sat back down in the lawn chair. Shelia edged up in her seat and rubbed the back of her head. She stared into the muddled ashes of the fire pit. Jack O' Lantern waited for her to leave, but she just sat there, not looking at him, but not moving either.

"Now what?"

Shelia sat up straighter and tossed her matted hair over her shoulder, bracing herself, but determined.

"Slim Jim said you'd give me two hundred dollars for helping you guys last night."

Jack O' Lantern burst out laughing.

"He said what?"

Shelia kept her head facing forward but let her eyes drift over toward him.

"That's what he said. I promise."

Jack O' Lantern couldn't believe he was even having this conversation. He reached over and gripped Shelia's arm, not forcefully like before, but firmly. She turned to him now, doing her best to look helpless, to look pitiful. Jack grit his teeth.

"Listen, Shelia. I don't know who the hell you think you are this morning, but let me remind you. You're a damn mama 'round here. You got it?"

Shelia nodded and cast her eyes down.

"And you don't like it? You can stop coming 'round. There's a line of whores behind you looking for a piece of this action. It's your call. Now get outta my sight."

Shelia pulled her purse higher up on her shoulder and stood up. Jack O' Lantern didn't watch her leave. He waited for about five minutes more and then hoisted himself up. He kicked over the flimsy chair and headed toward the clubhouse. It was time for everybody to wake their asses up and get down to business.

Felton watched the shadow of trees move across the dirt clearing in front of his camper. He had been sitting on the metal steps since mid-morning. Watching the sparse clouds meander across the blazing sky. Watching small lizards edge their way out into the sun, the males, prideful and parochial, raising their heads and blowing out their scarlet throats, desperate to attract a mate. Watching time draw out and elongate the puddles of shade created by the scraggly pines and sprawling oaks, woven together to create a dense barrier between his little island of sandy dirt, blistering heat and his only friends, his snakes and lizards and turtles and dinner mice, and the rest of the harsh, cruel world.

Felton had not been allowed inside either the church or the house since he had confessed to Sister Tulah. He had been afraid of her anger, afraid of her lashing wrath, but now he knew that she was taking a different approach with him. The one she took with people she no longer felt were useful. He had tried to steal the money from the Scorpions for the purpose of proving to Sister Tulah that he was capable and worthy of her trust. Instead, he was now even further distanced from her. Though he was sitting only acres away from Sister Tulah's tall, white house, he knew he had been cast into exile. Tulah would not confide in him, would not make him privy to her ideas, and certainly would no longer even consider listening to him. Until she was ready. For now, he would have to sit in his stifling camper, eating pimento cheese sandwiches and drinking warm diet soda, sleeping in the sweltering heat next to the brightly lit terrariums, and waiting out on the blistering steps until Tulah decided she needed him for something. At least he still he had his snakes. At least he still had his angel turtles.

Felton was about to get up and go inside the camper to see if he still had any barbeque potato chips left, when he heard the sound of twigs cracking and branches popping and knew somebody was coming down the narrow trail into the clearing. It had to be either Sister Tulah or one of the elders with a message. He was only halfway relieved when the forbidding form of his aunt stepped out into the sunlit clearing and strode toward him, arms swinging at her sides, huffing from the walk through the woods. He stood up and came down the steps, but waited for her to approach him. She stopped a few feet away and crossed her arms. Sweat was beading across her forehead and upper lip, but she didn't wipe it away. She glared at Felton, her pale eyes squinted to near slits against the brilliant sunlight, and caught her breath. Felton reached into his pocket and pulled out a white handkerchief, crusty with salt from his own dried sweat. He extended it out to her.

"Sister Tulah, I'm sorry. I'm still sorry."

She ignored the handkerchief and snapped at him.

"I don't care."

Felton slowly withdrew his arm and mopped his face with the handkerchief. He stuffed it back into his polyester pants and rocked back and forth on the soles of his shoes, waiting. He knew that if she hadn't come out here to forgive him, she must need something from him instead.

"I need something from you."

Felton nodded slightly. She handed him a small slip of folded paper. He took it and started to open it before she sharply reprimanded him.

"Don't."

"What do you need, then?"

Sister Tulah uncrossed her arms and put her hands on her hips.

"A snake."

Felton nodded again.

"What kind?"

"Rattler. Or something. It just needs to be dangerous and I don't want to see it. Just put it in one of your boxes and put that piece of paper in with it. Bring it up to the church and leave it out front. One of the elders will be by to pick it up."

Felton looked down at the folded piece of paper in his palm and then back up at Sister Tulah. Her mouth was twisted in a grimace of disgust. Felton knew she didn't like to even talk about snakes. Then he realized that whatever the snake was for, she might want it bad enough to bargain. It was worth a shot anyway.

"Okay."

She turned to leave and was halfway across the clearing before Felton called out.

“I’ll get you your snake, but what do I get out of it?”

Sister Tulah turned around. Felton thought for a moment that he had gone too far, but she only narrowed her eyes at him.

“You can come back inside the church. Not the house. But I’ve got the fans running in the church right now. I suspect it’s a mite cooler in there than in that serpent den you’re staying in now.”

Felton bobbed his head emphatically.

“Thank you. Thank you, Sister Tulah.”

She ignored him and walked away. Felton stood alone in the white hot sunlight and contemplated which of his snakes was worth sacrificing for a little cool air. It didn’t take him long. At least she wasn’t asking for a turtle.

CHAPTER 11

"SKIP THE BEER. I ain't got time for that watered down horse piss. Just give me a whiskey."

"Don't you think maybe you should slow down, son?"

"No. I don't. And I ain't your son. I ain't nobody's son. God, I wish to Christ I weren't nobody's son."

"That's a pretty tall order."

"Just pour the whiskey."

Judah had gotten the call early that afternoon. He had been wandering aimlessly through the hardware store, dipping his hands into bins of bolts and washers, fingering paint strips, halfway dreaming about possibilities, halfway fighting the urge to run out to the Bronco parked on the street and drive as fast as he could for the Florida-Georgia border without daring to look back over his shoulder. The past five days had been a whirlwind. After the stagnate confinement, the daily routine of boredom and survival, the predictability of every moment, every key turn, every food tray slid down the line, the hard cement ceiling meeting his eyes every morning, his return to Silas was overwhelming. He had moved through the past few days as if bobbing along in the ocean, a piece of Sargassum tossed about by the waves or warmed by the sun, but always at the direction of an element outside of himself.

He had assured Ramey, when she left him sitting alone at her kitchen table to return to her mundane job of stocking bait worms and flipping sandwiches at Buddy's, that he was fine. He was great, in fact. He had kissed her and mumbled something about needing time by himself to figure a few things out, get a few things in order. He had believed it when he said it, and become desperately terrified as he sat at the table and watched the digital red numbers on the stove clock change every sixty seconds. Too many decisions with too many outcomes had begun to whip through his head as he sipped his cold coffee and suddenly Ramey's kitchen had become claustrophobic and unbearable. He had grabbed the Bronco keys and set about aimlessly driving through town, not looking for answers, but rather, for distractions. His cellphone had buzzed in his pocket as he was staring at a selection of weed eaters.

When Judah had shown up at Buddy's, Ramey had been taking a customer's order, but she nodded her head toward one of the bright red plastic booths set against the windows. Judah had slid into the hard seat across from a man who seemed vaguely familiar. When the man introduced himself as Rooter, the bartender at Limey's across town, a fist had gripped Judah's heart and begun to squeeze. The only person who mattered to him who ever went anywhere near Limey's was Benji. He had been halfway out of his seat, heading toward the door, as soon as he heard the words *alive* and *First Memorial Hospital*, but Rooter had gripped his wrist and held him fast. When Judah twisted around in anger and met the man's eyes he realized that Rooter was scared. He said something about promising Sherwood he wouldn't tell nobody, and the situation instantly jumped into focus. Ramey had called after him as he pushed through the glass doors, but he had ignored her.

Burke, the bartender at The Ace, shrugged.

“Fine, you’re in a bar after all.”

“Damn straight.”

“You just seem pretty hell bent on tying one on as fast as you can.”

“That’s the idea.”

The hospital had been a nightmare, and now, after four beers and three shots of house whiskey, not much more than a blur in Judah’s memory. He remembered that a security guard had yelled at him for parking in the red zone, but he had refused to move the Bronco and continued stomping toward the emergency room entrance. He remembered an overweight receptionist in a tight white blouse repeatedly telling him that she didn’t know anything and to sit down and wait. He remembered nurses and doctors walking past the waiting room, laughing about something they had all seen on TV the night before, while he sat with his hands gripping the edges of a pale pink vinyl chair. And he remembered the pasty doctor with the slick haircut who had finally had the time to stop in the hallway long enough to explain to Judah what had happened. He only recalled pieces of the conversation now: *Benjamin Cannon, ICU, vehicle, critical, cerebral, bones, skin, coma, trauma, internal, immediate, no, no, he couldn’t see him, no*. And then he had stood alone in the septic white hallway with the calming beach scene paintings and the shining tile floor and realized that he was helpless. The doctors would save Benji, or they wouldn’t. That was all.

Burke set the whiskey bottle back on the bar and eyed Judah.

“You want to talk about it? Tell me what’s going on?”

“No.”

“Maybe has something to do with getting outta prison? I remember when your brother Levi got out the first time, he went on a bender that lasted for three weeks. His wife had to pick him up from where I dumped him in the parking lot every night. Every single night. It ain’t nothing to be ashamed of.”

“I’m not ashamed. And this has nothing to do with me getting outta prison. So why don't you shut your mouth and quit trying to be Dr. Phil. Can't a bartender just pour drinks instead of trying to be a therapist?"

He had sat in his illegally parked Bronco in the hospital parking lot and considered his options while he twisted his hands along the steering wheel and gripped a shaky cigarette between his lips. He could continue to sit in the waiting room and stare at the abstract industrial carpet and the grubby toys in the corner and wait for someone to tell him whether his brother was going to live or die. He could call Ramey and attempt to halfheartedly explain the bottomless well of his feelings. He could find Sherwood or Levi and try to kick the ever-living shit out of them. He could drive out to the Santa Fe River and throw himself in. Or he could go to The Ace in the Hole and try to make sense of everything with the aid of dim lights, smoky air, meaningless conversation and the best pain killer of them all: booze. By the time he had put the Bronco in reverse and squealed out of the parking lot, he knew where he was headed.

He had escaped into the safety of a darkly lit bar, his bar, with Flatt and Scruggs on the jukebox and a cold Budweiser pressed between the grip of his palms. It had been light out when he had walked through the door, jaw set, determined for a memory-obliterating binge, and now, though The Ace was a windowless tomb, he figured the sun must have already gone down. He wasn't exactly sure how many hours he had been sitting on the same stool and stewing in the same thoughts, but he knew it had been a while. He had stumbled to the bathroom at the back of the bar at least three times and his ashtray had been emptied twice. At one point he had hoped that Pellman and his cousin would show up, maybe argue about whales and space travel or something, but no such luck. Judah had picked up his cellphone from the bar half a dozen times, stared at the screen, even flipped it open and stared at the list of missed calls, but he always snapped it shut and set it back down next to his lighter and cigarettes. He knew it must be dark outside and he wondered if the stars were out. He wondered if Benji was still alive.

Things were not going well for Jack O' Lantern. He sat at the three-stool bar built into the back wall of the Scorpions' clubhouse and snapped open the top of his scratched Zippo lighter. He dropped the lighter on the bar and spun it around a few times. It was his favorite lighter, his lucky lighter; his wife, Cynthia, had stuffed it in the toe of his Christmas stocking many years ago. It featured a hand painted naked redhead on the front who Cynthia said looked like herself twenty years ago. Jack wasn't so sure about that part, but the lighter was his favorite anyway. He picked it up and rubbed at a long scratch on the bottom of it and then put it back in his pocket and rested his head in his hands. He didn't know what to do.

Slim Jim's cousin, Mack, had done some scouting down in Silas, but hadn't turned up much. The Cannon boy was in the hospital, he had reported, but there had been no sign of anyone who matched the description for the Cannon patriarch, Sherwood, or his eldest son, Levi. Mack said he'd seen someone peeling out of the hospital parking lot in a Ford Bronco who might have matched the description of the middle son, but it had been hard to tell. He knew Sherwood and Levi on sight, but apparently the other Cannon, Judah, had been in prison for the last three years and Mack couldn't remember what he looked like. It didn't matter so much, though, Mack had reassured him, Sherwood was the one calling the shots. If they had a beef with the Cannons, Sherwood was the one they needed to deal with.

Jack O' Lantern had sent Legs and Toadie to check out Cannon Salvage, but they had come back empty-handed as well. The place was locked down tight. The more he learned about this Sherwood character, the more uncertain he became. Christ, the man hadn't even shown up at the hospital when his own son was probably on his deathbed.

He had thought that going after the Benji kid would scare the piss out of Sherwood. Jack O' Lantern had envisioned something along the lines of Sherwood reaching out to him and then, when the Scorpions threatened the rest of his family, caving in and returning the cash. Sure, the man had been smart enough to set up the roadblock and heartless enough to watch his son shoot Tiny in the leg without flinching, but still, as far as Jack had known, he was just some old man with a scrap yard and a lack of scruples. He had counted on Sherwood not knowing how to handle himself after the shock of seeing his youngest son's face ground into raw hamburger. Now Jack O' Lantern was beginning to realize that the Scorpions were actually the ones who were in over their heads.

They had finally gotten the last of the girls out, but Jack had made it known that until the stolen money was recovered, all members needed to stay at the clubhouse. The prospects, Toadie and Ratface, were all about it; although they still weren't allowed to ride alongside the Scorpions on runs or take part it any decisions, they were excited to feel like they were contributing in some way, even if that way was cracking beers and unclogging the toilet. Legs had bitched a little, his old lady had been giving him hell about never coming home and was threatening to quit her job at the Waffle Hut, but Legs knew how to take an order.

Jack O' Lantern slowly swiveled around on the cracked leather barstool to survey the clubhouse. The prospects were sitting at the long kitchen table, cleaning the club's guns, and Legs was shooting a game of pool against himself. Long John, who couldn't ride but made up for it by spending days at a time in the trailer out in the woods off Highway 18 cooking up halfway decent crystal meth, was buried in a recliner in front of the flat screen watching *Ancient Aliens*. He wasn't too much use to anyone since he had lost his leg in a Ferris Wheel accident after a pint of vodka at the county fair, but it was always good to have someone else around to help hold down the fort if need be.

Jack O' Lantern slumped forward on the stool and let his gut sag out in front of him. He was tired and nervous. Only Slim Jim knew the urgency of their situation. Everyone else was understandably pissed about being robbed of the biggest payload in the history of the club, but they all seemed to have faith that Jack would rectify the situation and they'd have their money back by the end of the week. They didn't know what Sister Tulah was really like and they certainly didn't know about his conversation with her in the church. They didn't know where Jack O' Lantern had gotten the information on the Cannons and didn't care enough to ask. His club thought he was taking care of business as usual, not realizing that in reality he was only a few gasps away from drowning.

The front door of the clubhouse banged open and Jack O' Lantern jerked his head up. It was Slim Jim, scowling. He was supposed to be on watch, so it couldn't be good.

"Hey, Jack, there's somebody at the gate wants to talk to you."

"Did you tell him to screw off?"

Jack O' Lantern tried to crack a smile, but there was no reaction from Slim Jim. He leaned his elbows on the doorframe and stamped his boots.

"Yeah, but he's not budging. When I asked him who he was, all he said was that he was an elder. Whatever that means. Says he's got a message for you. From that crazy church. I figured you might want to talk to him."

Jack O' Lantern motioned for Slim Jim to shut up, but no one else was paying attention. He stood up from the barstool and followed Slim Jim out into the night. The gravel lot in front of the clubhouse was illuminated by motion sensor lights that flooded the ground with a sick yellow glow. Jack O' Lantern could see that there was dark colored SUV parked outside the chain link gate and as he got closer he saw a man get out of the passenger side. He was carrying something at his side. Slim Jim saw it, too, and pulled his .45 out of the back of his jeans. Jack O' Lantern glanced briefly at the gun, but didn't slow down. He slid open the gate but remained inside the gravel lot. The man stepped closer into the light, but stayed on his side of the gate as well.

Jack O' Lantern wasn't exactly sure what he had been expecting, but this certainly wasn't it. The man standing before him was ancient, tall and frail looking with a slightly stooped back. Even in the shadowy light Jack O' Lantern could see the blue veins popping up from the man's gnarled and translucent hands. His cheeks were sunken and his pale lips were so thin that his mouth appeared to disappear inside his narrow face. His skin was covered in age spots and his hair was snow white, the remaining strings of it raked back across his scalp. He looked like he should be sitting at a plastic table at an old folk's home, eating green Jell-O with a bib tucked into his long-sleeved dress shirt, not standing at the property edge of an outlaw motorcycle club. His only disconcerting feature was that he was wearing dark wraparound sunglasses at eleven o'clock at night. The old man was holding what looked like a wooden toolbox with a handle in his right hand. Jack O' Lantern waited for the man to speak, but he only looked straight ahead in silence. Jack O' Lantern put his hands in his pockets and leaned forward.

"Yeah? What do you want?"

The old man didn't speak. Jack O' Lantern wondered if maybe he was blind. Maybe deaf and dumb, too. What the hell was Sister Tulah pulling now? Jack O' Lantern looked over his shoulder, but Slim Jim only shrugged. Jack turned back to the old man and spoke loudly and slowly, as he would to some idiot from a foreign country.

"You got something to tell me? From Tulah? Well, get on with it. I ain't got all night."

The old man opened his mouth and from the angle of light hitting the man's face, Jack O' Lantern thought it resembled a black hole. He was beginning to feel uncomfortable.

"I have a message for you."

"Well, what is it? I just said I ain't got all night."

The old man raised the wooden box at his side and held it out to Jack O' Lantern.

"That's it? That's the message?"

The old man nodded slightly.

"Take it."

Jack O' Lantern reached out and grasped the handle of the box. He could see that it was tightly latched. As soon as Jack had possession of the box, the old man retreated to the SUV and whoever was driving it slammed on the gas. The SUV's tires spun and then the vehicle roared around and flew back down the sandy drive. Jack O' Lantern watched the receding taillights and then looked down at the box he had dropped to his side. Slim Jim came up next to Jack and eyed the box.

"That's a message?"

"I guess so. You sure that guy said he was from the church?"

Slim Jim nodded.

"That's what he said. Last steps to something or another church. What do you think is in there? A bomb?"

Jack O' Lantern rolled his eyes as Slim Jim wrenched the gate closed.

"No, I don't think it's a bomb, dumbass. What do you think, that old guy's a terrorist? I'm surprised he was able to stand up without falling over or pissing himself."

"Then what?"

"I don't know. Why don't you make yourself useful and hold the box so I can figure out how to open it?"

Slim Jim put his gun back in the waistband of his jeans and stretched out his arms to cradle the box while Jack O' Lantern fumbled with the clasp. It wasn't locked, but the metal was rusty and didn't want to open easily. Just as he popped the latch, though, Jack O' Lantern heard it. He understood the sound, but it didn't register with him fast enough. He slid back the top of the box and the snake struck.

"Jesus Christ!"

The serpent's long fangs missed Jack O' Lantern's hand, but he felt the soft scales under the snake's head graze his thumb. He jerked away and Slim Jim dropped the box on the ground.

"What the hell was that? You all right, man?"

Jack O' Lantern jumped back.

"Where is it? Goddamnit, Jimmy, where is it? Is it still in the box?"

They backed away from the wooden box, but they could still hear the unnerving rattle coming from inside.

"I don't know!"

"Well, shit, find out!"

"You find out!"

They heard the rattle again and as they watched, the snake's triangle head slowly inched out of the shadow of the overturned box and began to weave along the ground. Slim Jim was shaking, but Jack O' Lantern was clear headed enough to react.

"Give me your gun."

Slim Jim was transfixed. The snake was almost all the way out of the box and stretching out its long, thick body toward the fence.

"I said, give me your gun!"

Slim Jim didn't move. Jack O' Lantern grabbed the .45 out of the back of Slim Jim's waistband, took aim and fired. He missed the first time and the snake sprung back and began to coil, but the next bullet found its mark. The snake snapped up in the air, but could no longer do any harm. The headless body writhed for a moment more, the rattles still trembling and creating their haunting warning sound, but soon it fell still. Slim Jim couldn't take his eyes off of it. Jack O' Lantern handed the gun back and approached the box. He kicked away what was left of the snake and cautiously nudged the box with the toe of his boot. It appeared empty. He kicked it upright and peered inside. There was nothing else in it save for a folded scrap of paper at the bottom. Jack O' Lantern bent down and retrieved it.

"What is it, Jack?"

Jack O' Lantern shook his head and walked closer to the floodlights so he could see better. He unfolded the paper, turned it right side up and felt a cold hand reach out, take hold of his heart and begin to squeeze. In neat, black letters the paper read:

And these signs shall follow them that believe: in my name shall they cast out devils; they shall speak with new tongues; they shall take up serpents; and if they drink any deadly thing, it shall not hurt them – Mark 16:17-18

Jack O' Lantern read the words over and over and then closed his eyes. If he thought he knew what he was dealing with before, he now realized that he knew nothing.

CHAPTER 12

JUDAH HELD THE edge of the glass against his forehead for a moment and then sighed and gulped the whiskey down. He gingerly set the glass back on the bar and peered down into it. He studied the thin amber film on the bottom of the glass. For a moment he was lucid, aware that he was sitting in a bar, getting as wasted as he could, ignoring phone calls from the woman he cared about, disrespecting the man serving him drinks who he considered a friend, and beginning to embarrass the other patrons around him. He stared at the bottom of the glass and felt his throat close as he remembered the placid face of the doctor in the hospital hallway who had calmly let the words *Benji* and *chance of survival* pass between his lips. But as quickly as it had descended upon him, the moment of clarity evaporated and was replaced by the reckless anger and abandon brought on by a serious desire to get as drunk as possible. Judah picked up the empty glass before him and slammed it down on the bar.

"Another."

Burke hung up the phone at the end of bar and came down to stand in front of Judah. He crossed his knobby arms in front of his thin, bony chest and eyed

Judah. Judah eyed him back. Burke finally sighed and slid Judah's glass away from him.

"I ain't giving you another drink, son, 'til you tell me what's going on."

Judah reached for his cigarettes.

"I told you not to call me son."

"Does it look like I care? Now, you want another drink or not? I can just as soon have your ass thrown out of here. Free up some space."

"You gonna try to move me, old man?"

Burke picked up the glass and started to set it in the sink behind the bar. Judah lit a cigarette and waved the smoke out of his eyes.

"All right, all right. Give me the drink and I'll spill my guts. I'll yank my bleeding heart out and smack it down right here on the bar in front of you. Whatever you want. I don't give a shit no more."

Burke set the glass back in front of Judah and filled it with half a shot of whiskey. Judah watched the liquor dribbling into the glass and raised his eyebrows when Burke jerked the bottle up.

"Start talking, Judey-boy."

Judah squinted at the whiskey. He set his cigarette in the ashtray and wrapped his fingers around the glass.

"What is this? An interrogation or something? Are we bargaining here? You been watching too many spy movies."

"Believe it or not, I'm looking out for you. I've known you since you were in short pants. Hell, I knew your mother when she was in the hospital giving birth to you."

"Yeah, yeah. You told me the story a million times, Burke. And Sherwood was too drunk to be there. And you were the one who came in and saved the day."

Judah raised the glass to his lips, but didn't drink from it.

"Were you banging her, too? Probably shoulda been. Least she woulda got something outta life 'sides wasting away to disease and getting nothing but grief from Sherwood."

"You watch your mouth."

Judah grinned devilishly and downed the whiskey. He set the glass on the bar, but Burke made no move to refill it.

"You know, Judah, you sure turned into an asshole. I ain't seen you since they locked you up and now I really wish they'd kept you there."

"I'm sorry, I'm sorry."

Judah tried to reach across the bar to grab Burke's arm, but only succeeded in knocking over the ashtray. He tipped it back upright and tried to pick up the wrong end of his cigarette from the bar. He jerked his fingers back and rubbed them together. Burked watched him and shook his head.

"Man, something's got you messed up tonight."

Judah looked down at the polished wood of the bar and then up at the row of liquor bottles along the wall. He ran his hand over his face and exhaled loudly.

"I'm sorry for what I said about you and my mama. But damnit, Burke, Benji's in the hospital."

Burke leaned over the bar.

"What?"

"Something bad happened to him. Something real bad. They don't even know if he's gonna make it. Shit, this is Benji we're talking about. Benji. And we did it. We did it, Burke. Benji didn't do nothing. We did it. And he's lying in some hospital bed now 'cause of what we did."

"Whoa, hold on there, son."

"No, it's the truth. And I'm just as guilty as they are. I went along with it, again. I'm a stupid, stupid, cowardly worm who can't even think for himself."

Burke smacked the bar in front of Judah and leaned even closer.

"Watch what you're saying. You're drunk, you don't know what you're saying."

Burke jerked the whiskey bottle out of the well and filled the empty glass in front of Judah to the brim. Judah stared at it blankly. He shook his head and blinked a few times. Burke started to walk back down to the end of the bar.

"Drink that and get yourself together."

Judah eyed the glass. He shouted down to the end of the bar.

"I thought you wanted me to talk about it."

Burke had the phone in his hand and was punching in numbers. He cradled the receiver between his ear and shoulder and turned around to Judah.

"And I thought you wanted another drink. I just remembered that I gotta call Alma 'bout something. Give me a second."

Burke turned to face the wall and Judah looked at the glass in front of him. He closed one eye and squinted. The blurry double of two glasses focused into one. He reached for his cigarettes, but only rested his hand on the pack. The bar was beginning to spin around him. Judah looked over to his right and couldn't tell if the person sitting on the next barstool over was male or female. He let his eyes drift up the opposite wall, glazing over the neon Miller High Life sign. The blazing colors were a blur and made his head hurt. Judah gave up trying to orient himself and returned to staring at the full whiskey glass in front of him. Soon Burke appeared behind the glass and Judah raised his eyes.

"Everything okay with your wife?"

"Yeah, sure. Now you're not drinking or what?"

Judah squinted at Burke to keep the bartender's face in focus and then dropped his gaze back to the glass. He pushed it away, slopping half of the liquid onto the bar. It mixed into a rancid puddle with the cigarette ashes.

"It wasn't his fault, Burke. He didn't do nothing. Just being Benji. Same old Benji."

Burke began to mop up the mess on the bar with a ripped piece of towel.

"I think you need to stop talking, Judah."

Judah ignored him and began fumbling in his pocket for his wallet.

"Just same as always. Never doing nothing wrong. Just Benji. But it wasn't his fault. It was our fault. It was Sherwood's fault. That damn, stupid, motorcycle…"

Burke lurched across the bar and grabbed Judah's forearm with surprising strength. He jerked Judah close to him and whispered.

"Shut up, Judah. Just shut up."

Judah seemed to think about this for a moment and then threw back his head and laughed. Burke released him and Judah leaned back and slapped his palms on the bar. Burke continued to wipe the bar, furiously now, and kept his voice down.

"What's so funny?"

Judah slid off the barstool and steadied himself.

"You didn't just call Alma."

Burke tossed the rag into the sink and crossed his arms in front of himself.

"I don't know what you're talking about."

Judah laughed again. He clumsily grabbed his cigarettes and cellphone from the bar and stuffed them into his pockets.

"Don't know why I'm surprised. How much time you think I got 'fore they get here?"

The bartender raised his hands up in front of himself defensively.

"I don't know what you mean."

Judah reeled away from the bar.

"It's okay, old man. I'll try to make it to the parking lot. Spare you the scene."

Burke opened his mouth as if to say something else, but clamped it shut when the back door to the bar swung open. Judah turned around, stumbled, caught himself and then smiled grimly. He heard Burke mumble that he was sorry, but didn't look back as he walked out to meet Levi and Sherwood, waiting for him.

No one would meet Ramey's eyes when she walked into The Ace in the Hole. She let the heavy front door slam shut behind her, and although many heads were raised at the noise, the patrons at the bar and the surrounding tables quickly turned back to their intense contemplation of warm beers and scratched wood surfaces. Ramey adjusted the strap of her purse higher up on her shoulder and crossed her arms. She stood there a moment longer, beginning to understand what the silence and averted gazes meant, and then called out to Burke across the hushed bar.

"You want to tell me where he is or do I gotta raise hell to find out on my own?"

Burke glanced up briefly from the pint glass he was vigorously polishing. His voice was clipped.

"You need to go home, Ramey."

Ramey pursed her lips, but didn't move. She looked around the bar again, almost every face a familiar one, but realized no one was going to help. The jukebox had quit playing a little while back and the television in the corner was muted. The only sounds in the bar were the scuffling of nervous boots against the cement floor and the careful clink of glasses and beer bottles being carefully set down. The quiet was suffocating, but Ramey was prepared to wait it out.

"I mean it, Ramey. I ain't kidding. This ain't no place for you tonight. Just go on home."

Ramey continued to watch the hunkered old men and washed out winos at the tables.

"Where is he?"

For a brief moment she caught two older men, cousins who she regularly fed fried chicken and biscuits at Buddy's, look up at one another and then glance involuntarily toward the back door. That was all she needed. She gripped the strap of her purse in one hand and strode toward the back of the bar, ignoring

Burke's warning.

"I ain't gonna tell you again, Ramey. Do everyone a favor and just go on home."

She didn't look back at him.

"Shut up."

Ramey tried to push on the narrow emergency exit door, but it was stuck. Without hesitating, she kicked hard at the bottom of it and stepped out into the dark. She could hear them before she could see them and she bolted around Sherwood's parked pickup truck. She gasped and leaned on the still warm metal hood to keep from slipping in the dirt.

Sherwood stood a few feet away in the shadows from the orange streetlight, arms crossed, head tilted down and eyes expressionless as he watched one of his sons beat the shit out of the other.

He acknowledged Ramey's presence without even looking up at her.

"Go back inside."

The shock that had taken Ramey's breath away for a moment was fleeting and she began to yell. Levi took a step back when he heard Ramey's voice. Unlike Sherwood, whose face was a mask of business-like calm, Levi was sweaty and his mouth was twisted in a gruesome sneer. His eyes were blazing when he set them on Ramey, but he controlled himself for a moment. He also kept himself squarely in between Ramey and Judah, who was still curled up on the ground, clutching his stomach. Ramey couldn't see too much of what they had done to him, but she could tell that there was blood smeared across the side of his face and along the torn sleeve of his shirt. His eyes were open, but he was staring straight ahead. He didn't look at her. Levi glanced from Ramey to Sherwood, questioning what to do. Ramey was trembling, her eyes wide with fear and outrage, but she remained where she was. Sherwood sighed at her in disgust.

"I gotta tell you again? Go on back inside. This ain't your concern. This is family business."

Ramey ripped her eyes away from Judah's bleeding face and confronted Sherwood.

"Bullshit."

Levi took a step toward her, but Judah raised his head a few inches from the ground and spoke to her first.

"Stay out of it, Ramey."

She kept her eyes on Sherwood.

"No."

Judah swallowed thickly, but kept his head up.

"Go back inside."

"No."

Sherwood's eyes were twinkling and his lips curled up into a smirk. Judah wheezed and then spat out toward Ramey.

"For Christ's sake, get your dumb ass back inside. What's wrong with you?"

Sherwood threw back his head and laughed.

"That's great. A lover's quarrel to add insult to injury. That's just classic."

He nodded and Levi swung around and kicked Judah hard in the gut. Levi grasped Judah by the shoulders, as if lifting him up for another punch to the face, and Ramey didn't have to think about it twice. Both Sherwood and Levi had their eyes on Judah and she reached into her purse and wrapped her fingers around the gun. She yanked it free and pointed it toward the back of Levi's head. Her finger was resting on the 9mm's trigger.

"I ain't gonna raise my voice this time. Back off."

Levi glanced at her over his shoulder and saw the gun glinting in the streetlight. He dropped Judah in the dirt and turned around to face her. Sherwood didn't flinch.

"You got some balls, girly, but we both know you ain't shooting nobody."

She kept her arm stretched out and thumbed the safety off. The gun barrel was aimed right between Levi's eyes and she didn't waver.

"You want to keep going and find out?"

Sherwood laughed at her again, but motioned for Levi to step away. He backed up and wiped his bloody knuckles on the thighs of his jeans. Sherwood moved toward Judah and Ramey switched her aim to him, but Sherwood raised his hands up in defense.

"Easy there, darlin', I just got a last word for my son."

Sherwood walked over to Judah and leaned down. Judah kept his eyes on the dirt.

"You better take my meaning to heart, boy."

Sherwood stood up and walked past Ramey. She had lowered the gun, but still had her finger on the trigger. He came within an inch of grazing her shoulder and she tensed up.

"And you better start minding your own business, missy thing. You ain't no Cannon. And your daddy and me being friends back when he was still around or my son tapping your ass don't make you part of the family neither. You remember that next time it crosses your mind to point a firearm in my direction."

Ramey clenched her jaw, but didn't respond. She waited until Sherwood and Levi had gotten into the truck and driven off before she exhaled. She tucked the gun back into her purse and let the bag drop to the ground.

She crouched down beside Judah and touched the torn sleeve of his shirt. The smell of sweat, blood and alcohol was nauseating, but it didn't appear that Judah had any mind to get up on his own, so she leaned down further and slid an arm underneath his head. She wrapped her other arm around his waist and hoisted him into a sitting position. His head was loose on his neck and Ramey wasn't sure if it was the beating or the fact that he was piss drunk that was making him so difficult. She braced herself and finally managed to pull him to his feet. Judah swayed and then stumbled against her, blood from the cut over his eye smearing against her bare shoulder. She gripped him again and forced him to stand up straight. He wouldn't look at her, so she grabbed his chin and jerked his face toward her. She made him look her in the eye.

"You ever call me a dumbass again and I'll shoot you first. Got it?"

Judah's blank expression didn't change, but he slowly nodded his head. He swayed again and almost slipped back to the ground. Ramey groaned and picked up her bag.

"Come on."

She slung his arm around her neck and led him away.

CHAPTER 13

THE NAILS OF freezing cold water driving against Judah's face were a welcome contrast to the fevered headache and nausea he had awoken to. Judah opened his mouth and let the drops of water hit against his sticky teeth and dry tongue. He hadn't looked in the mirror before stumbling half-blind into the shower, but as he began to pay attention to his senses underneath the muting blanket of his hangover, he could feel the sting above his left eye. He pressed his hand to his forehead and looked down at the thin tendrils of watery blood on his fingers. He touched his skin again and winced as he probed the cut. Judah slowly turned the temperature in the shower up and then inspected the rest of his body. Mottled bruises wrapped around his torso and decorated his right arm and shoulder. He inhaled and felt an intense stab of pain along his right side. He knew that at least one rib must be cracked. The pain brought another wave of nausea crashing into him and he steadied himself against the plastic shower wall. He closed his eyes and let the warm water envelop him. He didn't want to open his eyes again.

Eventually, the water began to run cold and Judah knew he had to face whatever was waiting for him outside the bathroom door. He had woken up in an empty bed and had not even ventured to see if Ramey was still in the apartment before he had quickly disentangled himself from the sweat soaked sheets and staggered toward the relief of the shower. Judah stepped out of the low plastic tub and wrapped a damp towel around his waist. He ran his hands through his wet hair a few times but still didn't look in the mirror. Judah paused for a moment with his hand on the door handle, but knew that whatever he was going to have to deal with, he deserved.

Ramey was sitting at the kitchen table, a cigarette in one hand and a cup of coffee in the other. He didn't look at her and she didn't look at him as he walked around her to the coffee maker on the kitchen counter and slowly poured himself a cup. He turned around and looked at the back of Ramey's head. It was tilted slightly up as she kept her gaze focused outside the kitchen window, and he could tell that her jaw was clenched. He knew exactly what expression she had on her face. He knew her. She was pissed. She was volatile. She was going to be uncompromising. He gripped the coffee cup in both hands and sat down across from her.

She stared at him, her hazel eyes unflinching, her mouth set in a tight line. Judah's gaze fluttered back and forth between the stove behind her and the ceramic *Merry Christmas from Sunny Florida!* mug in her hand. He felt the nausea rise again, but did his best to ignore it. Finally, he took a deep breath and looked her in the eyes. He needed to get this over with.

"I don't remember exactly what I said to you last night, but I do remember you saying something about shooting me if I ever called you a dumbass again."

Ramey flicked her cigarette between her fingers, scattering ashes into the brown glass ashtray between them.

"Something like that."

"I'm sorry."

Ramey stared at him hard for a moment and he held her scrutinizing gaze.

She blew a final stream of smoke out of the corner of her mouth and crushed out the cigarette.

"I know. And you're bleeding again. That cut must've opened back up. Hold on."

Ramey stood up from the table and returned with a tin first aid kit from the bathroom cabinet. Without saying anything further, she began pouring peroxide and dabbing at his forehead with a cotton ball. Judah grimaced when she pinched the skin and pressed a butterfly bandage over the wound, but busied himself with trying to light one of her cigarettes while she worked on his face. Ramey took his chin in her hand, turning his face back forth a couple of times, and seemed satisfied.

"I don't think you'll need stiches."

"Good."

Ramey sat back across from him and stretched her arms out, palms upward.

"You want to tell me what happened?"

Judah looked down at her palms but didn't place his hands on hers. She drew back and wrapped her fingers around her coffee cup instead. Judah looked away from her. The sky outside the kitchen window resembled granite, the clouds flat and oppressive. He knew that if he were to step outside, the humidity would cling to him like a second skin. He turned back to Ramey. She was still staring at him intently and he conceded.

"Benji."

Ramey nodded.

"I heard. Flipped his truck or something coming home from Limey's Monday night."

"Is that what they're saying?"

"I figured if you were anything like you used to be, you'd be neck deep in a bottle of whiskey, so I came looking for you. I guess Sherwood and Levi got to you first."

Judah examined the burning cherry at the end of his cigarette.

"Yeah."

They sat in silence. Judah finished his smoke and ground it out. With nothing else to occupy their hands, they both gripped their coffee cups as if their lives depended on it. Ramey finally made a move.

"So, then. You want to tell me what happened for real?"

He stared at the grains of wood running through the surface of the table.

"Not really, no. It don't matter."

Judah squeezed his eyes shut. Deep down, he considered himself to be a righteous man, a man who would go to the death to defend what he believed in, but he was also a man whose family had defined his moral code and convinced him of its legitimacy. He had stayed with Cassie, moved to Colston and been a father to Stella, because his Aunt Imogene had told him that men were supposed to do so. You didn't run out on a woman carrying your child, even if she was running around with half the town in front of you. He had refused to give up Sherwood and Levi to the judge because Sherwood had told him that blood came before all else. Before God, before the law, before the well-being of anyone outside of the Cannon clan. You never turned your back on your family and you never dared to go against them. Judah had spent his life being swayed by one family member or another and had little time to work out his own system of judgment. And Ramey knew this.

"So you ain't never gonna open your eyes, huh? You ain't never gonna believe that you can think for yourself, that you could maybe have some ideas running contrary to Sherwood's?"

Ramey pushed back her chair, scraping the legs against the scratched linoleum floor. She stalked across the kitchen and slammed her cup down into the sink. Judah jerked his head up. She leaned back against the counter, locking her elbows, and gripped the edge. Judah watched her every move.

"Look. I've known you Cannon boys my whole life. I grew up with my daddy and your daddy sitting in one or the other of our living rooms cooking up God only knows what illegal, half-assed scheme to make a buck. I grew up with Levi teasing me out of his pickup truck on my way to the bus stop and Benji being all moony-eyed over me wearing a short skirt and you being my best friend in this whole messed up world."

"Ramey."

"Shut it. I ain't finished."

Judah ducked his chin a little, but still kept his eyes locked with hers.

"Now, I don't claim to know what's going on between you and me. But I think it's something good. Maybe something that was always meant to be or maybe we just got lucky. But I think it's good. You believe that, too?"

Judah nodded. He could see that Ramey's knuckles were white. She took a deep breath and looked away; when she spoke again, her voice cracked.

"Then there's only one way this works, you hear? I don't know what the hell you got yourself into this time, but I can imagine. And I'm gonna tell you right now, I ain't gonna be like Susan. With her doublewide and her pile of fat Chihuahuas and her Home Shopping Channel. Strolling around the grocery store with her coupon binder like none of what's going on with Levi exists. Like it's all one more show on satellite TV."

Ramey paused and fixed Judah with a dead level stare.

"So either you tell me everything. Or you tell me nothing and get the hell outta my house."

Judah rubbed his hand along his stubbled cheek and winced.

"Ramey, it's complicated."

She set her jaw.

"No. It ain't."

Judah narrowed his eyes at her. She was giving him an ultimatum, but one that would ultimately set him free. He knew it and she knew it and it was up to him to decide what to do about it. They glared at one another until Judah finally swallowed and gave in. He whispered.

"As you please."

Ramey let go of the edge of the counter. She slid back into her seat and folded her arms across her chest. Judah picked up the pack of cigarettes between them and tapped the corner on the table top.

"Saturday night. When I left with Sherwood and Levi and came back Sunday morning talking about money."

Ramey nodded.

"It was a holdup. Typical Sherwood style. Found somebody else with a score and decided it was his. The take was a hundred and fifty thousand. The mark was a motorcycle club outside of Kentsville. The Scorpions. We ambushed them on the road and took it all. Everything. I wasn't kidding about that fifty grand."

"No shit."

Judah leaned back in his chair.

"But it was stupid to think it wouldn't come back on us. Benji didn't flip a vehicle. He got dragged behind one. Rooter from Limey's told me he saw the skid mark where they dumped him. It was bike tread. Those assholes went after Benji as payback for us taking their money."

Ramey raised her hand to her mouth.

"Oh my God."

Judah tossed the pack of cigarettes down and then spun it around on the table.

"Yeah."

Ramey blinked a few times as she began putting it all together.

"And what does Sherriff Dodger think happened?"

Judah laughed.

"Dodger thinks whatever Sherwood's pocket wants him to think. You remember how this all works."

"Well then. What about last night?"

"I guess Sherwood was worried I was gonna start talking. Must have Burke up at The Ace on his payroll and he called in when I started running my mouth. I'm so damn stupid I don't even know how I survive sometimes."

Ramey leaned back in her chair and cocked her head.

"And the beating in the parking lot?"

Judah grinned bitterly.

"Just a warning. To keep my mouth shut, for one."

Judah took a deep breath and then exhaled quickly. He winced from the pain in his chest.

"And then two, not to have no stupid ideas about wanting to go after the Scorpions."

"Seriously?"

Judah stared at the table in front of him.

"They don't want to do nothing about it. Nothing. Lay low. Wait it out. Think about the cash at stake."

Judah slapped his palm down on the table.

"Think about the cash? What about thinking of Benji lying in a hospital bed with half his face missing? What about that? They knocked him out, tied him up and dragged him down the highway. Benji, for Christ's sake. Wasn't even there when we took the money. Didn't even know about it. Didn't know a damn thing. And now he's in the hospital and I'm just waiting for a phone call to tell me that he's dead. And Sherwood wants me to shut up and think about the cash."

Ramey nodded slowly. She waited, but it was clear that Judah had said his piece. He was sitting with his back hunched against the chair, staring intently down at the table before him. She reached over and this time Judah took her hand.

"What do you want to do about it?"

Judah shook his head.

"I want blood. I want to make them pay. And I want them to know that they can't do nothing like this ever again. Because if we let them, they will. Then it'll be someone else. It could be you. And I can't let that happen. I can't let this happen again."

Ramey squeezed Judah's hand and he looked up at her. Her mouth was twisted in worry, but her eyes were hard and determined.

"And you're gonna go against Sherwood?"

Judah released her hand and slumped back in his chair. He considered her question for a moment and all the weight that it carried, all that it meant. He made a decision.

"I'm gonna try."

CHAPTER 14

"TAKE ONE MORE step and I'll blow your brains all over the windshield of that clown car you got the balls to park in my driveway."

Judah paused halfway out of the passenger side of the Cutlass and slowly raised his hands. He looked over his shoulder at Ramey, who shook her head and killed the engine. She wrenched open the driver side door and got out.

"You stupid or something? I ain't kidding, and I ain't averse to shooting no woman neither, so don't think you can use her as some kinda decoy to…"

"Relax, Hiram, it's me. It's Ramey."

The old man with the long, stringy gray hair, matching mustache and red Hawaiian print shirt didn't lower the M16 he had trained on Judah's head, but his bloodshot eyes shifted over to Ramey. Judah's leg was starting to cramp from the half-standing position he was frozen in and he hoped Ramey knew what she was doing.

During the long drive up to Union County, Ramey had tried to explain Hiram to Judah. It had been Ramey's idea to visit him and, realizing that they had no better leads, Judah had agreed. Hiram was a second cousin, or something along those lines, Ramey wasn't entirely sure, of Lyle's. She hadn't offered more when he had pressed her about the connection and Judah had left it at that.

The man shifted the rifle on his bony shoulder and twitched his head to the left.

"Ramey? Ramey. Not sure it's ringing a bell, sister."

Ramey walked around the front of the car, her palms lowered and her steps light, as if approaching a wounded animal with a sharp set of teeth.

"I met you at a cookout a few years back. Over in Silas. Out on Dilly West's spread. We played a few mean games of horseshoes."

Hiram seemed to relax his grip on the barrel of the rifle slightly, but his mouth was still puckered in a suspicious grimace.

"We kin or something?"

Judah slowly stood up straighter, trying not to make any sudden moves. His eyes darted back and forth between Ramey's slender back and the barrel of the illegal automatic assault rifle that was pointed straight at her chest. He was beginning to think this wasn't such a good idea. Ramey had mentioned that Hiram could come off as crazy, but not bat-shit crazy. His .45 was underneath the passenger seat of the Cutlass and he tried to calculate how quickly he could swivel around and grab it. Ramey just kept walking toward Hiram, steadily.

"No. I was there with Lyle. Lyle Dryven. I met you a few times in his company. That's how I knew where to find you. He mentioned visiting you out here once."

Hiram narrowed his eyes.

"You Lyle's old lady?"

"Lyle's dead."

Ramey said it matter-of-factly, without a trace of emotion in her voice. Judah reckoned he could have his gun in his hand in less than five seconds. He bent his knees, ready to spring.

Hiram gave Ramey one last good, hard look and then quickly pointed the rifle at the ground.

"Guess that's why you're with this winner here, huh?"

Judah was too relieved to respond to Hiram's sarcastic tone. Hiram motioned over his shoulder for them to follow him and Judah and Ramey began trudging through the thick, tangled grass to the singlewide set back away from the rocky driveway in the middle of the empty, cleared piece of land. Judah caught up with Ramey and took her hand. He squeezed it and whispered.

"Next time you decide to scare the shit outta me, think maybe you could give me a heads up?"

Ramey raised her eyebrows and let go of his hand.

"I wouldn't be scaring the shit outta you, then, would I? Come on, we need to keep up. This field's supposed to be full of booby-traps and we need to follow in Hiram's footsteps or we could get blown up. Or skewered."

Apparently, Hiram's mood was apt to change on a dime, because now Hiram was in tour guide mode, listing off the various traps and security systems he had installed across the ten-acre field. He wasn't exactly pointing them out, though, so Judah followed Ramey's advice and watched Hiram's tracks closely.

Hiram gestured vaguely around himself as he spoke, ticking off security measures that ranged from the latest high tech military surveillance equipment to homemade setups made out of trip wire and sharpened sticks.

"Some guy tries to be sneaky and come across that ditch over yonder, he trips a line and wham, a pallet rises up and he's got so many spikes sticking outta him he looks like your Grandma Effie's pin cushion. Then, he tries coming at me from the south, I got a damn near minefield set up in one quadrant. Set off by lasers. He crosses past one of those beams and boom, I've got enough C-4 buried that when the smoke clears there won't be pieces of him left big enough to find."

Judah glanced around the open field, surrounded by pine forest on all sides.

"Who exactly are you worried about trespassing?"

Hiram stopped short and whipped around to face Judah.

"You serious, brother? You one of them deluded zombie citizens walking around in an unsuspecting daze believing every lie the government spoon feeds you? Lulling you to sleep so they can take away your rights, your freedom, your very humanity?"

"Uh?"

Judah looked to Ramey, but she just widened her eyes and shook her head in warning. Hiram stepped closer to Judah and waved his arms over his head.

"The Man, brother! That's who I'm worried about. The Man! But that's okay. All you dumb sheep will just walk blindly over the cliff and I'll be the one sitting here in my fortress, with all the water and food and weapons I need. I'll be surviving, brother. And you'll be wishing you had the foresight your friend Hiram here had."

Judah looked over Hiram's shoulder at the singlewide they had almost reached. The windows were painted black and a dozen spikey antennas were perched at odd angles across the narrow roof. Strings of razor wire wound their way around the aluminum siding, reminding Judah of a strange sea urchin he had once seen in a tank at Marineland. Judah wasn't sure what good the wire was going to do in case of an attack, but he was pretty sure Ramey was going to kick him in the shins if he asked any more questions, so he acquiesced and nodded to Hiram.

"Well, it's sure as hell that no one's getting through here if you ain't want 'em too."

Hiram hefted the assault rifle over his shoulder and nodded back.

"Damn right!"

Hiram turned on his heel and finished leading the way to his fortress.

Once inside, Judah and Ramey squeezed next to a pile of gas masks and hoses and sat on the edge of a moldy pullout couch. While Hiram was banging around in the refrigerator hunting for beers, Judah tried to get his bearings in the cluttered trailer. If he had thought the trek across the field was odd, he was completely unprepared for some of the sights accosting him in the claustrophobic singlewide.

The guns leaning in every corner weren't unusual. This was the country after all. Most every house, trailer, barn and garage had at least one rifle hanging on the wall over the TV or stuffed behind the couch. Judah's Aunt Imogene, who had stepped in and helped raise the Cannon boys after Rebecca's death, always slept with a loaded shotgun on the dusty floor underneath her bed. Judah remembered getting the tar whipped out of him by Imogene when he dragged it out once to inspect it. She hadn't been mad that he was playing with guns so much as she was concerned he would have forgotten to put it back.

Judah had expected the piles of survival gear as well. Hiram had stacks of canned goods and MREs piled up underneath the blackened windows in addition to the water filtration kits, flashlights, gutted radios, computer parts and twisted lengths of wire. Three alien-looking contraptions that Judah thought might be Geiger counters were carefully laid out on top of a waist-high pile of instruction manuals from the 1970s.

What Judah wasn't prepared for, however, were the stuffed squirrels. Every which way he looked tiny glass eyes were staring back at him. The trailer was filled with stuffed squirrels in various poses and costumes. One, balanced on top of the television set in the corner, was dressed as a crusader; it held a tiny banner emblazoned with a red and gold cross. Another squirrel on one of the shelves of a teetering bookcase wore a Civil War uniform, rebel gray of course, and another was dressed as a World War II paratrooper. A tiny deflated parachute was strung out behind it on the mounting board. The most unsettling of all was the animal posed in the middle of the coffee table amid scattered stacks of *Soldier of Fortune* magazines. The squirrel seemed to be staring directly at Judah, a bandolier slung across its chest and a tiny AR glued to its outstretched paws. The squirrel's head had been fixed so that its jaws were pried open with its tiny yellow teeth on display. The rodent appeared to be in a rage, an angry squirrel warrior in the process of gunning down its enemies. Judah couldn't look away.

"I see you like my collection, huh?"

Hiram slammed the refrigerator door and secured it closed with a bungee cord around the handle. He came stomping out of the kitchen with three cans of Schlitz under his arm.

"That one you're looking at there's my favorite."

Hiram pointed to the squirrel on the coffee table as he handed around the beers.

"I call him Rambo."

Judah cracked open his beer.

"Oh."

Hiram settled into the ragged armchair across from Judah and Ramey.

"Yeah, I used to have dogs. Raised coonhounds nearly all my life, but with the end times approaching it seemed like they was just too much trouble. I didn't want to be starving and have to resort to eating Bo or Sam. Didn't want to be tempted. So I set 'em loose and started on these little guys. They make a helluva lot better pets and help to pass the time, too. I learned how to sew their outfits on YouTube."

Judah couldn't even begin to think of an appropriate response, so he was relieved when Ramey set her unopened beer on the coffee table and took control of the conversation.

"As much as we admire your handiwork, that's not why we came out here."

Hiram crossed his leg over his knee and leaned back in his chair.

"Suppose maybe we get to the point and you tell me what you want, then."

Judah was unnerved by the ease with which this man went from casual to confrontational, but Ramey didn't flinch. She clasped her hands on her knees and leaned closer.

"We need information on a motorcycle club that runs up near Kentsville."

Hiram slurped his beer but didn't respond.

"Lyle mentioned a few times that you used to ride with the Jackals over in this part of the county. I figured you must have known all the clubs in the area."

"Maybe."

"And we need to know more about this one. It's important. Anything you could tell us about them would be appreciated."

Hiram raised his eyebrows.

"You drove all the way out here to ask me that? You telling me there ain't nobody up in your neck of the woods you coulda asked? It wouldn't of taken you too long to find somebody knows the Scorpions."

Judah and Ramey exchanged glances.

"It's important and it's also a tricky situation."

Hiram grinned sourly.

"Meaning you ain't want nobody to know you're looking into 'em. That about right?"

Ramey nodded.

"That's about right."

"And why exactly you want to know 'bout them? Your friend here looking to grow a pair and try to prospect?"

Judah grit his teeth and leaned forward.

"If I were you, I'd keep my mind off my balls. And this club we're talking about almost killed my little brother. Strung him up and dragged him down the highway. He's in the hospital and we don't know if he's gonna wake up. That answer your question?"

Ramey touched her hand to Judah's knee but kept her eyes on Hiram. Judah crossed his arms and leaned back into the mashed couch cushions.

"He's telling the truth, Hiram. We don't want to involve you in any way. But this kid who got hurt is the last person on earth who deserved it. We just need any information you can give us and then we'll be gone."

Hiram tapped the lip of his beer can against his brown teeth and squinted his eyes at Ramey. They sat in tense silence for a moment until Hiram abruptly slammed his can down onto the coffee table. Beer flew over the pile of magazines and Rambo wobbled slightly.

"Fine. I'll help you out. But it's not 'cause I like the look of this loser sitting over here."

Judah started to lean forward, but Ramey elbowed him sharply.

"It's 'cause I don't like the new guy they got running that club. Pansy ass kid who probably has to whistle when he takes a shit so he knows which end to use."

"So the Scorpions' leader ain't as tough as he might seem?"

Hiram scoffed.

"Jack, they call him Jack O' Lantern or something stupid like that. I guess 'cause he's got a big old pumpkin head. He's not exactly a bad guy, I don't think, just ain't his uncle Oren. Back when I was riding with the Jackals, 'fore they got torn apart by the Mongols and I had the good sense to get out while I could, the two clubs used to meet up for runs. The Scorpions weren't never no big club. I don't think they even had more than the one charter outside of Kentsville, but Oren, man, he was something else."

Judah drummed his fingers on his knee.

"So, he used to be the Scorpions' president?"

"He used to be mightier than Thor."

Hiram laughed.

"He had a reputation for cold-heartedness that could freeze the tits off a witch at midnight. Chill guy, usually. Funny as hell when he was wasted. He'd get lit to the gills and then start walking up and down a line of bikes, pissing on 'em. Just pissing. Said he was christening 'em. Like he was the pope or something. But when it came to getting something done he was all business."

Hiram picked at the loose threads on the arm of his chair.

"Oren had no qualms about offing somebody got in his way. Even one of his own members. Bikers ain't generous, but we take care of our own. Oren didn't give a shit. Take 'em to The Pit, he'd say, and that was that."

Ramey cocked her head.

"The Pit?"

"This place not too far from their clubhouse. Weren't really a pit, but that's just what the Scorpions called it. It was just this old abandoned limestone quarry at the end of Devil's Beggar Road. Maybe that's why they called it The Pit. Some kinda Biblical nonsense. The Scorpions always got off on being dramatic. But they all knew that if they were taken to The Pit, it was lights out forever."

Hiram had a faraway look in his eyes, so Ramey tried to snap him back to attention.

"So, this new guy, you said his name was Jack O' Lantern, he ain't as tough as Oren was?"

Hiram scratched the side of his nose with a long, brittle fingernail.

"Nah. I think he done his best to fill Oren's shoes once Oren met his maker, but he just don't got that ruthless spirit, I don't think. I only knew him when he was younger, mind you, 'fore he became president, but that's just my opinion."

"You know anything about the Scorpions now?"

"I heard some rumors 'fore I moved out here. Tried to distance myself from that world once I realized I had to start preparing for the great war headed our way. But I remember somebody saying something about the Scorpions' numbers being down. Back in the day, they were like any other club, riding high and tight, four abreast, ten deep, tearing down the highway. But last I heard they were half that. Barely an enterprise no more. With that kind of manpower, they probably just sell drugs to junkie teenagers to make enough money to buy beer. Oren could get you any gun you wanted in a week's time, a whole shipment without even blinking an eye. Jack can probably get you a gram of crystal in about the same time. Pathetic, if you ask me, what kids are into these days."

Ramey shifted on the couch next to Judah and met his eyes, questioning. Judah cleared his throat.

"You think the clubhouse is still in the same location as before?"

"Don't see why they woulda changed it. It was in the perfect spot, the only place at the end of this long drive off Highway 225. Lightning Strike Road, I think. See what I mean about a flare for the dramatic? They loved it. But you couldn't even see the clubhouse from the highway and it was easy to control access to. I never actually been out there, but the Scorpions were always bragging about it like they cleared the road themselves or something."

Judah nodded and rubbed his hands up and down the thighs of his jeans. He was anxious to get the hell out of the creepy trailer, anxious to get started on the next step of the plan.

"Anything else you think we should know?"

Hiram furrowed his brows.

"No. Now, I don't know what you two got planned, and, honestly, I don't want to know and I don't care. I got enough to worry 'bout trying to make sure I survive what's coming. Anybody asks on either of our ends and this conversation ain't never happened."

Judah stood up.

"Fair enough."

Hiram stood as well and parted his lips in an ugly smile.

"But if you're planning on doing anything like what I think you might, I gotta ask if you're packing enough heat."

"Meaning?"

"Meaning if you got the cash, I got a storage shed out back that would put the National Guard's armory to shame."

Ramey stood up next to Judah and put her arm around his waist. Judah couldn't read the expression on her face, but her next words gave him a strange thrill.

"All right, Hiram. Let's see what you got."

CHAPTER 15

JACK O' LANTERN banged the gavel down on the long plastic table. Back in Oren's day, the table for church was a massive slab of oak that reportedly had been hewn and carved by Oren's great-grandfather back when Bradford County was just being settled. It had been a beautiful piece, lacquered to a high shine and nearly indestructible. When Oren had died, his wife had been forced to sell the table to pay off his creditors who had begun firing shots into her kitchen at night. The table was sold, the harassment eventually stopped, but Jack never forgave his Aunt Belinda for selling off the most enduring piece of the Scorpions' history. Now they were left with dwindling numbers and a table that could be folded up and jammed behind a couch.

Jack slammed the wooden gavel down once more and the flimsy table wobbled. It got everyone's attention, though, and the men sitting before Jack turned away from their side conversations and focused on him. Because their numbers were so small and their decisions so few, church had become a rare occurrence. Usually, Jack O' Lantern only conferred with Slim Jim, on occasion with Legs or Long John, and then told everyone else what to do. But Jack knew the situation with the Cannons was different. Something had to be done, and he needed everyone on board.

Jack O' Lantern surveyed the table. The men sat in their metal folding chairs and waited for Jack to speak. Slim Jim was at his left, hands flat out on the table, the puckered scars across his knuckles standing out pink against his taunt, sallow skin. Legs and Tiny sat opposite him, both fidgeting with lit cigarettes, and Long John occupied the seat to Jack's right. Long John sat stolidly on his chair, his prosthetic leg straight out in front of him and his hands resting on his thick thighs. Toadie and Ratface weren't allowed to sit at the table, but they were in the room, leaning up against the wall with arms crossed in posed nonchalance. Jack O' Lantern rested the gavel in front of the large glass ashtray in the middle of the table and grunted.

"This everyone?"

A sarcastic smile came to Slim Jim's face.

"Yep."

"What about Grundy and Junior?"

"Still out in Phoenix, checking on their cousin in rehab. I tried calling 'em but I can't get nothing."

Jack frowned.

"And Kippy?"

Slim Jim shook his head.

"Still in the hospital with that gallbladder infection. Don't know when they'll set him free. His old lady wouldn't even let me in the room to talk to him. Started raising hell, squealing like a stuck pig, so I left it alone. You want me to try again?"

"Don't bother. His organs picked a helluva time to go out, but if they won't let him outta the hospital, then he ain't no use to us right now."

Jack O' Lantern looked into the faces of his men. Long John couldn't fight, and after being shot, Tiny was pretty much useless. Toadie and Ratface weren't much more than testosterone-soaked teenagers looking to either fight or screw anything within barking distance. At least he had Legs and Slim Jim. Jack rubbed his forehead with the palm of his hand and then coughed. It was time to get to business.

"All right, boys. The Cannons. Let's go over what we got."

Legs stubbed out his cigarette.

"They run Silas. No one's willing to give 'em up. They must have everyone scared. I even tried talking to some folks on the street. Housewife types. They acted like they ain't never even heard the name Cannon. Looked at me like I had three heads for asking."

Jack O' Lantern nodded.

"Okay. What else? Slim, anything?"

"I told you 'bout the scrap yard. I know that's where they gotta run from, but the place's been locked up since yesterday morning. I got my cousin watching, but I don't think they're gonna show."

Slim Jim sparked his lighter.

"And we can't figure out where they're staying. Found the older son's trailer, but no one in it."

"We got names for these people yet? Any kinda info?"

Slim nodded, his raw Adam's apple bulging as he spoke.

"We know Sherwood. My cousin said he's been around. Got a reputation for being a real asshole. Professional. Unforgiving type."

"Fantastic."

"And the older son's name is Levi. He's even bigger asshole. Likes to pick fights, bust heads just to see 'em bleed. He's got a wife and kid, but he must've moved 'em somewhere."

Jack O' Lantern frowned.

"And the kid. But he don't matter no more. Who's the other guy?"

"Sherwood's got another son. Judah. My cousin thought he was in prison, but maybe he just got out or something. Don't know nothing on where he's at, though."

Jack sat in silence for a moment while the rest of the Scorpions watched his face, waiting. Finally, he ran his hand through his curling orange hair and then slammed his fist down on the table.

"This place is on lockdown. Nobody gets in and nobody leaves, 'less I know about it. Long John, how's that new batch of crystal going?"

Long John cleared his throat.

"It's a waste if I can't get back out there to finish it."

"Fine. We need that score. Head back out to the trailer, but stay there. Don't go driving around and don't go home. That's the same for everybody. The Cannons are planning something. They gotta want revenge for that kid. They're gonna come after us sometime and we need to be ready. As soon as they show themselves, we gotta be ready to strike so we can get our money back."

Legs leaned forward and rested his elbows on the table. It wobbled and shifted against the added weight.

"So we're just gonna sit here and wait for them to invite themselves to dinner? They got our money. We need to be out there, tracking 'em down."

Jack shook his head.

"No. This guy Sherwood's gotta be smarter than that. That's what he's expecting us to do. Be spread out and vulnerable. He's gonna hit us here soon. We mighta killed his son, for Christ's sake. He's gotta come after us. We stay here, we don't show our numbers and we draw him to us."

Jack O' Lantern eyed the men around him.

"Unless someone else has a better plan?"

No one spoke. Legs looked as if he were about to, but then stared down at the table instead.

"All right. Long John, get outta here. And remember what I said; don't leave the trailer 'til you hear from one of us. Tiny, take Ratface and Toadie and load up on grub. Legs, get out to Wal-Mart, you're in charge of ammo. Slim, you're with me. I'm locking the gates in an hour, so everybody had better be back by then. Questions?"

Slim Jim had a dark look on his face, but he kept his mouth shut. Jack O' Lantern waited through a moment of silence and then pounded the gavel on the table.

"All right. Let's move."

THE AIR CONDITIONER in Ramey's Cutlass had been broken since last summer. Even with all four windows rolled down, it was sweltering inside the car. The sun seemed to radiate off the black vinyl interior and dash, intensifying the stifling heat. They were driving down Highway 18, taking the back way up to Kentsville, and Judah had cautioned Ramey not to exceed the thirty-five mile an hour speed limit. The last thing they needed was to be pulled over by the police on their way to stake out the Scorpions' clubhouse. Consequently, there wasn't much of a breeze.

Judah leaned back in the passenger seat and laced his fingers behind his head. He loved watching Ramey drive. Considering the circumstances of the day, her grip on the wheel was surprisingly relaxed. She hung her right wrist over the steering wheel and leaned her left elbow out the window. Her hair was swirling about her bare shoulders and collarbone in wispy tendrils. She was wearing sunglasses against the afternoon glare and though she wasn't exactly smiling, her lips had the trace of an ease that did not often favor her. She was lost in the rhythmic lull of stretching asphalt and passing trees and for a moment Judah thought to himself that maybe this could work. They could make a go of it; they could really have a chance. Ramey turned to him, a frown creasing her forehead and tightening her lips, and the moment was forgotten.

"You sure you know what you're doing?"

Judah reached into the plastic cup holder between them for his pack of cigarettes. He fitted one between his lips before mumbling.

"No."

Ramey pushed in the cigarette lighter for him.

"I just want to make sure I got this right. You want me to drop you off a mile north of Lightning Strike Road and just wait for you to call me while you're trekking through the woods, getting to within spying distance of their clubhouse and watching them to see what they're all about."

The cigarette lighter popped and Judah touched the orange coil to his cigarette.

"That's pretty much it."

Ramey snatched the cigarette from Judah's fingers and brought it to her lips. He gave her a sour face and then fumbled with the pack for another one.

"And you don't think that's the least bit risky?"

Judah squinted against his cigarette as he lit it. He inhaled deeply and blew the smoke out of the side of his mouth.

"Of course it's risky."

Ramey turned to him, her eyes going back and forth between Judah and the road.

"I don't like the idea of you going out there alone. What if they see you? What if something happens and they get ahold of you? I'd have no way of knowing. You'd be screwed."

"Do you remember our senior prom?"

Ramey turned her attention back to the road and pressed both palms against the steering wheel.

"Don't change the subject."

Judah looked out the open passenger window at the scrub pines and turkey oaks drifting by.

"No, I'm serious. Just listen. Do you remember?"

Ramey took another drag of her cigarette, holding the smoke inside her lungs as long as she could. She exhaled, blowing a stream toward the windshield.

"I remember going stag and you going with that tramp Marcy McLean."

"You coulda gone with any guy in the whole school."

"I didn't want any guy in the whole school."

Judah slapped his thigh.

"Man, you were proud. And stubborn, my God. I think you went by yourself just so you could break as many hearts as possible."

Ramey pursed her lips.

"I don't think I was breaking many hearts in that puke green number I was wearing. Aubrey picked it out for me. She read in some magazine that a green dress would set off my hair. She called the color chartreuse. I called it a pale shade of baby vomit."

"I think you looked good in it."

Ramey cracked a wry smile.

"You say that now."

Judah grinned.

"And I thought you looked even better with one sleeve torn off your dress and a cut above your eye."

Judah knew the scar was still visible, torn into her skin by Marcy's cubic zirconia ring. The one he'd bought for her at Penny's.

"She came out a lot worse."

"I remember."

Ramey threw her half-smoked cigarette out the window and then pulled her hair back with one hand.

"And she deserved it. Dumb whore. Made out with that loser John Green right in the middle of the dance floor. That guy was like a twenty-two-year-old senior or something. And you standing right there, next to the spiked punch bowl."

Judah smiled.

"I think I was too drunk to even know I was still at the prom."

"Well, there was no way I was gonna let her get away with it. She's lucky I didn't permanently disfigure her face."

Judah reached over and rested his hand on her hip. He hooked his finger through the belt loop of her jeans and tugged.

"See, that's what I'm talking about. You always had my back. You were always willing to risk everything for me. Even at the expense of that chartreuse dress."

Ramey reached down and squeezed Judah's hand. Her mouth was set in a fierce line.

"Always."

"So that's what I need you to do."

Judah leaned over and tucked a wafting strand of hair behind Ramey's ear.

"Trusting me to take care of myself is a risk. Letting me do what I need to do is a risk. But that's the way it's gotta be. And that's the risk I need you to take."

Judah leaned back against the passenger side door and watched Ramey's lips. Just as he knew she would, she bit the bottom one, held the edge of it between her teeth for a moment and then set her jaw in a hard line.

"I know."

Judah turned in his seat slightly so that he was facing the road again.

"Whatever happened to Marcy anyway?"

A slight grin played at the corners of Ramey's mouth.

"She went through three husbands, got as big as a house and is addicted to video poker."

Judah turned his gaze back to the windshield.

"Well. I guess I dodged a bullet with that one."

CHAPTER 16

THREE CROWS SCREAMED in indignation as they sliced through the ashen sky above. A dull wash of clouds had rolled in, shrouding the sun but offering no relief from the smothering heat. Jack O' Lantern shrugged his shoulders, trying to create some air flow underneath his cut. The worn leather vest was sticking to his broad back and making him itch between his shoulder blades. He pulled a bandanna out of his back jeans pocket and mopped his face with the damp rag before taking one last look around the gravel lot. There was no way in except through the sliding chain link gate and he had recently strung razor wire along the top of the nine-foot fence after a pack of local teenagers had climbed over and tried to break into the clubhouse. They were most likely just looking for beer and a place to vandalize, but the incident had left Jack feeling vulnerable. Oren would never have let something like that happen.

Jack O' Lantern heard footsteps crunching in the gravel behind him, but didn't turn around. He kept his eyes on the long, white road beyond the gate and waited for Slim Jim.

"Everything secure?"

Slim Jim put his hands on his hips and glanced around the lot.

"Fences are good. Camera three is down again, but there's nothing we can do 'bout it right now. I bet a damn squirrel chewed through the wires again."

Jack O' Lantern grimaced.

"Perfect."

Slim Jim twisted around and looked at the clubhouse.

"The motion sensor lights are still working, though. And we'll have someone out on watch. Don't break a sweat on it."

Jack O' Lantern grunted and shoved his hands in his pockets.

"You call my old lady and tell her what was what?"

Slim Jim squatted down on one knee in the gravel.

"Yeah, I told her. Cynthia didn't seem too thrilled, though. Something about your kid's soccer game tonight."

"Shit."

Slim Jim picked up a piece of scuffed quartz and twisted it between his fingers.

"Shelia called again, too."

Jack groaned.

"I don't even want to know."

Slim Jim spat on the quartz and rubbed it with his thumb.

"She ain't a bad broad, Jack."

"On her knees, no."

"I'm serious."

Jack kicked a spray of gravel toward Slim Jim.

"Great, then wife her up so she'll shut up and stay home."

Slim Jim rocked back on his heels and stood up.

"She bite your dick off or something? What you got against her now?"

Jack O' Lantern took a cigarette out of the pack in his back pocket and clenched it between his teeth while he waved the flame of his Zippo over it and inhaled deeply. He pointed a finger at Slim Jim and spoke around the cigarette.

"Let me tell you something, Jimmy. She's calling 'cause of that Cannon boy she helped you string up. Either one of two things is going through that bottle blond head of hers."

Jack took the cigarette from his mouth and rolled it between his thumb and forefinger.

"Either she's trying to hit me up for money to keep her trap shut, which ain't gonna happen, or she's started feeling bad about it and she wants someone to talk to. Which ain't gonna happen neither."

Slim Jim looked off into the woods beyond the fence.

"I guess."

"See, the problem with a girl like Shelia is that she's not dumb enough for her own good. She's not smart enough to find something else to do that doesn't involve hanging around a pack of dirty bikers to make a buck, but she's not quite dumb enough to just take it lying down."

"Maybe she wants something better than what she's got."

Jack O' Lantern flicked his half-smoked cigarette onto the gravel.

"Maybe you should take it to Oprah. Now, anything else? Anything important?"

Slim Jim pocketed the quartz and turned back to Jack O' Lantern.

"Like I said, everything's good. The boys are on their way back. I just talked to Legs and he cleared out the ammo at the Wal-Mart in Kentsville and the one over in Starke, too. Got a bunch of stuff we don't need, but maybe that makes up for the fact that Tiny's gonna show up with twelve cases of beer and a jar of pickles."

Jack O' Lantern laughed.

"I guess we can live on that."

He turned to walk back to the clubhouse, but Slim Jim cut him off. His face was grave.

"We ain't doing all this for the Cannons."

Jack cocked his head.

"What do you mean?"

Slim Jim crossed his arms in front of his chest.

"I mean, this whole batten down the hatches act ain't 'cause you're worried about Sherwood Cannon."

"All right."

"Maybe it'll draw them out to attack us like you said, and we'll get them and the money and we can all go on living the American dream. But I saw that snake last night, Jack. And I saw your face when you came back from that church on Sunday. This ain't just about the Cannons. This is about that Bible thumping bitch. She's got you scared so bad I bet you ain't taken a shit in three days. What'd she say to you?"

A tinge of heat rose to Jack O' Lantern's face, but he kept his mouth straight and stared back at Slim Jim with a level gaze.

"If you needed to know, I woulda told you by now."

Jack pushed past Slim Jim and walked toward the front door of the clubhouse. Slim Jim waited a moment and then called after him.

"Well, are you gonna wait to tell me once it's too late?"

Jack O' Lantern kept walking.

"Maybe."

RAMEY STILL HADN'T been happy about letting Judah go off into the woods by himself, but he had smacked his palm down on the top of the Cutlass twice and turned his back. He heard the tires of her car pull away from the sandy shoulder of the road and he knew that she was driving away, albeit slowly. He had promised to be back before nightfall. The late afternoon sunlight filtered down through the canopy of pine needles and oak leaves, but the twilight was long and languorous this time of year and he figured he had at least four good hours of light left in the day. Judah adjusted the rifle strapped over his back and headed west toward the Scorpions' clubhouse. He had judged the distance at no more than three miles, and if he kept up his pace through the twisting underbrush, he figured he could be in a good surveillance position in under an hour.

The going was slower than he had anticipated, though. He'd been living inside concrete walls for too long and had forgotten much of what had been second nature to him as a child growing up in the woods of Bradford County. He had forgotten which palmettos slid over clothing and which stuck their long points into a sweat soaked T-shirt and jabbed through the cotton. He had forgotten, too, that no matter the heat, a T-shirt was a poor choice for going deep into the woods. His arms and neck were benighted by long-legged mosquitos that left thick splats of blood on his skin when he was quick enough to smack them. Pestering gnats hovered around the crown of his head like a halo. There were a few early yellow flies out as well, leaving welts the size of dimes when they managed to alight on his slick skin. He careened through spider webs that left him searching his hair and shaking out his shirt and he flipped a thick black snake out of its hiding by accident. It slithered over his boot and disappeared as quickly as it had been seen. Birds, squirrels and who knew what else bolted through the tangled tree roots, waist-high bushes and clinging weeds and briars. It wasn't nearly as easygoing as he had imagined, and the rifle was giving him trouble as well.

At first, when Hiram had offered Judah and Ramey a chance to pick over his stockpile of weapons, Judah had been cautious. Between the two of them, they had only the .45 Sherwood had given Judah and the 9mm Ramey always hid under her bed or carried in her purse. What he wanted was a rocket launcher, maybe a handful of grenades. What he had access to was two handguns. And not enough money to buy anything else. But he had followed Ramey's lead and agreed to humor Hiram by looking at some weapons before leaving. They couldn't very well have left on their own anyway; they needed Hiram to take them back through the minefield maze.

Judah had expected Hiram to take them out back to a storage shed of military surplus weapons, but just as they were about to descend the trailer steps, Hiram ordered them back inside. Judah had eyed Ramey warily from the kitchen as Hiram began pushing his coffee table back against the wall and rolling up the fake Oriental rug underneath. Ramey had raised her eyebrows, but seemed unfazed by any of Hiram's erratic behavior, so Judah had tried not to be alarmed. He was half expecting Hiram to trigger some switch that would blow them all to high heaven, when the old man pried up a piece of the floor and shoved his arm up to his shoulder down into the dark hole. The gun he finally latched onto and dragged out from underneath the trailer almost made Judah laugh. When Hiram sprang up and tossed it at Judah, he was so surprised he almost didn't catch it.

"No need to look at nothing else, brother. That there's all you need."

Judah looked down with wide eyes at the M14 rifle in his hands.

"What the hell is this? A gun from a Civil War reenactment?"

Hiram was busy moving the coffee table back into place and didn't see the expression on Judah's face.

"Best gun in the world for what you'll be needing it for. Accurate, never jams, standard military issue."

Judah turned the gun over in his hands and whispered to Ramey.

"Issued before electricity was invented?"

Ramey only smiled and shook her head.

Hiram marched over to Judah and took the gun from him. He ejected the clip, blew on the magazine and slammed it back into the gun. He rubbed his fingers fondly down the length of the wooden stock in a way that made Judah uncomfortable. Hiram obviously loved the gun. He touched the barrel to his cheek for a moment and then thrust it back into Judah's still outstretched hands.

"Don't even need to look at no others. That's the one for you."

Judah protested.

"I don't mean to be rude, but I need something that can actually fire a bullet."

Hiram ignored Judah and walked past them through the tiny kitchen. He held the screen door open and motioned them out.

"Best gun you'll ever own there, brother. They used those back in Vietnam. Still use 'em over in Iraq and Afghanistan today. Sniper rifle. Don't even need no scope 'cause those iron sights are dead on. Take it, it's on me. I got five more under there. Though I guess I'll have to move 'em now that you know about that particular hiding spot."

Hiram had been serious. Judah had looked to Ramey again, but she merely shrugged and had taken the gun off his hands. She had thanked Hiram and followed in his footsteps until they reached the safety of her car. Once out of the minefield, Judah had turned to Hiram to shake his hand, but the old man had quickly held his arms up, indicating that he didn't touch people. Ramey was already in the driver seat, so Judah merely said thanks. Hiram had nodded, but had one request for Judah.

"If you get a chance, blow the dick off that peckerwood Jack O' Lantern. I don't mean kill him or nothing, but since he ain't got no balls in the first place, you might as well even him out."

Judah had said he would do his best.

As yet another low lying branch got hung up on the tip of the gun's barrel rising high over his shoulder, Judah was starting to regret bringing along the rifle more and more. Ramey had insisted he take two guns with him, however, and he wasn't going to saddle her with a relic that looked like it belonged in a museum of ancient history. He had come to realize that she didn't like being without her 9mm, either.

He had been too drunk the night before to be surprised when she pulled the gun out of her purse and aimed it at his father, but now that he was able to reflect back on it, it did seem like a pretty ballsy move. Had Ramey always been like that? As he stumbled over snapping pine boughs, wincing at the cracking sound echoing through the woods, he remembered another time she had threatened Sherwood. It had been not long after Judah's mother had passed away and upon coming over to visit him Ramey had noticed yet another dark bruise running down the length of Judah's face. She had spotted it from where she was still straddled across her bicycle in front of the Cannon's house. Judah had been coming down the steps to meet her, making a wide circle around Sherwood, sitting on an overturned five-gallon bucket on the porch, and knew the instant he saw the storm in her eyes that something bad was going to happen. He didn't have time to stop her; he barely had time to duck. The chunk of cinderblock missed Sherwood's face by only an inch. If he hadn't turned his head to spit a drip of tobacco off the porch she would have nailed him in the eye. And later that night, Sherwood made Judah very cognizant of that fact. Judah never told Ramey of the repercussions of her act, though. Instead, he had always let it make him smile. So, yeah, maybe Ramey had always been like that. And it made Judah smile even more now.

A motorcycle engine growled up ahead and Judah was startled from his reverie. He instinctively crouched down in the palmettos and held his breath. The engine continued to rumble, but now Judah could tell it wasn't as close as he first thought. He was definitely nearing the clubhouse, though, and began to take his steps cautiously. A few more yards and he was able to glimpse open space up ahead and a flash of metal beyond that. The engine sound cut off swiftly and the chattering noises of the woods crept back to his ears. Judah took a few more steps and looked around for a suitable tree to climb. He hauled himself up a sprawling live oak and found a half-decent perch in between two branches. Judah unslung the rifle and bridged it between two smaller branches while he folded his legs underneath him. He brought the binoculars dangling around his neck up to his eyes and adjusted them until he could see more than only various shades of green. Judah settled himself and began to survey the clearing before him.

Over the next hour, Judah watched the Scorpions move around the gravel lot surrounding their clubhouse. Every club member he saw was carrying, and the two men at the metal chain link gate were brandishing AK-47s as they scanned the drive leading up to the clubhouse. Judah also noticed that the men seemed slightly awkward with the rifles as they tried to balance them on their shoulders or lean them against their legs to light a cigarette. He figured they weren't as familiar with the rifles as he had previously assumed outlaw bikers to be. While he watched, though, two men replaced them at the gate and seemed to handle the guns with ease. It was hard to tell for sure, but one of the men on the second shift had the same stringy build as one of the bikers on the highway Saturday night. Judah realized he was dealing with at least two different levels of competency.

In addition to the skinny man who took over one of the posts at the gate, Judah recognized one of the club members who was fiddling with the engine of a motorcycle backed up against the side of the clubhouse. He was sitting on a cinderblock next to the bike with one leg stretched out stiffly in front of him, and Judah was sure he was the man Levi had shot. Finally, just as the light was beginning to slip from afternoon pewter to evening copper, and Judah was readying himself to climb down and head back, he saw the man he had been looking for. The bright orange hair was unmistakable. When Judah raised the binoculars to his eyes and caught the man's face in his sights, he was sure. It was Jack O' Lantern. Judah followed him through the lenses as he walked across the gravel lot toward the gate. Judah hadn't thought much of him when he had been pointing his gun at the back of his head in the rain, but now he noted Jack O' Lantern's every movement. His shoulders were tense and his hands balled into fists, but almost unconsciously so, as if he wasn't angry, but merely ready to spring. Nervous. Prone to making rash decisions and stupid mistakes. Or at least Judah hoped.

Judah watched him walk to the fence and talk with the tall, skinny man. The skinny man kept pointing down the road and then back at the clubhouse while Jack O' Lantern crossed his arms and shook his head. Judah thought they must be arguing. He continued watching until Jack O' Lantern turned away and walked back to the clubhouse, hands deep in his pockets with his shoulders hunched and his head downcast. It was a good sign. Judah slipped the rifle strap over his head and situated the gun between his shoulder blades before dropping down to the ground. As soon as he was sure he was far enough away from the clubhouse, he pulled his cellphone out of his pocket and powered it back on. He ignored the three missed call alerts and dialed Ramey's number in the darkening light.

CHAPTER 17

JUDAH'S CELLPHONE VIBRATED on the kitchen table between them and Ramey glanced down and rolled her eyes. It continued to vibrate, edging closer to the open takeout containers in the middle of the table with every muted ring. Ramey reached for her beer.

"You gotta answer it sometime."

Judah kept his eyes on the pulled pork sandwich he was eating. He didn't look at Ramey and he didn't look at the phone. Finally, it stopped buzzing. The silence grew loud and was broken only by the feathery crinkle of paper napkins and the jarring clink of beer bottles. Ramey picked up a piece of greasy garlic toast, but only tore it into pieces on the paper plate in front of her. She rubbed her fingers together and then wiped her hands on her jeans. She drew one leg up onto the chair she was sitting on and rested her chin on her knee.

"So you think the Scorpions are setting a trap?"

Judah popped the last bite of sandwich into his mouth and rifled through the plastic takeout bag for another napkin.

"I don't know for sure."

He pulled out the last napkin and mashed it between his fingers, trying to soak up some of the sauce. Judah wadded up it up and tossed it back in the bag before reaching for his Budweiser. He wrapped his hand around the bottle's neck, but didn't pick it up.

"I think this guy, Jack O' Lantern, he's gotta know we're coming at them for Benji. And they want their money back. They didn't go after Benji 'cause they thought he robbed them; they went after him to rile Sherwood up. They were trying to rattle him so they could flush him out and find a way to get the cash back."

Ramey ran her nails up and down the length of her leg.

"But that's exactly what Sherwood's not doing."

Judah raised his beer and took a swig.

"I know."

"And exactly what you are."

He set the beer down and picked at the wet, peeling label.

"Your point?"

Ramey stretched her leg out and sat up straight.

"My point is, if you go after them, you're playing right into their hand. You're doing exactly what they want you to do."

Judah still wouldn't look at her.

"Yeah."

Ramey spread her hands out on the table, palms down.

"Sherwood may be a real dick, but he's playing it smart."

"And I'm playing it stupid."

"That's not what I said."

"No, that's what I said."

Judah finally raised his eyes to Ramey. He reached out across the table and placed his hand over hers.

"Look, Ramey. I know that the smart thing to do would be to act like

Sherwood."

Ramey cocked her head to the side, but only listened.

"Lay low, wait 'em out, whatever. If I gave a damn about the money, that is. But it ain't about the money. It's about what they did to this family. It's about making sure that no one thinks they can mess with the Cannons. Ever."

Judah gripped Ramey's hand, then released it and leaned back in his chair, his dark eyes boring a hole in the table before him.

"So, it's about pride?"

Judah's head snapped up and his eyes smoldered at Ramey.

"It's about justice. It's about what Benji deserves. It's about doing the right thing now. What I think is the right thing. You're the one who said I needed to open my eyes. Think for myself. Well, this is what it looks like when I think for myself. It's stupid and it don't make no sense, but it's all I got. Gut feelings, not brains."

Ramey's eyes were soft.

"I'm not arguing. I said I was with you, and I'm with you."

Judah squeezed his hands into fists.

"I can't just leave it alone. I can't."

"I know. But what's the plan? We just ride up in there, guns blazing, maybe launch a grenade or two and take down who we can?"

Judah ignored Ramey's tone and grin. He looked past her out the kitchen window, into the orange streetlight glow.

"I need to know more before I can make a decision. Before I can make a call."

Ramey shook her head.

"I don't know who else we can go to."

"We go to them."

He turned back to Ramey.

"If they're gonna set a trap for us, we need to trap them right back."

Ramey narrowed her eyes, questioning, but before she could speak, Judah's cellphone vibrated again. They both glanced down at it. It buzzed twice and Ramey reached for it. Before she could snap it open, though, Judah grabbed her hand.

"I got it."

He took a deep breath and answered the phone. It was Sherwood and he wasted no time.

"Where the hell you been, boy?"

Judah raised his eyebrows at Ramey and then twisted around in his seat. He rested his elbow on the edge of the table and let his eyes wander to the warped linoleum floor.

"Around."

"I been calling you all day."

"I misplaced my phone. I've been laying low like you said to."

Sherwood made a sound that was somewhere between a phlegmy cough and a growl. Judah wasn't sure if Sherwood bought it or not, but he continued.

"But you got me now, so what do you want? You want to meet me in another parking lot so you can get Levi to crack another rib? Or maybe you want to take a swing at me yourself, for old times' sake?"

Ramey touched Judah's arm, but he pulled away from her. Sherwood just laughed.

"No, I think we're all done with that. Any word on Benji?"

"Why, you still ain't been by the hospital to see him? Too much trouble to drive all the way out there?"

Sherwood's tone was edgy. Dangerous.

"You are walking a narrow line with me, son."

No one spoke for a moment, and then Judah conceded.

"Ramey called up there earlier. Still the same. Multiple fractures, brain swelling, massive abrasions. They got him in some kinda induced coma or something."

"So he'll make it?"

Judah grit his teeth.

"They still don't know. That all you called about?"

"I called to make sure you'd taken last night's conversation to heart."

"Yeah."

Sherwood didn't seem convinced.

"I mean it. We'll handle it, Judah. In good time. Without making the situation any worse than it already is. So you just keep laying low, keep playing house with Ramey or whatever it is you're doing right now, and I'll let you know if we need you when we make a move."

"If you need me?"

Sherwood wheezed.

"You been gone awhile, son. You did okay Saturday night, but right now this ain't your game. Take some time, get your head straight. Figure out your priorities. Talk to that girl of yours, for Christ's sake. She's wild, but maybe she can convince you to do the right thing."

Judah tried to make his voice resigned.

"Which is to let you handle it."

"Yes. Let me handle it."

"All right."

"I mean it, Judah."

"Me too."

There was a long pause and then the line went dead. Judah looked down at the phone in his hands, then snapped it shut and tossed it on the table. He turned back to Ramey and managed a slight grin.

"I hope he bought that."

Ramey smiled. She picked up her beer and raised it to her lips.

"So, we were talking about a trap?"

CHAPTER 18

THEY KNEW IT was a different kind of night. Wednesday nights usually lacked some of the energy and theatrics of Sunday, as most of the congregation arrived after working long hours, and some children, who still couldn't be pulled from the secular public school system, were permitted to stay home and sleep. Although Wednesday nights were not the endurance marathons of Sunday, the services didn't start until nine and could go on long past midnight.

An odd weight settled on the church members as they found their seats on the long wooden benches and joined in with the rhythmic clapping. The usual opening songs were sung as minivans and pickup trucks pulled into the parking lot and a few testimonials were shouted as the air grew warmer and warmer with the press of bodies still smelling of cooking grease, cleaning products and dried sweat. When Sister Tulah finally emerged from the door at the back of the sanctuary and ascended the low stage, they understood the change in the air. The sharp points of Sister Tulah's mouth were turned down and her pale, milky eyes appeared hooded and shadowed. She held her arms out stiff in front of her with her hands formed into fists, as if she were flexing an invisible switch between them. There would be no holy laughter tonight, no laying on of hands to heal the sick and sad, no running and falling in the aisles. The Holy Spirit would be walking amongst them tonight, but only in Sister Tulah's shoes.

Felton had been greeting members as they filtered through the front doors, but once Tulah assumed the stage, he scanned the parking lot for headlights and then closed the doors and locked them. He stood with his back leaning against the far wall of the room and he stuffed his hands deep into his pockets when the clapping ceased. Felton, better than most, knew what the strange tension in Sister Tulah's shoulders and forearms meant. He tapped his foot nervously on the floorboards and held his breath with the others until Sister Tulah decided to speak. When she finally did, her voice came out like the crack of a whip, each word slow and biting, with the burning sting of the lash.

"'*Ye shall do my judgments, and keep mine ordinances, to walk therein: I am the Lord your God.*' Does anyone know what book of the Bible that's from?"

Most everyone in the congregation knew, but no one would be foolish enough to speak. Several women nodded their heads, but the rest of the church kept their necks stiff and their gazes trained like beams of light on Sister Tulah's face. Their eyes followed her as she began to stomp across the stage, but their heads did not move.

"It's from Leviticus, chapter eighteen. And if you didn't know that, then you'd better go home tonight and spend the next twenty-four hours praying on your knees with your Bible held over your head asking God to forgive your ignorance. I will say it again, '*Ye shall do my judgments, and keep mine ordinances: I am the Lord your God.*' Did you get it that time?"

Sister Tulah raised her fist in the air.

"God didn't say maybe. He didn't say consider, He didn't say think about it a little while. He said do! He is telling you right there, plain as day, plain as breathing, what you need to do. You need to obey. Let me say that again. Obey."

Felton shifted uncomfortably against the wall, snagging the shoulder of his dress shirt against the rough plaster. Sister Tulah's pale eyes were roving among the congregation, but Felton didn't need Tulah's glare to feel her words stamping themselves deep into his chest.

"God didn't say to obey Him because it's fun. God didn't say to obey Him because you have nothing better to do. God didn't say to obey Him because it's what you want to do."

Sister Tulah banged her right fist down into her left hand.

"God said to obey Him because '*I am the Lord your God*!' Let me repeat, '*I am the Lord your God*!'"

Sister Tulah scanned the rows of followers. Her gaze lingered on a few, probing for weakness, searching for even the minutest lapse in attention. She slowly ambled her way around the stage to stand behind the pulpit. Her severe pauses could be even more commanding than her words, and she was well aware of this. No sound, no movement, was uncalculated by Tulah.

"God tells you to do something and you do it. God says to repent and you repent. God says tithe and you tithe."

Tulah picked up the mason jar of clear liquid balanced on the edge of the pulpit and held it aloft.

"God says you drink poison and let me tell you, you're going to drink poison."

A few muffled affirmations rose from the crowd, but Sister Tulah's cutting gaze quickly silenced them.

"Let me tell you something else it says in Leviticus. If you read chapter twenty, God says, '*Ye shall therefore keep all my statutes, and all my judgments, and do them; that the land whither I bring you to dwell therein, spew you not out*.' Do you hear that? Do you know what that means?"

Felton's hands were trembling inside his pockets. He clenched his fingers into thick balls and pressed his fists against his legs. Sister Tulah seemed to be sucking all of the air inside the church into her lungs, and Felton was finding it difficult to breathe. His eyes darted around the church and he could tell that while their faces did not reflect it, many of the members' chests were beginning to heave with the same struggle.

"You!"

Sister Tulah pointed to an awkward boy, all legs and scraped elbows, who was folded up like an accordion between his sweating parents.

"Do you know what that means?"

The boy's rapt face didn't change, but his small hand edged its way into his mother's. Sister Tulah jabbed her finger toward the row behind the boy.

"Do you? Do any of you? Well, spew means to cast out. It means to vomit. God is telling you right there what is going to happen to you if you even think about disobeying Him. If it even crosses your mind for a second. He is going to vomit you out away from Him and straight into the waiting arms of the devil. Straight into the gnashing teeth of Satan's army."

Sister Tulah raised her chin and in the shadowy light, her eyes found Felton's and stayed for a moment.

"Do you?"

Sister Tulah smashed her fist down on the wooden pulpit and the clear liquid in the Mason jar sloshed against the glass sides.

"Is that what you want? You want to be disobedient and dance with the devil? You want to think for yourself and feel those scorching flames licking up the sides of your body for the rest of eternity? You want to not listen to God, you want to ignore His orders, you want to do things your own way and think you can get away with it? Well, let me tell you, when you die, your children are going to wake in their sleep from nightmares, because they are going to be able to hear your screams all the way from Hell."

Sister Tulah walked to the very edge of the stage, the toes of her white Reeboks hitting the wooden lip of trim. To Felton, her pupils seemed like two tiny points of pure darkness peering through the globes of white. He wanted to look away but, like the people seated on the rows before him, he knew that was impossible. His fingernails were cutting into the soft, doughy flesh of his palms, but he couldn't unmake his fists. He suddenly had a burning need to urinate, but moving was not only impossible, it was unimaginable. If a warm stream began to trickle down the inside of his pants leg, so be it. It had happened before. Sister Tulah's voice sank dangerously low.

"And let me tell you what happens before you even get to Hell. You might be thinking right now that you don't have to worry until you die. Oh, no. God tells us exactly what He's going do to you in Deuteronomy. What He's going do to you right here on earth. He says, '*If a man abide not in me, he is cast forth as a branch, and is withered; and men gather them, and cast them into the fire, and they are burned.*'"

Sister Tulah's face reddened and she screamed out at her congregation. The piercing sound seemed to suck all the air, all the light, all the essence of humanness from the room and left it in an empty, dark void.

"They are burned!"

JACK O' LANTERN was awoken by a great whooshing sound, followed by shouts and the sound of doors banging and boots pounding on the floor. He immediately rolled off the twin bed in one of the back bedrooms and was on his feet, careening in his boxer shorts down the narrow hallway to the main room of the clubhouse. He raced around the corner and slammed into Legs, whose eyes were wide with fear. He had his pants in one hand and a fire extinguisher in the other; he seemed unsure which item was more essential to the situation. Jack ripped the pants from Legs' grasp and pushed him forward with the extinguisher. Legs bolted out the open front door and joined the shouts and curses. Jack O' Lantern followed him, but stopped short when he beheld the chaos before him.

His men were running to and fro like addled lemmings, unsure of which cliff to run off first. Tiny hobbled past him, dragging both his leg and a shovel. Ratface and Toadie were untangling the garden hose from the side of the building and Legs was trying unsuccessfully to pull the pin out of the extinguisher. He had it clamped between his knees as he yanked and cursed in frustration. Slim Jim, who had been standing still with his hands on his hips, caught Jack O' Lantern's eye and slowly walked over to the steps. He looked up at Jack and crossed his arms. They watched it together.

A ring of fire had been lit around the clubhouse. Jack could tell from where he was standing that it was in the shape of a perfect circle, completely encompassing the building. The flames rose almost to the men's shoulders and the air around them was laced with a toxic smell. Oily black smoke wafted upwards in the still night, and with the absence of any wind the wall of fire remained vertical, burning straight upwards. The ring stood about ten feet from the doorway and Jack could feel the wave of heat assaulting his skin. Any closer and the fire would have taken the clubhouse. As it was, it stood no chance of catching anything else ablaze as long as the summer air remained still and the Scorpions didn't do something stupid to fan the flames in the wrong direction. The fire was a warning, a threat, not a failed attempt to burn them out. Jack O' Lantern raised his hands to his face and stared wide-eyed through his fingers. It was Wednesday night. He had expected a phone call, maybe another snake in a box. He had not expected this.

Jack O' Lantern whispered between his hands.

"Holy mother of God."

Slim Jim nodded.

"Exactly."

"THEY ARE BURNED, brothers and sisters! They are burned, my fellow saints!

They are not chided, they are not scolded. They are burned and the skin is scorched from their bodies and the flesh on their bones is cooked and their very bones are blackened."

Tears had begun to roll down the faces of the few children in the congregation, but they did not dare close their eyes or look away or wipe their runny noses on their sleeves. Felton watched Tulah pace back and forth across the stage as her voice cracked and strained and he knew that something terrible was happening tonight. Not there, not in the church, and whatever it was, it wasn't going to involve him. But he recognized the flushed tinge to Sister Tulah's cheeks and the curl of her thin lips. Someone, somewhere, was getting what Tulah thought they deserved. And she was loving every moment of it.

"How can He do that, you ask? He can do that because He is the Lord your God."

Sister Tulah's yellow teeth were revealed behind her grotesque smile. She grinned down at her followers while pointing in the air above her.

"He says, '*I am the Lord your God*.' I am the Lord your God! Do you hear me? Brothers and sisters, do you hear me? I'm not up here tonight for my own benefit. I know my place is next to our Lord. I know where I'm going to be standing when God spews you out. When He starts that fire. When He casts the backslidden, disobedient filth into the flames. I'll be standing right next to Him, secure in my place. I'll be standing right next to Jesus Christ himself, shaking my head in sorrow, but comforted by the fact that I've done everything I could to save those poor burning souls."

Sister Tulah's eyes were glazed over, but not from tears. Felton knew. He had seen the same sheen in her eyes the night the brakes went out on Melville Sheppard's Cadillac and he almost sank along with his new car to the bottom of Lake Rowell. The night Luanne Bradshaw found her mother cold and lifeless in the Longflowers Nursing Home with the cord to her ventilator unplugged and kicked under the bed. The night Mayor Clifton's daughter turned up missing and was found only after a sizable check was made out to Sister Tulah to pray for the girl's safe return. Tulah was not lost in sorrow. She was lost in ecstasy. Felton finally tore his eyes away from her livid face, but he couldn't block out her screeching voice.

"Let me tell you, my dear brothers and sisters. The Lord God is a just God. The Lord God is a merciful God. But the Lord God is not stupid. He knows when your obedience to Him wavers for even the blink of an eye, and during the Latter Days, He will remember. He will seek you out and He will not be forgiving. So I am warning you now. You must obey Him. You must cleave to Him. You must fear Him."

Felton stared down hard at the scuffed leather of his loafers. He wished he was alone in his camper. He wished he was with his snakes and his turtles. He wished he was far, far away, and yet, there was a small sliver of him that wished he was closer. Sister Tulah was his flesh and blood. She was his only family. If she possessed such uncontested power, before the eyes of man and before the eyes of God, why couldn't he have just the tiniest glimmer of that power inside of him, too?

"Think on these words, my saints. God says to you, '*Behold, I set before you this day a blessing and a curse.*' A blessing and a curse. Which will you be the recipient of? Will you stand shoulder to shoulder with myself and Jesus Christ as we look down from the safety of Heaven and survey the carnage inflicted on the wicked during the end times, or will you be kneeling in the rivers of blood and wailing your lament, asking yourself why, oh why, did you not heed Sister Tulah's warnings? For the righteous and the obedient will be reclining in the land that flows with milk and honey and the headstrong and disobedient will be as branches, gathered and cast into the fire."

Felton raised his head and stared into the bottomless eyes of Sister Tulah. Over the tops of the church members' heads her gaze held his alone. He dug his nails into his bleeding palms and straightened his shoulders. He looked back at her without flinching. Sister Tulah raised both of her arms above her head and closed her eyes. The congregation bowed their heads and followed suit.

"Let us pray, brothers and sisters. Let us pray for the strength to obey God's will."

Only Felton remained with his eyes wide open.

CHAPTER 19

Jack O' Lantern snapped his lighter shut and shoved it deep down into his pocket. He inhaled deeply and kept the smoke in his lungs as long as he could. When he finally blew the stream of smoke out, it caught in his throat and he bent over, wheezing and coughing. The group of men standing near the row of bikes glanced his way, but he shot them a dirty look. He needed time to think and they weren't helping.

The smell of smoke had finally dissipated and the ground was cool to the touch where the fire had burned, but a strange black ring remained around the entire circumference of the clubhouse, smudged in places but still clearly visible in the hazy morning light. The unnaturalness of the dark mark bothered him, as well as its placement. How had it been done at all? Jack O' Lantern shook his head and turned his back to the clubhouse.

The woods beyond the fence were already alive with the sounds of cicadas and other summer insects. The increasing heat was bringing them, and their racket, to life. Over the din, Jack could hear traffic in the distance from the highway. Behind him, he could hear gravel being scuffed and kicked around as the Scorpions stood about in the yard, drinking watery gray coffee and inspecting each other's bikes. Ratface and Toadie began shadow boxing each other and creating a rolling diatribe of insults to each other's sisters, mothers and girlfriends. They were restless and trying to find a way to shed their nervous energy. Jack tilted his head upward. The morning had started off with a heavy blanket of stifling, dirty clouds, but they were slowly thinning. A faint stain of blue was beginning to bleed across the sky. A buzzard circled lazily on an air current, but otherwise the endless space above him was empty. Only in the sky could one find silence. He watched the buzzard until he heard a single engine plane droning in the distance and then he gave up. He couldn't get her voice out of his head: *If I don't get my money before the evening service on Wednesday, you will experience baptism by fire. And after that, well, there is always dynamite. Do you understand?* Jack O' Lantern pulled his cigarette from his lips and stomped it into the gravel. He understood all right.

Slim Jim sidled up next to him and clapped him on the shoulder.

"We gotta talk about this, Jack."

Jack O' Lantern shrugged Slim Jim's hand away.

"What do we know about last night?"

Slim Jim scratched the side of his face. The sticky air was already causing both of them to sweat.

"What we know is shit."

Jack O' Lantern turned on him.

"What does that mean, Jimmy? Where were the guys on guard? Whose ass do I need to feed to the wood chipper?"

Slim Jim looked over at the men standing around the motorcycles. Everyone was quiet now, standing still, pretending like they didn't care what Slim Jim and Jack O' Lantern were talking about.

"Tiny and Ratface were supposed to be on the perimeter. Tiny said he ducked inside to pop some more Percocet, and Ratface didn't know Tiny had left so he went inside to take a leak. I guess the fire started just about as he was shaking his dick off. They couldn't have been inside for more than five minutes."

"Are you kidding me? What is this? The damn Boy Scouts would do a better job watching this place. A guy's gotta take a piss, he can use the side of the house! Jesus H. Christ!"

Jack's face was becoming the same shade as his hair. He turned his back on the Scorpions and marched over to the edge of the lot. He stood with his hands in his pockets for a moment, his shoulders hunched up, and then he lashed a kick at the chain link fence. It sprung back and wobbled and Jack kicked at it again. Slim Jim waited patiently for Jack O' Lantern to come back to him. When he did, his face was still flaming, but Jack seemed to be doing his best to keep his temper under control. He ground his teeth and stared down at his boots.

"All right. I'll deal with Tiny and Ratface later. What about the security cameras? They had to record something."

Slim Jim shook his head slowly.

"That's the thing, Jack. I been over all the tapes. I could even see Ratface walking up the steps into the house. Then, they all go blank."

"What do you mean, they all go blank?"

"I mean, on camera two, thirty seconds after you see Ratface go up the steps, the tape goes blank. They all do, at the same time. Nothing but snow. The next thing you can see is us running around like a bunch of retarded ants trying to put the fire out."

Jack O' Lantern glared at Slim Jim.

"You have got to be shitting me."

"I'm serious, man. And that's all we got. I don't even know how they got in here. Our padlock was still on the gate and I already checked the whole fence. Nothing's been cut. It don't make no sense."

Jack O' Lantern looked up at the top of the fence, strung with razor wire.

"Could they have gone over?"

"Maybe. I'm not sure what difference it makes. All that matters is that in less than five minutes some freaks got through the gate, drew a perfect circle around the clubhouse with God knows what, lit a match and got out without us knowing a thing. Who does that preacher bitch have working for her?"

Jack O' Lantern looked sharply at Slim Jim.

"You gotta quit saying that. We don't know who it was."

Slim Jim shook his head in disgust.

"Come off it, Jack. We gotta stop playing around. These guys got a right to know who they're dealing with. They're not dumb enough to think this was just the Cannons. Or, well, not all of them are dumb enough. Either way, they deserve to know what's going on. You got Toadie over there talking about voodoo and ghosts and God knows what else. Some of the guys are freaked out, man. You gotta deal with that."

Jack O' Lantern glanced up at the group of men trying not to look at him.

"Okay."

"I mean it. You tell them about Tulah, or I will."

"I said okay!"

Jack O' Lantern took a deep breath to calm himself and then walked over to the line of motorcycles. Toadie and Legs moved aside and Jack joined the ragged circle. Slim Jim stayed standing slightly behind him. Jack O' Lantern looked into the faces of his men and realized Slim Jim was right; they were scared. These were men who were comfortable with slashing tires and banging skulls. They were not men who knew how to handle waking up inside a ring of fire. The prospects looked like they were on the verge of deserting, if only they had the key to the padlock on the fence, and Legs wore an expression somewhere between being pissed off and needing to puke. Tiny was crunching on another pain pill as he wobbled on his crutches and seemed only half aware of what was going on around him. And this was it. This was his crew. Two scared kids, two men questioning his judgment and a guy with a bum leg and a pocket full of dope.

Oren would have walked straight up to Ratface and punched him in the jaw. Then he would have kicked Tiny's good leg out from underneath him. He would have stood there with his thick arms crossed over his barrel chest and roared, asking if anyone else wanted more of the same. Jack O' Lantern had seen it happen many times before. Oren would have cowed the Scorpions into doing exactly what he wanted; he would have made them afraid. And most importantly, Oren wouldn't have let some crackpot woman preacher get the best of him. Jack O' Lantern was pretty sure if his uncle knew about the fire, he'd be rolling in his grave. Or clawing his way up out of the pine box to strangle Jack for letting it happen.

Jack O' Lantern spit on the ground at his feet and met the eyes of the club.

"I don't want to talk about blame right now."

Legs rolled his eyes and shot Ratface a dirty look. He mumbled something under his breath, but Jack ignored it.

"I don't want to talk about the fire neither, because that just goes back to blame and we don't got the time or the man power to start playing that game. We gotta focus on what we're doing right now. What we're doing today. You hear me?"

Tiny shifted his weight awkwardly and cleared his throat.

"Are we talking 'bout the Cannons? You think it was the Cannons?"

Jack O' Lantern kept his voice steady.

"I think it was the Cannons."

Jack could hear Slim Jim huffing behind him.

"So we need to deal with them."

Legs grunted.

"And how we gonna do that, huh? Stay holed up here all day again, shooting pool and taking turns being on the lookout for arsonists? Standing around with our dicks in our hands? That ain't working, Jack."

Jack O' Lantern nodded.

"I know. So we're not sitting around no more waiting for them to just show themselves or roll up on us."

"Then what?"

"We're going old school, boys. It's time we quit playing around and we got back to basics. Practice is over. It's time we set the trap."

JUDAH CLIMBED OVER to the passenger side of the Bronco and leaned his elbow out the window.

"You want to go over it again?"

Ramey bit her bottom lip and then nodded from the driver seat of her car. The two vehicles were parked side by side in the same turnoff where Judah and Levi had hidden their truck in only a few days before. The Bronco and the Cutlass barely fit abreast in the narrow drive, but both were hidden far back enough from the main highway by the low hanging pine boughs and high scrub. Ramey slid her hands up and down the steering wheel a few times before looking over at Judah through her rolled down window and reciting the plan back to him.

"We hear the first set of motorcycles take off and listen for which way they're gonna go."

"From the sounds I heard in the woods yesterday, they're most likely gonna head north again. They probably have a set run, a set route they take for trying to lead someone on."

Ramey picked at the rubber seal on her window.

"Right. So the bikes take off, we listen and then I take off after the first group."

Judah glanced toward the highway.

"Yep. Just tail 'em. Don't get too close, but make sure they know you're back there. Make sure they know you took the bait."

"Okay."

"I should be able to hear the next set of bikes not long after you leave. They'll be following behind the first set, hoping the lure worked and they hooked someone on the line. So, again, don't go too fast. You want the guys behind you to have seen you so they think they've got you sandwiched between them."

"All eyes on me, huh?"

Judah reached across the space between them and tapped the lip of her window.

"Don't worry. I'll be right behind the second set. Far enough back that they'll think I'm just another car on the highway. They should be so focused on thinking their trap worked, that they snared you, hopefully, they won't be concerned about another car way back behind them."

"Hopefully."

"Ramey, I mean it. I won't let those bikes outta my sight. They're not gonna get to you."

She nodded slowly, watching the road through the glare of her windshield.

"And I just keep following the first two guys."

"Until you get up near Kentsville. When you see the sign for the Wal-Mart right off the highway, you turn sharp. Turn into the parking lot but stay on the outer edge so your car is still visible. As soon as you see the bikes come up behind you, drive up to the front. The Scorpions won't want to roll up on you that close to the store. They'll hang in the back of the lot, trying to figure out what to do, and I'll be right behind them."

Ramey shook her head and frowned.

"Judah, I don't know. If there's two of them and you're by yourself..."

He cut her off.

"It'll be fine. It works because I'll have the element of surprise. The whole time they thought they were trapping you, I'm actually trapping them. And it's not like we're going to OK Corral it out among the minivans. They're gonna want to talk to me, remember? It's just gonna be on my terms now, not theirs."

"Is that what they wanted to do with Benji? Just talk?"

Judah sighed.

"Look at me."

Ramey shifted in her seat so she was facing Judah across their open windows. Her lips were turned down in worry.

"Nothing like that's gonna happen to me. You gotta trust me, okay? I'll handle it."

"And you think you're gonna get the answers you need from them?"

Judah shrugged his shoulders slightly.

"I hope so. I don't know what else to do. You just get to that Wal-Mart and stay up by the front. You get scared, you leave your car in the fire lane and get your ass inside the store. Get around people and you should be safe."

In the distance, they could hear the faint roar of a motorcycle engine. Ramey started to speak, but Judah held up his finger for her to be quiet. Ramey touched her keys hanging from the ignition and listened to the sound grow loud for a moment and then begin to fade again. She looked to Judah and he nodded once.

"The sound is going away from us, so they turned north. All right, you got this?"

Ramey turned the ignition but didn't answer him. Judah reached out through the window and grabbed her hand.

"You got this?"

Ramey looked Judah in the eyes and forced a tight smile to her lips. Judah squeezed her hand.

"Ramey?"

She let go of his hand and gripped the steering wheel.

"I got it."

Ramey put her foot on the gas and swung out onto the highway. When she curved around the bend, she could see the two motorcycles far up ahead on the straightaway. She sped up until she gauged that she was at the right following distance and then held steady. Ramey didn't look down Lightning Strike Road as she passed it, but she was hoping she'd been seen; she only wanted to go through this once. The bikes ahead of her swung around a lazy curve and when Ramey followed, she could no longer see the stretch of highway behind her.

For five minutes she saw only the bikes in front of her. The road was continually twisting and she lost sight of the motorcycles a few times, but with her windows rolled down she could always hear their engines growling, and whenever she came upon a straight track of road she could glimpse them up ahead. Neither Scorpion was wearing a helmet and one had a long ponytail whipping behind him. She kept shifting her eyes back and forth from their dingy red and white Scorpion patches to the empty road behind her reflected in the rearview mirror. A light blue work van passed by too close as they went around a tight curve, but that was the only other vehicle she saw until they came upon a long straightaway with a fallow field stretched along one side. She swerved to avoid yet another deep, pitted pothole, and when she glanced back up at the rearview mirror she caught a glimpse of what she'd been looking for: about half a mile back, two more motorcycles were obviously on her tail.

Ramey's heartbeat sped up but she took a deep breath and forced her eyes back on the road in front of her. It had worked; the Scorpions had taken the bait and now all she had to do was keep it steady until they bumped over the railroad tracks and she could swing off into the store parking lot. She tried not to think about the fact that she was now trapped between four dangerous bikers who most likely thought she was Sherwood Cannon. She knew that what she was doing was risky. A hundred different things could go wrong and it felt like Judah had stayed up half the night with her, listing them and coming up with backup plan after backup plan. Ramey had begun to suspect that he was trying to offer her a way out from going along with him, but she never took it and so he never outright said it.

She came up to another long straightaway and Ramey realized that they were almost there. It had been years since she had been up to Kentsville, and even longer than that since she had come by this route, but she approximated the distance and figured they were only about three miles away now. It was mostly a straight shot, with only a few more curves, and she knew she'd be seeing the bikes behind her again. She checked her speed, trying to decide how close she should let herself get to both sets of Scorpions. They were about a mile down the straightaway when Ramey began to get uneasy. Every time she glanced up into the rearview mirror she saw only the road. Where were the motorcycles behind her? How had she gotten so far ahead?

Ramey slowed down and kept her eyes on the mirror. The uneasy feeling was growing into uncertainty. Judah had told her to just focus on what was ahead of her, to only worry about getting to the parking lot, but she knew that she should have been able to see the bikes behind her now. Just as she was coming up to the curve ahead, she heard the sound of motorcycle engines roaring and realized it was coming from the bikes in front of her. She sped up, but as she went through the lazy S-bend in the highway, the uncertainty escalated into stabbing panic. Something was definitely changing. She stomped down on the gas, but when she came out of the last curve the straightaway ahead of her was empty. Ramey's jaw dropped. They were gone.

Judah had told to her to get the parking lot no matter what, but now Ramey slowed down to a crawl. She had lost the Scorpions she was following and she had no idea what had happened to the ones following her. She knew it was dangerous to wait, but she pulled off parallel to the road in the entrance to a sandy driveway. She craned her neck out the window to look behind her, but the motorcycles were nowhere in sight. She picked up her cellphone from the cup holder between the seats and dialed Judah. The phone rang six times, but there was no answer. Ramey snapped the phone shut. Her heart was racing and she could feel the blood pounding in her temples. She looked straight ahead down the road in front of her and then twisted back around to look behind her again. The road was deserted in both directions. Even if something had happened to the Scorpions tailing her, she should have been able to see Judah by now. Her breath was coming in short gasps and she blinked her eyes rapidly as she tried to decide what to do.

She looked down at the cellphone in her lap. Something had gone wrong with the plan, she knew, but why wasn't Judah answering his phone? Why hadn't he called her if there was a change? She picked up the cellphone and stared at it like it was poisonous. She was afraid to call again. Afraid she would hear only the six rings and then silence. Ramey squeezed her eyes shut and opened them again to look down the road. Empty. She hit redial and brought the phone to her ear. No answer. It kept ringing. No answer. No answer.

Ramey didn't give herself time to think. She snapped the phone shut and threw it up on the dash before stepping on the gas and peeling out in a U-turn. She wasn't sure where she was going or what she was going to find. She only knew that she had to do something.

CHAPTER 20

SISTER TULAH SLID her plastic tray down the metal rack and stopped at the roast beef carving station. A tall black man in a Brooks Brothers suit with a crew cut was in line ahead of her. The man stared at the slab of meat being hacked away at by the teenager in the smeared white apron and did not acknowledge Tulah's presence until she spoke.

"You come all the way to Kentsville just to end up at Golden Corral?"

"I like the soft serve ice cream."

Tulah smacked her lips together and smiled an ugly smile. The man in the suit shook his head when offered a slice of beef.

"No, give me a different one."

The teenager rolled his eyes and slapped the meat back on the cutting board. Sister Tulah laughed.

"Are you always this picky? Seems like a man like you wouldn't presume to be disagreeable in these parts."

The man in the suit turned and looked down at Sister Tulah over his tinted glasses.

“Really? Seems like you might be the one wanting to walk a little more carefully right about now.”

This time he held out his plate when the thick piece of rubbery meat was offered. He waited for it to be doused with a ladle full of gravy before sliding his tray down to the mashed potatoes. Sister Tulah scooted into his place.

“What exactly is that supposed to mean, Mr. Reynolds?”

Mr. Reynolds scooped up a mound of gloopy potatoes and plopped them onto his plate.

“It means that you have some steps to take, preacher lady. And soon.”

The teenager held out a piece of roast beef to Sister Tulah, but she ignored him. The man in the suit had already moved down to the creamed corn and fried okra and Tulah slid her tray along the line. She pushed herself up against him and whispered hoarsely.

“What are you talking about?”

“You’re from around this podunk popsicle stand, aren’t you? What do you think is better, fried okra or sautéed okra? There’s this place up in New York that serves the best sautéed okra you ever put in your mouth. Some kind of Moroccan spices on it or something. Like nothing you ever tasted. What do you think?”

Sister Tulah pursed her lips together and gripped the edge of her plastic tray.

“All right, city boy, you’ve proved your point. Now get to business. What sort of steps are you talking about?”

“I’m talking about the upcoming vote on a certain phosphate company’s permits.”

“What about it?”

The man turned to her and chuckled.

“See, if you were as smart as you claim to be, you would be spending less time down here waving snakes around and hollering about fire and brimstone, and more time keeping an eye on what's going on up in Tallahassee."

Sister Tulah hissed.

"I know everything I need to know."

Mr. Reynolds shrugged and speared a log of boiled corn with a serving fork.

"Then you'd know that the vote got bumped up on the timeline. You wouldn't need to be paying me to stop by on my way up there to tell you."

Sister Tulah smacked her hand down on her plastic tray, rattling the silverware.

"And if you want to get paid, then you'd better start talking. I don't have time for your games, Mr. Reynolds. When is the vote going to be now?"

"Monday."

Sister Tulah's eyes widened.

"This Monday?"

Mr. Reynolds slid his tray down to the end of the line and picked through the soggy pile of cornbread triangles.

"This Monday. As in, Friday, Saturday, Sunday, vote. You feel me, sister?"

"We've got everyone we need on board, right?"

He shrugged again.

"You need Kirkland in order to get the rest, and he's still holding out. That's why I'm here. To pass along the message."

Tulah frowned.

"What does he want for the vote?"

"Fifty thousand. In his bank account, before Monday morning. Otherwise, he's voting against the permits and swaying the others to do the same. And let me tell you, PRB Industries is not keen on waiting any longer. Word on the street is, if those permits are denied, there'll be a mine popping up in North Carolina next year, not in Florida. The deal's just not sweet enough for PRB to hold on to the proposal here."

"What do the others say?"

The man picked up his laden tray and moved over to the dessert bar. Tulah grimaced and followed him.

"There's no doubt that you hold the key properties and stand to make the most money on the mineral rights, but with men like Gripes and Josten, well, if this deal doesn't go through, they have twenty other projects in the works. They told me to tell you that they've put enough into this already. Kirkland's your problem. If you want this deal, then you had better come up with the cash. Pronto."

Sister Tulah looked down at her empty tray. She gripped the edges again, then let go and smoothed her hands down the sides of her flowered dress.

"You tell Mr. Gripes and Mr. Josten not to worry. Kirkland will have the money by Monday."

Mr. Reynolds nodded and pushed his tray down to the ice cream machine.

"Oh man. They have the swirl kind. This is just my kind of day."

Sister Tulah abandoned her tray and stalked out of the restaurant.

CHAPTER 21

So far, the plan seemed to be going well. About a minute after Ramey pulled out onto the highway, Judah again heard the growl of motorcycle engines in the distance and he knew that the trap had been set. The second set of Scorpions must have seen Ramey go by, following the first group, and they had taken off behind her. He waited about thirty seconds and then put the Bronco in gear. Judah was cautious at first, hoping to give the bikers ahead of him time to set the pace and be focused on Ramey, not the vehicle slowly approaching behind them. About two miles past Lightning Strike Road, on a long stretch of highway, Judah saw two of the Scorpions up ahead. He was far enough back, and driving slow enough, that he hoped he would be taken for just another car on the road. He was betting everything on the Scorpions' assumed incompetence. They had been robbed of a hundred and fifty thousand dollars by an old man and his two sons, after all, and Hiram certainly didn't place any confidence in Jack O' Lantern's ability to lead. Judah didn't think he was too far off in believing that he would be able to out-trap the Scorpions.

He tried not to think about Ramey up ahead. He tried not to think about

Benji lying unconscious in a hospital bed or Sherwood hiding out with Levi. He tried not to think about all of the little things that could wrong in the Wal-Mart parking lot when he confronted the two Scorpions led there by Ramey. He had left the rifle in the backseat of the Cutlass, but he had his .45 under the seat, ready to go. He hoped he wouldn't have to use it. He kept his eyes on the road and tried not to think.

About halfway to Kentsville, Judah swerved around a curve and saw that the bikers in front of him had left the main highway. He caught a glimpse of them turning down a side road leading off into the trees and then they were gone. Judah stepped on the gas and tried to ignore the sinking feeling in his gut. Something had obviously changed in the plan, and as Judah approached the side road, he had only seconds to make a decision. He could forfeit his chance to get to the second group of Scorpions and meet up with Ramey or he could stick with following the bikes ahead of him. And what had Ramey done? If the first two motorcycles had turned off as well, had Ramey stayed following them or had she stuck with the original plan? Or had something else gone wrong?

The turn was suddenly upon him and Judah had only a split second to decide. He took a deep breath and yanked the wheel hard to the left, fishtailing off the asphalt. Once Judah became aware that he was on a sandy back road, lined with encroaching oak trees and canopied by overhanging, entwined branches, he slowed down. He didn't want to get too far behind the Scorpions, but as he continued down the narrow, winding road, Judah became more and more nervous about his decision. The road was graded and he could tell he was gradually going downhill, as if heading into a ravine. He went around curve after curve and then the roar of the motorcycle engines abruptly ceased. The sudden quiet unnerved him and he stomped on the gas. He spun around the last bend and slammed on the brakes to keep from crashing into the two motorcycles parked in the middle of a dead end clearing. High rock walls, blinding in the noon sun, surrounded him on all sides. He knew it instantly. He had just driven into The Pit. The two Scorpions were standing in front of their bikes and each had a gun pointed directly at him.

Judah slammed the gearshift into reverse, but before he could step on the gas he saw a flash of sunlight reflect off another vehicle behind him in the rearview mirror. He whipped his head around just in time to see a mud spattered Dodge Ram pull up behind him and cut off the only entrance and exit to the quarry. Judah started to duck down for the .45 beneath his seat, but a bullet blasted through the glass of his windshield and exploded into the passenger seat of the Bronco. Judah froze.

"Next one's going through your head, jackass."

Judah raised his hands slowly above his head. He heard the truck's door slam behind him and then the sound of a shotgun being racked. The tall, skinny Scorpion Judah remembered from the robbery on the highway waved his gun slightly, indicating for Judah to get out of the Bronco.

"And easy does it, buddy. You even think about reaching and we'll blast you six ways to Sunday."

Judah kept his hands over his head and met the biker's eyes. They were dark and narrowed against the glaring sunlight. The man from the truck came up behind Judah and opened the driver side door. He slowly slid out of the Bronco, keeping his eyes on the man who had spoken to him and ignoring the man with the shotgun barrel pressed hard between his shoulder blades. From the center console of the Bronco, Judah's cellphone began to ring. The man behind him sniggered.

"I think you should probably let that one go to voicemail, friend."

Ramey could hear the voices now. She crept forward on her stomach and inched her way up to the lip of the quarry. The M14 was slung over her shoulder awkwardly, the strap choking her as she crawled, and though it would have been easier to move without the 9mm gripped in her right hand, she didn't dare put it away. Ramey had no idea what she was going to see when she looked over the edge, and she knew that she had to be ready for anything.

Once she had determined that something had gone wrong with Judah's part of the plan, Ramey had turned around and raced back toward the Scorpions' clubhouse. She had been frantic, her mind galloping in a thousand directions, when she came up on a side road she hadn't previously paid any attention to. The road sign had been hidden by low hanging branches when she had been coming from the other direction, but now she could read the name: Devil's Beggar Rd. She had slammed on the brakes and sat with the Cutlass idling in the middle of the blistering pavement as she realized what had just happened to Judah. In the same instant, she understood why the road name had sounded vaguely familiar when Hiram had mentioned it the day before.

When Ramey had been nine years old, the summer that her mother had left a note on the fridge telling Leroy that she'd found true love in the form of an ice cream truck driver and was moving with him to Texas, she and her sister had been hustled out of the way to stay with relatives in Kentsville. Her cousin Opie had been in charge of occupying them during the long, sweltering days and his idea of fun was to take Ramey and Aubrey with him down to what he called The Hole. Ramey and her sister had spent most afternoons collecting rocks while Opie and his friends smoked pot, drank beer and tried to scale the towering quarry walls.

Once Ramey had realized she knew The Pit, knew every inch of it and the high limestone ridge above it, she knew what she had to. She had pulled the car over to the shoulder of the highway and leaped out. She had stuffed the 9mm into the back of her jeans and slung the rifle from the backseat over her shoulder before bolting through the woods.

Ramey finally edged her way to the rim and, using a scraggly pine tree for cover, was able to look down. Part of her was terrified, but part of her was relieved as well. She wasn't sure exactly what was happening to Judah, but at least she knew where he was. Ramey figured she had pretty good coverage from her vantage point; she remembered as a kid how the light had reflected off the quarry walls and made it difficult to look straight up and see a person scaling down. She pushed herself up so that she was squatting on her heels and surveyed the scene beneath her.

She could see how they had trapped Judah. A large, white pickup truck was blocking the only exit and she understood that once Judah had entered the quarry, he had been unable to leave. Two motorcycles were parked in front of the Bronco so that it was essentially surrounded. Three men were standing in the middle of the quarry. The heavy man with a full beard had a shotgun gripped in both hands. He wore a sleeveless flannel shirt that left an inch of his white, flabby belly exposed over his cut-off jean shorts. Ramey decided he wasn't one of the bikers, maybe only hired help, and she hoped she could use that to her advantage. The other two men were obviously the Scorpions who had initially been following her. Their black leather vests gleamed in the sun. One of them was hanging back, closer to the bikes, and she took the other one, a tall, skinny man with a bad haircut, to be the man in charge. He seemed to be the one doing all of the talking.

In the middle of the three men was Judah. He was leaning against the hood of the Bronco and Ramey could tell he had already been in the dust once. His left side was streaked with dirt and she could see a line of blood running from the corner of his mouth. Other than that, though, he looked unharmed. He stood with his arms crossed in front of him and a stubborn look on his face. His mouth was firm and his shoulders were thrown back. Ramey knew that posture. He wasn't going to give them anything. She held her breath, but could only make out the echo of voices, not the actual words.

The tall man kept gesticulating with his hands, but she couldn't see Judah's lips moving. He just kept shaking his head. The heavy man with the shotgun came up behind Judah and pushed his shoulders like a schoolyard bully, but Judah kept his footing and only swayed. The tall man indicated for the heavy man to stop. He pulled a cellphone out of his pocket and stepped away from Judah for a moment. Ramey watched him nod his head several times. The other two men seemed to be getting restless and Ramey knew she didn't have much time left. She put the handgun down; at this range there was no telling what she'd hit if she pulled the trigger on that one. She eased the M14 over her shoulder and held it level between her hands. Though it seemed she had been pulling a gun out a lot lately, it had been a while since she had actually fired one. And definitely not at a human being.

She slid her hands up and down the barrel of the rifle. Judah was right, it did look prehistoric, but Hiram had been right, too. She remembered shooting this type of gun once at a family reunion with Lyle and Hiram. It was more accurate than anything she had ever fired before, but she was still at least two hundred yards away. She sighted down the barrel, tried to keep her hands steady and waited.

The tall man snapped the phone shut and walked over to the other biker. He spoke to him for a moment and then gestured to the man with the shotgun. The heavy man pushed Judah with the butt of the gun, forcing him to move, while the two Scorpions turned and began walking back to their bikes. She realized that they were going to put Judah in the truck, most likely to take him back to the clubhouse, and Ramey knew it was now or never. She waited until Judah was on the other side of the Bronco, lined up the sights and fired.

The first shot hit the rocky sand right next to the heavy man's sneakers. At the sound of the gunshot, everyone in the quarry scattered. Ramey's chest was pounding and her hands were shaking, but she forced the fear from her mind and fired at the motorcycles. The bullet hit one of the bikes, but ricocheted off the metal into the shoulder of the shorter biker. He screamed and grabbed his arm and she fired again, hitting the ground about a foot away from the skinny man. Judah had ducked down behind the Bronco as soon as the first shot was fired and Ramey hoped he would stay there. She had been right about the blinding effect of the white rock walls. The tall biker pulled out a gun and fired a few shots in her direction, but they weren't even close. They couldn't see her, and from the way the men were looking around themselves in all directions, the weird acoustics that the quarry created were acting in her favor as well. She took aim and fired again.

As soon as the shooting had begun, the heavy man had immediately run for his truck. Ramey had been right in thinking he wasn't invested enough to risk being part of a gunfight. After the blind shots at the quarry wall, the Scorpions ran for their bikes as well. The motorcycle Ramey had hit was toppled over in the dirt, so they jumped on the other bike together. The man on the back of the bike fired wildly behind him with his good arm as they followed the pickup truck out and the shots exploded into the quarry wall. Ramey fired back and shot out the back windshield of the truck. She lined up the sights one final time and aimed for the back of the already wounded biker, but didn't pull the trigger. She didn't need to. It was over.

Ramey tossed the rifle aside and looked for Judah. She had seen where most of her shots had landed, but she wasn't sure. Then his head appeared above the hood of the Bronco. There was dirt in his hair and a wild look in his eyes. Ramey called down him.

"Judah!"

His head snapped up as he tried to follow the sound of her voice. Judah stepped out from behind the Bronco with an astonished look on his face. He shaded his eyes with his hand as he slowly looked up to the edge of the quarry.

"Ramey?"

She stood up and waved her arm in the air so he could see her. His forehead was creased and his mouth hung wide open. He couldn't believe what he was seeing. Ramey couldn't believe what she had done.

CHAPTER 22

Felton stood in the spacious foyer and looked up the carpeted stairs. His bedroom was up there. With the same twin bed he had slept in all his life and the same brown oval rug and the same single window that looked out over the driveway with a view of the church, the highway and the rangy woods beyond. The window had been nailed shut when he was a child, and even as a teenager he had never been able to pry it open. As an adult he hadn't even bothered to try. There were posters of reptiles ripped from the pages of *Ranger Rick* magazines he had stolen from the Kentsville Public Library and a mobile he had once made out of hollow tortoise shells hanging above the child's size desk in the corner. And there was air conditioning. And a bathroom right down the hall. Felton gazed up the flight of stairs and wondered how long he was going to be banished to his camper this time.

"Are you coming in, Felton?"

He turned away from the stairs and stepped into the dining room. It was bright outside, but the heavy, velvet curtains had been drawn against the afternoon heat and sunlight. The room was full of darkly lacquered wood and shadows. Felton recognized the ever-present smell of potpourri and Pinesol. A line of Hummel figurines eyed him from the sideboard and several pastel portraits of Jesus stared accusingly at him from all sides of the room. At the end of the long dining room table that could seat ten, but had only ever hosted three, Sister Tulah sat with hands clasped, mouth puckered and pale eyes shining through the gloom. Felton edged his way around the table and sat down in an uncomfortable wooden chair. Only Tulah's chair at the head of the table was allowed to have any padding.

Felton rested his hands in his lap and stared down at them. He waited for Tulah to clear her throat and speak.

"Do you like sleeping out in that tin can camper with all of those disgusting reptiles?"

Felton didn't raise his eyes.

"They're my friends."

Sister Tulah exploded into cruel laughter.

"Sometimes I can't even believe we're kin. I can't believe we're of the same flesh and blood."

Sister Tulah smacked her thin lips, but Felton said nothing.

"Maybe it's a good thing your mother's dead. Saved Rowena the pain of having to see how unnatural you've become."

Felton slumped his shoulders and sighed. He had heard it all before.

"What do you want from me?"

"And to think how hard your Uncle Walter tried to raise you up like a man before he died. Well, maybe it's not entirely your fault. Walt wasn't much of a man himself."

Felton sat up straight and looked at Sister Tulah. He kept his face flat and emotionless.

"What do you want?"

Tulah narrowed her eyes at him and rubbed her palms together.

"It's funny, Felton, hearing you address me like that. Considering the world of trouble and pain you've caused me as of late. I'd expect a little more humility from somebody who has made the mistakes you've made. From somebody who is ultimately such a pathetic, lazy screw-up."

Felton shifted in his seat, but kept his gaze on Tulah. He knew what this was all about, he knew the routine: she wanted something from him, but had to go to lengths to shame him before she could ask. He had a feeling that this was something bigger than the snake, though. Otherwise, why would she have invited him into the house when he was supposed to be banned from stepping foot in it?

"I can't believe I've even let you back through my front door. Can't believe I've let your sniveling, cowering self sit at the same table as me. It's a disgrace. Really, just a disgrace."

But Felton wasn't sniveling. It had begun to dawn on him that Tulah wasn't coming to him this time because it was convenient, but because it was necessary. He had something she not only wanted, but needed. He felt a strange flush creep into his face and he tried to keep the corners of his mouth from turning upwards. Felton quickly looked away from Tulah and kept his eyes cast down as she continued to berate him.

"To think that I used to hope that one day you would outgrow your weak ways and your peculiar inclinations. To think that I used to believe that one day you could be somebody. To think that I once thought you could have even half a chance of ever beginning to fill my shoes. I must have been delusional the day I ever looked at you as a child and thought I could make something out of you."

Felton wasn't listening. He suddenly jerked his head up and met Sister Tulah's eyes. They went wide when she realized how he was looking at her. Felton kept his voice steady.

"What do I get?"

"What are you talking about?"

"What do I get in return for whatever it is you want from me?"

Sister Tulah glared hard at Felton and did not look away. She seemed to be waiting for him to recant, but he kept his gaze level and his mouth shut tightly. She couldn't see that underneath the table Felton was squeezing his hands together so hard he was starting to loose circulation in some of his fingers.

"Fine."

Tulah smoothed her hands across the embroidered placemat in front of her. She traced her thick fingers slowly across the knotted pink roses.

"Today just seems to be the day for everybody else to think they have the upper hand. But that's okay. You reap what you sow, you know, you reap what you sow."

Felton, with his new found sense of importance, was undeterred.

"What do I get?"

Sister Tulah bared her teeth in a grotesque grin.

"Do you want to be allowed back in the house?"

Felton nodded.

"Then you'd better start telling me everything you know about the man who has my money."

"ARE YOU SHITTING me?"

Jack O' Lantern ran his hand over his face and then slammed it down on the plastic foldout table. Slim Jim sat opposite him but kept his composure. His mouth was drawn into a grim line and his eyes were sunken, tired. Whereas Jack's face was aflame with frustration, Slim Jim's cheeks sagged and his face had a gray cast to it. He sat still, with his shoulders slumped forward, not defeated, just exhausted.

"I'm sorry, Jack. We had him, but then they had us."

Jack O' Lantern turned to Toadie, sitting at the corner of the table, blood seeping through the white gauze Legs had pressed against his wounded shoulder. Sweat was beaded across his forehead and upper lip in thick drops and his skin was taking on a waxy sheen. His eyes were still bright with adrenaline, though, and he didn't seem to notice Legs at his side.

"How many shooters?"

Toadie rolled his head toward Jack O' Lantern and though his eyes were glittering, Jack could tell that they were going in and out of focus. He was looking at a point over Jack's shoulder.

"I don't know, at least two. Had to be at least two. Maybe more. They were high up on the rock wall and we couldn't see 'em."

Jack's mouth twisted in disgust.

"Save it."

Toadie winced as Legs lifted the gauze to inspect the wound. He turned his head awkwardly to try to look down at his shoulder. His teeth were chattering and his skin was slick with cold sweat. Jack O' Lantern turned back to Slim Jim.

"Which one of the Cannons did you actually have?"

Slim Jim shook his head.

"He wouldn't say his name."

Legs looked up from the bloody mess he was trying to hold together.

"Big beefy dude?"

"Nah."

"Musta been the other brother, then. Didn't your cousin say the older one was a real bull? Built like a freight truck or something."

Slim Jim's mouth sagged into a frown.

"We don't even know if it was the Cannons. The guy wasn't saying nothing. I loosened his jaw up for him, but he still kept his clam shut. We were just about to bring him back when the shooting started."

Jack O' Lantern slammed his palm down on the table again. He was shaking and Legs backed away from the table slightly, afraid that Jack was going to toss it. It had happened before. Jack spoke through clenched teeth and glared at Slim Jim.

"It was the Cannons."

His blue eyes were shooting daggers at Slim Jim, but Legs took advantage of the pause. He pulled away the gauze from Toadie's bloody shoulder to show Jack O' Lantern.

"Hey, boss? The bullet's still in there. We gotta get him to a hospital."

Jack's eyes didn't leave Slim Jim.

"Nobody's going anywhere right now."

"I'm telling you, he needs a doctor."

Jack O' Lantern kicked his chair back, the metal legs screeching against the concrete floor. Toadie raised his head sharply at the sound, but only looked off into the distance.

"And I'm telling you, no hospitals! You want to be the one explaining this in the police report? You're just gonna have to do what you can here. He ain't gonna die from a bullet in the shoulder. Now, everybody get out of here and give me some Goddamn room to think!"

Legs put his arm around Toadie and helped him up. They lurched away toward the couch across the room. Slim Jim stood, but didn't move away from the table.

"Jack."

Jack O' Lantern stood up and leaned across the table on his knuckles. His voice was low and dangerous.

"I don't want to hear another word. It was the Cannons."

Slim Jim nodded and put his hands in his pockets, causing his bony shoulders to arch up.

"I know. But it's not about that. Shelia called me while Toadie and I were waiting for that second car."

Jack O' Lantern closed his eyes. Slim Jim could see his jaw muscles clenching and unclenching as Jack tried to maintain some form of cool. When he opened his eyes, they were livid and his voice was trembling with anger.

"I don't want to hear about that dumb whore either. What's wrong with you, Jimmy? Don't tell me you answered the call."

"I did."

Jack O' Lantern stood up straight and ran a sweaty hand through his hair.

"I gotta explain what we're dealing with right now? I gotta draw you a picture or something?"

Slim Jim's face was expressionless.

"Jack."

"We got a family of psycho hillbillies who stole a hundred and fifty thousand dollars right outta our hands and are now taking pot shots at us like they're hunting squirrels. I got two guys laid up now and I got snakes and fire showing up on my doorstep. I don't got time for Shelia's sorry-ass phone calls, and I certainly don't got the time for you to be taking them."

"She knows about that Cannon boy. I think she's starting to feel bad about the whole thing."

Jack O' Lantern laughed.

"Tell her to take it up with her therapist."

Slim Jim's eyes were wary.

"You're not worried about her talking?"

"So what if she does?"

Jack O' Lantern pulled his lighter out of his pocket and flipped it open and closed.

"I think today proved that the Cannons know what we did to that kid and they know where we are. She can go squawking all she wants to them and it don't make no difference now."

Slim Jim considered this for a moment and then nodded once. He relaxed his shoulders slightly.

"Fine."

"And, Jimmy, if she calls you again, you damn well better not answer it. You understand?"

Slim Jim met Jack's blazing eyes and then quickly looked away.

"Yeah. I got it."

Jack O' Lantern flipped the top on his lighter a few more times and then shoved it back in his pocket. He waved his hand at Slim Jim.

"All right. Now go make sure tweedle-dumb and tweedle-dumber are actually standing at the gate, doing their job. Jesus Christ, what the hell is going on around here?"

THE OLD MAN stood in front of Tulah's desk in the tiny church office. It was getting late, past twilight, but the man had entered the church wearing dark, wraparound sunglasses and he kept them on inside. Two white bars of florescent light were reflected in the black lenses as the man stared straight ahead at the wall just above Sister Tulah's head. His long-sleeved white shirt was immaculately pressed and, though he stood with his narrow shoulders stooped and his thin hands hanging down, clasped low in front of him, he gave off the impression of standing at attention. He licked his thin, chapped lips with the tip of his colorless tongue and waited.

Sister Tulah finished shuffling through tax forms and stacked them together neatly in a pile to her right. She rested her elbows on the edge of the table and leaned back in her reclining desk chair. She surveyed the space in front of her, to make sure that everything was in the right place, and then she finally looked up at the elder.

"I need you to do something for me."

There was no response. Tulah picked up a ballpoint pen and tapped it on the pile of papers.

"Tell me. Are you familiar with the book of Mathew?"

The old man nodded slowly.

"Chapter twenty-one? Verse twelve?"

The man spoke in a voice completely devoid of tone.

"*Then Jesus went into the temple of God and drove out all those who bought and sold in the temple, and overturned the tables of the money changers and the seats of those who sold doves.*"

Sister Tulah waved her hand at him.

"Continue."

"*And he said to them, it is written my house shall be called a house of prayer, but you have made it a den of thieves.*"

Only the man's mouth had moved; his body stood like a statue in the center of the office. Not even the rising and falling of his chest could be noticed. Sister Tulah's nose wrinkled in a smirk.

"Correct. It seems that there are so many dens of thievery nowadays, wouldn't you say? Popping up all over the place like mushrooms after a storm."

The man didn't answer her. Tulah tapped the pen again and then pointed it at the man.

"Now, Deuteronomy. That's one of my favorites. One of my absolute favorites. All kinds of crazy events occurring within those pages. We can read Deuteronomy and feel that God is really speaking to us, you know? How about it? Do you happen to know chapter thirty-two, verse twenty-two? That's a real mover and shaker."

The old man's lips parted.

"*For a fire is kindled in my anger, and shall burn to the lowest Hell; it shall consume the earth her increase, and set on fire the foundations of the mountains.*"

Sister Tulah nodded and her pale eyes narrowed as she looked up at the man.

"Do you know what you need to do?"

The man dipped his chin slightly to indicate that he did. Tulah leaned back in her chair and swiveled slightly from side to side.

"Good. In the morning, then. And make sure you call him and have him meet you there."

Sister Tulah lavished a ghoulish grin on the old man and rapped her fleshy knuckles on the desk.

"I want him to see it."

The elder bowed his head and slowly crept out of the room.

CHAPTER 23

JUDAH PULLED A ribbed white undershirt over his head and let Ramey's screen door bang closed behind him. The wave of heat that assailed him was like walking into a brick wall. He had cursed the rattling window air conditioning units in Ramey's apartment when he woke tangled in suffocating, sweat soaked sheets, but now he was tempted to duck back inside and press his face against the flimsy plastic slats for relief. The sun was just now beginning to climb in the sky, it couldn't have been much past nine, but already the cracked thermometer tacked to the side of the apartment building was pushing ninety. He rubbed his hands over his eyes and then through his hair, though he knew he was probably only making it worse. He fixed the cuffs of his jeans over his bare feet and then stood to take in the scene around him: an empty street already beginning to steam in the heat, a yappy dog barking somewhere in the distance as if its tiny life depended on it and Ramey, eyes closed, chin in her hand, elbow on her knees, sitting on top of the patio table in the open area outside her apartment. Judah walked across the hot pavement and slipped a cigarette out of the pack sitting next to her. She didn't open her eyes.

"You know those things are gonna kill you."

Judah lit the cigarette and squinted upwards through the smoke. A hawk, buoyed up by the rising heat waves, was slowly skimming across the sky.

"When I was a kid, I thought you should only smoke cigarettes when it was cold."

He sat down on the table next to her.

"I thought it was like some kinda device to warm you up inside. Like a little tiny space heater for your face or something."

Ramey opened her eyes and crushed her cigarette out in the overflowing plastic ashtray between them.

"Wow. I guess that explains a lot."

Judah stared across the street.

"I couldn't never figure out why everybody was smoking all the year round. It just didn't make no sense to me."

"You ever tell this theory of yours to anybody?"

Judah smiled.

"I asked Sherwood about it once. He was buying a carton down at the convenience store and I asked him something about why he needed to warm himself up when it was near a hundred degrees outside."

Ramey turned her head to look in Judah's direction.

"He laugh or smack you?"

"Both, I think."

Ramey turned away from him and they stared out at the empty road in silence. Judah finished his cigarette and reached for her hand. She tried to pull away, but he laced his fingers through hers and held her firmly.

"We gotta talk about this, Ramey."

She wouldn't look at him.

"We do?"

"You ain't put more'n ten words together at one time since we left The Pit.

I know you were up half the night sitting at that kitchen table, just smoking cigarettes and trying to find the answers on the walls. Trying to find answers that don't exist to questions you don't even have in your head yet."

Ramey tried to yank her hand away again, but Judah gripped her tighter. She sneered at him.

"You're quite the philosopher this early in the morning. Haven't even had a cup of coffee yet and you already think you know everything that's going on in my head."

"No."

Judah's voice was low and steady.

"I don't know what's going on in your head, Ramey. But I know you're hurting. And I don't know if yesterday scared you, or made you mad, or what, but I know it made you feel something."

The smoky gray cat with the mangy tail came out from underneath a parked car across the street and sauntered down the road. Judah watched its shoulders move through its ragged fur and kept his eyes on the animal so he wouldn't have to look at Ramey.

"And I know this show ain't over. There's still a rough road ahead of us and you keep saying you want to go down it with me. But if we're gonna do this, if we're gonna walk side by side to wherever this leads us, then we got to be honest with each other. That's what you been telling me all along."

Judah watched the cat and waited. The animal slipped underneath the shade of another car and Judah watched the space where it had been. A skein of sweat was forming between his and Ramey's palms, but still he wouldn't let her go. Finally, he looked up into her face. Her mouth was set in a rigid line and her eyes were lost. Judah sighed.

"Ramey Barrow, if you never pick up another gun. If you decide to just walk away. If you decide to walk away from me right now, and never look back, and never have no more to do with me in all your life, I'm still gonna love you as much as the first day I saw you, when you were five years old and you showed up in my yard, chucking rocks at squirrels. You understand?"

Ramey's shoulders heaved and then her hand relaxed against Judah's. Some of the tension went out of her face and her arms and she rested her head on Judah's shoulder.

"When I started shooting, I wasn't thinking. It was just you. And the gun in my hand. And they went together somehow. I had to stop them from hurting you. That was all."

"You mighta saved my life, Ramey. I know you don't want to think about it like that, but I might not be sitting here with you right now if you hadn't started shooting."

Ramey's voice was quiet.

"I coulda killed those men. I coulda killed you."

Ramey lifted her head from Judah's shoulder and let go of his hand. She lit another cigarette and slid off the table. Judah watched her back tighten again.

"I wasn't aiming to, but that don't mean it couldn't have happened. Or I coulda shot you. Or one of them coulda shot me. Jesus Christ, one of them could show up here right now and put a bullet in us both. What the hell have I gotten into?"

"I mean it. You can still walk away."

Ramey waved her cigarette in the air, as if she was lecturing the empty pavement before her.

"I've carried a gun on me most of my life. Daddy made sure I knew how to shoot by the time I was ten. I been to ranges, I shot deer, I plunked away at tin cans and beer bottles like it was nobody's business. I even pulled that little 9mm out a time or two."

She turned back to Judah and crossed her arms over her chest.

"But I've never pulled the trigger with another human being standing in my way."

Judah shrugged.

"Well, now you know. It ain't the same thing as just taking a gun out and waving it around and saying a few words. And shooting at people ain't like they show it on TV neither. It's something different. You gotta be right with the fact that you might take a life, even if you don't intend to. And you gotta be aware that once you pull the trigger, you've set your own self in the crosshairs for somebody else."

Ramey narrowed her eyes.

"How would you know? You ever shot somebody before?"

Judah shook his head.

"No. But with my family, with some of the things I've done, I had to think it through enough times. It's something I had to come to terms with a long time ago. I guess I've just been lucky so far."

"I guess I just ain't."

Judah stood up and shoved his hands in his back pockets.

"I wish I could say I could make it better. I wish I could say, let's run away. Let's get outta here. Let's pick up, go somewhere, let the chips fall, try to be happy. All those things you probably want me to say, even if you won't admit it."

Ramey opened her mouth to speak, but Judah wouldn't let her.

"I wish I could. But you know I can't. And you know I won't. But there's a reason that Levi's wife lives in a fantasy world of soap operas and little dogs. And that my mama would clean Sherwood's guns, but never ask questions. I heard my mama tell my Aunt Imogene once that the less she knew about what Sherwood did, the better."

"I ain't gonna be like that."

"I'm just saying…"

Now Ramey wouldn't let Judah speak.

"I know what you're saying. And you can save it. I made my choice when I showed up at The Ace last week. I made my choice when I took you to Hiram's and I made my choice when I started tailing those bikers and when I pulled the trigger at The Pit, and now I'm making it again. I'm with you."

Ramey's eyes were dark, but her voice was strong.

"Am I rattled? Yeah. And I'm scared. And I'm pissed off. More than you know. But I'm with you. And this is the last time I'm gonna waste breath explaining that to you. Now, do you understand?"

Ramey dropped her cigarette to the hot pavers and stamped it out. Her jaw was trembling, but she held her chin up defiantly. Judah wanted only to take her into his arms and hold her, to run his hands through her hair, down her back and tell her that it was all going to work out. That it was all going to work out in the end. Instead, he squinted up in into the sun-blasted, piercing blue sky and frowned.

"You know this is gonna turn worse 'fore it gets better."

Ramey nodded.

"I know."

"And I can't promise you a happy ending. I want to, but I can't."

"I know that, too."

Judah watched a second hawk swoop into the wake of the first. He finally looked away and met Ramey's eyes. Behind them were fear, and determination, and the fierce gaze of unwavering loyalty. Judah had no choice but to accept what she was offering and be grateful for it.

THE WAITRESS WHO greeted Sherwood at the Mr. Omelet on Friday morning was one of his favorites. She had long legs, long hair and wore her shirt unbuttoned one lower than the restaurant uniform required. Add to that a push-up bra and barely legal status, and Sherwood had all the eye candy he needed for nine o'clock in the morning. He watched the butt of her tight black pants as she languidly led him across the restaurant to his usual booth in the back. He pinched her upper arm as he slid into the maroon vinyl seat and she winked at him before slapping the plastic menu down in front of him and turning on her heels. Sherwood craned his neck to watch her walk away and then smiled to himself.

He flipped the sticky menu over to the breakfast side and ran his eyes down the list of items. He knew the menu by heart, could recite it forwards and backwards in his sleep, but he still read it every morning and considered his options. He had just decided to order the number twelve special when a voice spoke from the booth behind him.

"Do you know who I am?"

Sherwood gently set the menu back down on the table in front of him and slid to the edge of the seat. He was bracing himself to stand up when he heard the voice again.

"I wouldn't do that, Mr. Cannon."

The voice was slow in rhythm, but biting in tone. It belonged to someone who had utter confidence in herself and her actions. Someone who had the upper hand and knew it. Sherwood froze.

"I have a man sitting in a vehicle out in the parking lot with the window rolled down and a gun pointed at the entrance of this establishment. He knows what you look like and he's been instructed to shoot you on sight if you walk out of that door before I do."

Sherwood didn't move.

"There's a man on the back exit as well. So sit down and don't do anything stupid."

Sherwood considered this for a moment and then slid back to the middle of the seat. He clasped his hands on top of the plastic menu and waited. The back of his booth shook and then a heavy woman with strikingly pale eyes meandered around the seat and wedged herself into the space across the table from him. She, too, rested her bloated hands on the table top, so Sherwood knew she was playing fair. At least for the moment.

One of the waitresses started to come by the table to drop off a mug of coffee and take Sherwood's order, but he shot her a warning look. The girl abruptly went to another table and Sherwood turned his attention back to the woman sitting across from him. She licked her pale pink lips with a gray tongue before speaking again.

"Now I'll ask you again. Do you know who I am?"

Sherwood nodded.

"I'm gonna assume you're Sister Tulah Atwell, that crazy preacher lady from up in Kentsville. You run one of them Bible-thumping, snake-swinging churches."

Sister Tulah frowned.

"I don't swing snakes, Mr. Cannon."

Sherwood leaned back against the booth.

"Well, then, what do you do?"

"I deliver people's souls to God. And I look after their business interests."

Sherwood sneered.

"You mean your own business interests."

Tulah's pale eyes flashed for a moment.

"So you do know who I am."

Sherwood leaned over and glared at Sister Tulah.

"I know enough to know that I should be reaching across this table right now and wrapping my hands around your fat neck."

Sister Tulah returned the glare.

"And then you must also know enough to be aware that engaging in such capricious actions would be unwise."

Tulah glanced around the restaurant before turning her eyes back on Sherwood.

"I offer my condolences for your youngest son, Mr. Cannon. Such a tragedy.

I heard there's a possibility he might not live. I'll be sure to pray to our Lord for his survival."

Sherwood grit his teeth, but didn't miss a beat.

"What do you want, you old hag?"

"My money."

Sherwood's face was blank.

"I don't know what you're talking about."

"Oh, yes, you do. And you're going to return it to me. Unless you want one of your other boys ending up lying in the hospital next to his brother. Or in the ground, for that matter."

A tinge of color rose to Sherwood's cheeks.

"You gonna threaten me?"

"Do I need to?"

They stared at one another for a moment, neither one looking away, neither one backing down. Finally, Sherwood cleared his throat and settled himself on the squeaking vinyl.

"You're a smart woman, preacher lady. And you've obviously done your homework on me, so try again. What're you offering?"

Sister Tulah pursed her lips together and narrowed her eyes.

"Fine. I want that money back. Now. And in exchange, I'm extending the invitation for you to enter into business with me."

Sherwood laughed.

"Do you even know how much money we're talking here? Maybe you don't, since I don't recall you being present when it came into my possession."

"I am fully aware of the amount in question, Mr. Cannon."

Sherwood picked up the edge of the plastic menu and snapped it a few times against the table.

"Business with you, huh? What, like being an altar boy or something? Maybe you want me to feed the snakes or stand around and catch people when they start falling over like bowling pins?"

Sister Tulah's jaw tightened.

"I said before, there are no snakes in my church."

"Oh, right, right. No snakes. Maybe you just cut the heads off of chickens or sacrifice goats or something."

"I think you are mixing up your religions, Mr. Cannon. And I, for one, don't find it funny. God's work is not something to be trifled with."

Sherwood grinned darkly.

"You mean your work."

Tulah dipped her chin and huffed impatiently.

"Perhaps you have time to sit here and play at this all day long, but I do not. Again, if you know as much about me as you claim to know, then you are aware of what I'm offering."

Sherwood thought about this a moment and then tilted his head to the side.

"How do I know I can trust you? How do I know you ain't just blowing smoke up my ass?"

"Because, money aside, I could use someone like you. Someone who can take care of things that need to be taken care of. Someone who isn't afraid to partake in certain questionable situations. I have societal obligations that prevent me from taking part in all aspects of my business and it would be beneficial to me to have someone like yourself on my staff."

"Someone to do your dirty legwork for you?"

"Someone who would like to earn a lot more money than they currently do."

Sherwood waved a waitress over to the table and pointed to the number twelve special on the menu. When the girl asked Tulah if she wanted anything, she received only a dangerous stare for an order. Sherwood waited until the waitress had left to continue the conversation.

"I want twenty percent of every gig I'm involved in. No matter how small my role is. Blanket twenty percent."

Sister Tulah laughed.

"Absolutely not."

"Fifteen."

Tulah's pale eyes narrowed again.

"You do understand how generous I am being here, correct?"

"How so? I have the money you want."

"And I am agreeing to leave your family alone. To look past your sin of taking from me what is rightfully mine. I'm allowing you to walk away from this building alive."

Sherwood started to speak, but clamped his mouth shut as the waitress brought a ceramic white mug to the table and poured steaming coffee into it. Tulah glared at the girl until she scurried away again. Sherwood raised the cup of coffee to his lips and blew on it.

"Ten percent, then."

Sister Tulah nodded.

"That's better."

"And I'm keeping ten thousand of that cash for myself. Ten percent and ten thousand. Deal?"

Sister Tulah watched Sherwood slurp his coffee. Her mouth was curled in an expression of disgust, but eventually she dipped her head in agreement. Sherwood set his coffee down and reached across the table to shake on it. Tulah looked down at his hand as though it was a worm writhing on the table.

"We have an agreement. Bring the money to the Last Steps of Deliverance tomorrow afternoon and come alone. I know that I don't have to worry about one of your sons, but I had better not catch even a glimpse of the other two. And mark my words, Mr. Cannon. It would be extremely imprudent to not hold up your end of the bargain."

Sherwood withdrew his hand.

"You threatening me again, lady?"

Tulah slid awkwardly out of the booth and stood next to the table, eyeing Sherwood with that same look of disgust.

"I don't know if you believe in God, Mr. Cannon. And I don't know if you've ever been baptized."

Sister Tulah leaned down so that her face was uncomfortably close to Sherwood's.

"But trust me, you have no desire to ever, ever be baptized by me."

JACK O' LANTERN pulled his motorcycle up next to Long John's Cadillac and cut the engine. Slim Jim rode up too far on the other side of him and then backed his bike up parallel to Jack's. Slim Jim switched his motorcycle off and they sat together in silence, straddling their bikes and eyeing the dilapidated singlewide wedged back into a stand of pine trees. To reach the trailer, Jack and Slim Jim had ridden along the back roads, down a cow path and a winding dirt trail that twisted through the tangled oak, pine and palmettos. Even though the place was technically out in the back end of the middle of nowhere, Long John was paranoid and had made sure the trailer was as camouflaged as possible by the heavy, drooping pine boughs. The trailer was beige and white, with rusted trim and black garbage bags stretched and duct-taped across the windows. It was balanced precariously on a row of cinderblocks and had a ramp made of plywood and two-by-fours leading up to the front door. The smell of ammonia and burnt plastic reached them even from fifteen feet away and Jack's eyes began to water.

Slim Jim pulled out his cellphone and dialed a number while Jack O' Lantern scanned the trees, looking for movement. Slim Jim snapped the phone shut and shoved it back in his pocket. He frowned and looked over at Jack.

"He ain't answering."

Jack O' Lantern nodded, keeping his eyes on the trees.

"Could be right in the middle of a batch. 'Course, he never picks up his phone for shit anyway. Might as well just go on in."

Jack O' Lantern threw his leg over the seat, but Slim Jim didn't move.

"You ever walk in there when he's neck deep in fumes?"

"No."

Slim Jim shook his head.

"Trust me, you don't want to. I made that mistake once and he nearly flayed me alive. We don't go in there when he's working."

Jack O' Lantern looked at the closed trailer door and considered Slim Jim's advice. Slim Jim knew Long John better than anyone. When Slim Jim's father ran out on his family, back when he and Jack were just kids running around the clubhouse yard chasing each other with wrenches and screwdrivers, Long John had stepped in and been a father figure of sorts. He had helped Slim Jim build his first bike and taken him on his first run. He had vouched for him when the time came for him to patch in. Long John was from the old guard, he had been Oren's vice president, but had stepped down when Oren died. Before he lost his leg, he was considered the wildest man in a fight. Now, he stayed out of the fray, but had found a talent for chemistry. He could put down twenty beers on an all-night run, but stayed away from his own product. Long John said he loved to make it, but hated to taste it. Jack would have trusted no one else with the Scorpions' only reliable source of income.

Jack O' Lantern turned away from the trailer and pulled a pack of cigarettes out of his pocket. He shook one out and lit it. Slim Jim watched Jack's movements and stayed on his bike.

"Now tell me again what you think we're doing here."

Jack coughed out a stream of smoke and turned sharply on Slim Jim.

"Damnit, Jimmy, quit talking to me like I got all the answers stuffed up my asshole. I'm doing the best I can here, all right? That okay with you?"

Jack O' Lantern's face was red, but the color came more from a mix of shame and frustration than anger. Slim Jim was unfazed. He shrugged his shoulders, but shifted his gaze away from Jack's piercing, and desperate, blue eyes. He casually looked off into the woods.

"What'd that preacher lady's guy say on the phone?"

Jack sighed and rubbed his forehead with the side of his hand.

"He said to meet him out here at nine this morning."

"How'd she know 'bout this place?"

"I have no idea."

Jack O' Lantern closed his eyes.

"I have no idea how Tulah knows anything 'bout anything. But she does. She just does."

Jack O' Lantern opened his eyes and studied the glowing end of his cigarette.

"Anyway, this guy, his voice sounded something like that crazy old man who brought us the snake, he said to meet him here. He said that Tulah was willing to work out a deal. Taking product in place of cash."

Slim Jim snorted.

"And you believed him?"

"What else was I supposed to do?"

Slim Jim leaned forward and hung his long arms over the handlebars of his bike.

"What the hell is someone like Sister Tulah going to do with a load of crystal meth? She's a preacher in a loony bin church, for Christ's sake."

Jack O' Lantern's mouth twisted in a grim smile.

"Maybe she's gonna sell it to the church folks. Maybe that's why they're always whooping and hollering and acting like they've all lost their marbles. They're all higher than a kite."

Slim Jim did not smile back. Jack O' Lantern crushed out his cigarette.

"Or maybe she's got a distributor running it for her or something. I don't know."

"Seems like there's a lot you don't know."

Jack O' Lantern jerked his head up and his face flamed red again.

"I'd start watching my mouth if I was you, Jimmy. We may go way back, but you'd best not be forgetting what the patches on our cuts say. Got it?"

Slim Jim glowered at Jack O' Lantern and opened his mouth to say something, but changed his mind. He crossed his arms in front of his chest and leaned back, deliberately looking away from Jack. They waited, not speaking, for another five minutes. Jack O' Lantern checked the time on his cellphone and broke the silence.

"It's five after nine."

Slim Jim slowly turned his head toward Jack.

"Yeah? And?"

Jack O' Lantern stared down at the cellphone in his hand. Deep creases ran across his forehead.

"The man on the phone. He said exactly nine."

"So?"

"It was the way he said it. Like running late wasn't an option. And then it's past nine and he's not here."

Slim Jim gripped his handlebars.

"This is bullshit, Jack. We gotta go. We gotta get back to the clubhouse. You know Legs and Tiny can't handle nothing on their own, and those prospects are next to worthless. What if coming out here was just some kinda setup? Some kinda decoy? Think, Jack."

Jack O' Lantern nodded slowly.

"I am. They'll be fine. Let's go check on the crystal, at least. If Tulah's guy don't show up in the next ten minutes, we'll head back."

Slim Jim didn't move and Jack threw his hands up in the air.

“If we have even half a chance of paying Tulah off this way, and getting her off our backs, then we need to take it. You know that. Now come on.”

Slim Jim slid off his bike, but still didn’t make a move toward the trailer.

“Okay. But I mean it, Jack. We can’t just walk up on Long John when he’s working. I did that once and he said I was like to cause him to blow the whole place to high heaven.”

Jack O’ Lantern started walking toward the trailer.

“Well, he needs to get over it. I don’t have time to just sit around and wait for him to answer his phone.”

Slim Jim shook his head.

“I’m just saying.”

Jack O’ Lantern started to take a step forward, but wasn’t able to complete it. In the next instance, there was a deafening roar and a blistering wave of heat and a flash of blinding light. Slim Jim, Jack O’ Lantern and their bikes were blown backwards into the pine trees, and shards of glass and tiny pieces of burning plastic rained down upon them. Jack O’ Lantern had squeezed his eyes shut against the blast and when he opened them he saw the dark pine canopy overhead and the deep blue morning sky through the leaves. And then smoke and glowing cinders caught up in the haze. Jack O’ Lantern couldn’t hear anything, though he could see Slim Jim’s mouth moving, opening and closing furiously as he scrambled to his feet. Jack clapped his hand on Slim Jim’s shoulder to haul himself up as they slowly turned to view the wreckage before them.

There wasn’t much left. Twisted pieces of scorched metal and melting plastic were strewn through the woods like confetti, and where once the trailer had stood there was now only a blackened, hollow shell with a mist of greasy smoke rising from the remains. Pockets of flame were still billowing up in places, but it was clear that nothing was untouched; no one could have survived the explosion. Jack O’ Lantern sank down to his knees in the pine needles and began to understand.

CHAPTER 24

Benji was not waking up. Judah squeezed his hand awkwardly, unaccustomed to touching his brother in any way other than firm handshakes or slaps on the back. He pressed Benji's limp, clammy fingers between his own and scrutinized his brother's face for a response. Benji didn't flinch. His eyelids didn't flutter and his lips didn't curl in that half smile that made all the girls swoon. Underneath the crusting streaks of healing road rash, Benji's face was flat and gray. Without his customary grin and twinkling eyes, without movement to make his blond hair flop over his forehead and without ruddiness in his cheeks from continually grinning, Benji too closely resembled the rest of his family members. Bereft of the lightness that was always present in his features and his voice, he had fallen eerily into line with the rest of the grim faced Cannon brethren.

Judah released Benji's hand and set it gently back on the edge of the hospital bed. He let his forearms dangle between his knees, but raised his head to look up at Ramey, standing on the other side of Benji, studying the numbers and blinking lights on the respirator.

"You know what all those lights and beeps and shit mean? Does it tell you what's wrong with him?"

Ramey crossed her and shook her head.

"Not exactly. I mean, the machines say he's stable, but that's about it."

"What's stable mean?"

Ramey blew a stray strand of hair out of her face and turned to Judah. His eyes were desperate, haunted. He needed concrete answers and she had none to give him.

"It means that he's breathing. His heart rate is steady. He's okay for the moment."

Judah stood up from the narrow chair and shoved his hands in his pockets. He clenched his teeth.

"For the moment. Well, when the hell is he gonna wake up?"

Ramey looked at him sadly, but had nothing to say. Judah wondered if she, too, noticed how much Benji now looked like the rest of the Cannons. She touched the bandage running across Benji's forehead, being careful not to disturb the tube snaking down his throat or graze the line of stiches running alongside what was left of his ear and across his jaw.

"If we wait around long enough, a doctor's gotta show up. We can ask then. Get more details."

Judah chewed on the inside of his cheek for a moment, but shook his head emphatically and rocked back on the heels of his boots.

"No, we can't stay here. It was dangerous enough showing up in the first place. This is exactly the place the Scorpions would try to find us if they were looking. We gotta leave now."

Ramey nodded and needlessly adjusted the rough hospital blanket on Benji's chest. She tucked it in under his side and came around the bed. Ramey started to put her arm around Judah's waist, but stopped herself when she saw Judah's eyes riveted on Benji's motionless face. Instead, she ducked her head down slightly and walked past him to open the hospital room door. Ramey stood out in the empty white hallway and waited.

Judah ground his teeth together and felt his jaw popping with the force. He wanted to say something to Benji. To tell him that he was going to make them pay. Make them all pay. He wanted to tell Benji that he was sorry he hadn't been there to protect him this time. And sorry that he had been the victim of a crime he had nothing to do with. He wanted to tell Benji that he had screwed up in the quarry, but that he wasn't finished. He wasn't giving up. He was going to make sure no one would ever mess with him again; no one would ever dare go after another Cannon again, not after he was finished with them all. Whoever they might be. But he didn't. Not because Ramey was only a few feet away, or because a nurse or doctor could walk in at any moment, but because he didn't know how to say it. He didn't know exactly how to put words to the anger and frustration and helplessness raging around inside him in a muddled storm of emotions. And he was pretty sure Benji couldn't hear him anyway.

Judah turned on his heel and joined Ramey in the cold hallway. They closed the door behind them and navigated their way through the twisting corridors and reception areas, all the while keeping an eye open for people watching them. No one seemed to notice their presence, though, and they slipped quietly through the sliding glass doors of the emergency room exit. The noonday heat radiated up from the black pavement of the parking lot and blasted them as they crossed to the line of cars shimmering in the hazy air. Judah scanned the parking lot for motorcycles and was just about to tell Ramey that it was all clear when a high-pitched voice rang out behind them.

"You one of the Cannon brothers?"

Judah whirled around, ready to fight even though it was clearly a woman's voice calling to them. He cautiously eyed the tall blonde leaning up against one of the hospital's sandstone pillars. The woman was dressed in a tight denim miniskirt and hot pink tube top that needed to be yanked up a few inches higher. She was wearing strappy, high heeled sandals and her thick, bright makeup was beginning to ooze through the sheen of sweat on her forehead and upper lip. She crushed out her lipstick smeared cigarette beneath the *No Smoking* sign and crossed the pavement to Judah and Ramey. Judah could see a slick of sweat on her sunburned chest and across her collarbone. She stopped about two feet away from them and adjusted her leopard print purse on her shoulder. Ramey immediately crossed her arms in hostility against the woman. Judah looked her up and down, noticing her long legs and sagging but full, cleavage, and narrowed his eyes. The woman appeared to be waiting for an answer, but neither Judah nor Ramey spoke.

"Fine. You don't gotta answer me. It don't take a rocket scientist to know who you are. You might not be as good looking as that Benji kid, but you still look like him."

Judah stiffened and clenched his fists at his side. He took a step toward the woman.

"Who the hell are you?"

The woman ran her hand up and down the strap of her purse nervously.

"Not that it matters to you, but my name is Shelia. Now, you gonna tell me yours or what?"

"No."

Shelia glanced at Ramey, but saw that there was no sympathy on that front either. She took a deep breath and held her head up higher.

"All right. You can be that way if you want. I didn't come here looking for trouble. I ain't aiming for a fight."

Judah looked over his shoulder at Ramey, whose stony glare was fixed on Shelia. He turned around and eyed the woman again. Her words countered it, but he could see that she was scared. She carried herself like a woman who was used to speaking her mind, but was always braced for the resulting blow. She kept her arms in close to protect herself. Judah sighed.

"Well, then why don't you tell me what you did come here looking for,

Shelia."

She twisted her hand around her purse strap.

"I been waiting out here."

Shelia looked around the parking lot, as if unsure how to explain even to herself what she was doing.

"I been waiting, thinking maybe there was a chance I'd run into one of Benji's brothers. I heard he was laid up at this hospital. I knowed that he had two brothers, so I thought, maybe, I'd find one of 'em here. You know, visiting him like. And I guess it worked."

Judah nodded and relaxed a little.

"It worked. So, what are you, one of his girlfriends or something?"

Her eyes shifted again.

"Kinda. Something like that I guess."

Behind Judah, Ramey huffed.

"But you ain't from 'round here, are you?"

Shelia looked at Ramey and then lowered her gaze again.

"No. Not exactly. I been through Silas a couple times. I been around."

"I bet."

Shelia jerked her head up and she and Ramey eyed one another. The last thing Judah needed was a cat fight, so he quickly drew the woman's attention back to him.

"Look, I ain't got time for this. Tell me what you want and be on your way, all right? If you want to see Benji, go on in. No one's gonna stop you."

Shelia bit her lip.

"I said I ain't exactly Benji's girlfriend. Truth be told, I just met him one night. This past Monday night."

Judah opened his mouth, but Shelia rushed through what she had to say.

"I was with the Scorpions. I got Benji to come outta that bar so they could grab him. I ain't seen what they done to him, but I know it had to be bad. I'm sorry."

She flinched right before Judah grabbed her by the throat. She put her hands around Judah's wrists, but didn't put up too much of a fight. He dragged her behind the closest vehicle and slammed her against the side door of a Ford Econoline. Her head banged dully against the door, but she didn't make a sound. He jerked her body again and she instinctively let her limbs go slack. She knew she would sustain less bruises that way.

Judah brought his face down close to hers, forcing Shelia to look at him, and began to squeeze her throat. Ramey's voice, sharp but calm, cracked behind him.

"Judah."

He didn't let her go, but he didn't squeeze any further.

"This piece of trash might not look like much, but I don't think she's stupid neither. She's gotta have a reason for showing up here, more than just a guilty feeling in her heart."

Judah considered this for a moment and then slammed Shelia once more against the side of the van before letting her go. She started to drop to the ground, but Judah grabbed her by the shoulders and forced her to her feet. He stepped away from her and watched her gasp and clear her throat. He didn't take his eyes off of her.

"She better be right about you. You better have something more to say than a sniveling apology. Otherwise, I think she's gonna be just as unforgiving as I am."

Shelia picked her purse up from where it had fallen to the ground and hiked it up on her shoulder. She caught her breath and nodded fiercely.

"I do. I do, I promise."

Judah stepped back next to Ramey and crossed his arms, waiting.

"I didn't come here just to say I'm sorry. I am, I mean it, but that's not why I come. I know you think it was all the Scorpions' fault. What happened to Benji.

But you need to know that there was someone else. Someone who had 'em do it. Honest, I swear."

Judah shook his head.

"Wow. They send you down here to tell me that? Try to whine their way out of it? Man, they are a sorrier bunch of pussies than I thought."

Shelia gingerly felt the back of her head and looked at her hand for signs of blood.

"No. They ain't know I'm here. And they didn't tell me nothing when they asked me to get Benji outta that bar Monday night. I didn't know nothing 'bout that woman Tulah 'til this morning. I swear."

"Tulah?"

Judah glanced sharply at Ramey and she shrugged in reply.

"Who's Tulah?"

Shelia started to comb out her mussed hair with her fingers.

"Just listen to me for a second, okay? I swear, it'll make up for what I did to Benji. I know your daddy don't want to get no revenge, but I figured one of Benji's brothers might, so that's why I'm here. But you gotta promise me you're not already working with Sherwood and Tulah. Otherwise, I might as well start digging my own grave. Promise me."

Judah stared at Shelia.

"What do you know about Sherwood?"

"Promise me."

Judah nodded slowly. Shelia tossed her hair back over her shoulder and began to tell her story.

"Now, just listen. I come down to Silas because, well, it's a long story with the Scorpions. But anyway, I come down here 'cause I was feeling terrible about Benji. I mean it. Sincerely. I had to know what happened to him."

Judah shifted restlessly and Shelia spoke faster.

"Anyway, this morning I was in this breakfast joint I always go to when I'm down here. Over on Central. They got this two ninety-nine special that ain't too bad."

"The Mr. Omelet?"

Shelia bobbed her head.

"Yeah. So I was in there just having some coffee. I was bored, so I was listening to conversations around me. Comes kinda natural. Never know when you're gonna pick up something useful. I heard the name Cannon pop up, so I started paying attention real hard. Thinking somebody were talking about Benji and I could find out if he was okay. Turns out it wasn't just somebody. It was your daddy. And this other woman. He called her Sister Tulah."

"And they were talking about Benji?"

"Just at first. Then they started talking about money. It was that money you stole from the Scorpions. I knew 'bout that already. Then this Tulah woman said she'd make a deal with Sherwood. If he gave her the money back, she'd make him some kinda partner or something. And they'd let bygones be bygones about Benji."

Judah spoke through clenched teeth.

"And he agreed?"

"Oh yeah. He seemed all about it. They struck up some kinda agreement. Tulah said to bring the money to the church up in Kentsville tomorrow afternoon. He said he would. Then she left. And he left right after that."

Shelia faltered for a moment.

"I thought, I thought it weren't right. It sounded like your daddy knew it was Tulah who told the Scorpions where to find Benji. And then he just forgot about him like that. It weren't right what was done to him, but it weren't right for no one to care about it neither. So I thought, I thought maybe if I told someone who did care, it might make things square. With me, I mean. Make up for what I helped do to him."

She looked back and forth between Ramey and Judah. Ramey's face was more skeptical than angry, but Judah still wore a mask of fury. Shelia kicked up her leg and fixed the strap on her sandal, watching Judah warily for a sign. They still didn't speak to her and Shelia swung her purse to the other shoulder.

"So, that's what I got. You gonna let me go now or you gonna bash me against the van a few more times?"

Ramey crossed her arms and jutted out her chin.

"Just seems a little too convenient to me. You being in the exact same restaurant as Sherwood this morning."

Shelia's eyes flashed at Ramey.

"It ain't exactly like there's much to choose from around here. Or maybe you hadn't noticed?"

The raw hatred had not left Judah's eyes.

"You're still responsible for Benji laying up in that hospital bed in there. You did that to him."

Shelia dipped her head.

"I know. I ain't arguing with that. But you need to know something. I didn't want to do it. To do that to Benji. And neither did any of the guys. The Scorpions. It was all their president, Jack. You know him?"

Judah just stared at her.

"They call him Jack O' Lantern. He's got red hair, you know. Hard to miss. I didn't want to be a part of hurting Benji, but he made me go along. And the other guys, I heard them. They didn't want to do it neither. They just wanted to rough him up a little. Scare him, so he'd take the message back to Sherwood. But Jack's president, so they couldn't say no. He made us all do it."

"Why are you telling me this? Why do you think I care?"

"I just, I thought you should know. About your daddy and Tulah. And about Jack. I thought you should know everything. For Benji's sake."

Judah continued to stare at her. Finally, he broke his gaze and turned away. He started toward the Bronco without looking back, and Shelia looked to

Ramey, waiting. Ramey wrinkled her nose and turned on her heel.

"Get the hell outta here. Get the hell outta Silas and don't never come back."

Ramey stalked off behind Judah and left Shelia alone in the blistering heat.

SHELIA SWERVED HER battered Grand Am into the abandoned lot of a boarded-up convenience store and jerked the gearshift into park. She let the engine idle while she stretched her neck back and forth and then adjusted the rearview mirror so she could inspect the mottled red band around her throat. She pressed the skin gingerly and realized that it wasn't as bad as she thought. Judah had been angry, but he didn't have naturally angry hands. Shelia had seen it in his eyes, though they had been momentarily clouded by bloodlust; he was a man who was uncomfortable with hitting a woman. Shelia thought about this with a mixture of admiration and pity for him as she dug into her purse for a compact of concealing powder. She craned her neck in the mirror and swiped the powder on, then reapplied her thick mascara and magenta lipstick. She popped her lips in the mirror and decided she had done enough to cover up the damage. At the bottom of her purse, underneath used tissues and crusted bottles of nail polish, she located her cellphone and flipped it open. There was no answer the first time and she immediately dialed the number again. When it was answered, she didn't wait for hello.

"Don't hang up, Slim. I got some information about your stolen cash that, trust me, you really, really want to know."

CHAPTER 25

JUDAH SAT IN the driver seat of the Bronco and didn't speak. He had left the windows rolled down while they were in the hospital, but the air inside the truck was still broiling. He sat still, with his hands gripping the bottom of the steering wheel and his eyes staring dead ahead, not seeing, blind with the overwhelming incapacity to deal with the emotions boiling over inside of him.

Ramey watched him warily from the passenger seat. She had witnessed this quiet rage from Judah before and knew it was best not to give into it. Not to coddle it and not to acknowledge the tense lump of fear it could lodge in her throat if she let it. Ramey watched Judah's swift, deep breathing, the way his chest was rising and falling in heavy arcs, and then forced her eyes away from him. She carefully slipped a cigarette from the pack on the dashboard and flicked her lighter, flinching when she heard Judah's fist slam into the steering wheel. She turned her head and blew a thin stream of smoke out of the open window and counted to ten. Two long-beaked birds were tearing apart a hamburger wrapper in the empty parking space next to the Bronco. Finally, she held the cigarette out to him, still keeping her eyes on the birds, and waited.

When the cigarette left her fingers, she knew it was time to speak.

"So, what do you want to do?"

Ramey slowly turned back toward Judah and pushed a wave of hair behind her shoulder. He had the cigarette clamped tightly between his lips and didn't answer her. His hands were on his thighs now, balled into tight fists. She knew that his mind was racing and she gave it another moment to focus before reformulating her question.

"Okay. So what are you going to do?"

Judah turned, though his eyes were seeing past her. He took the cigarette from his lips and handed it back to her. His voice was low and dangerous, and the slow, halting delivery of his words reflected the erratic development of his ideas.

"I can't believe. I mean, I can. I mean, I'm done."

"With Sherwood?"

"With dicking around."

Ramey nodded slowly.

"How do you know that girl was telling the truth?"

"I know she was. It's just the kinda thing he would do. Always talking about family, but really, it's always been about him."

When Judah's eyes finally met Ramey's they were dark and fierce. Unforgiving. There was a simmering brutality behind them. Ramey realized that something deep inside of Judah, in a place even she didn't know about, had just crossed over a line.

"I'm going after him. Sherwood. And this Tulah woman, too. And I'm gonna break them. I'm gonna make them pay for Benji. For walking away from him without even glancing back. I'm gonna make Sherwood wish he had never had sons. I'm gonna make him wish he had been castrated at birth. I'm gonna make him pay."

"How?"

Judah stared hard at Ramey for another moment and then fell back in his seat, letting his shoulders sag.

"He screwed Benji, so now we're gonna make sure he's the one with his ass up in the air. He decided to make a deal with the devil, so let's make sure that when the devil comes knocking, Sherwood's empty-handed."

"We make sure he doesn't have that money to give to Sister Tulah tomorrow."

"Exactly. I don't think this preacher lady sounds like too compromising a woman. If Sherwood was willing to give up all that money just to go into business with her, she must be some kinda rock star. Which means that if he goes back on the deal before their partnership has even started, I don't think Sister Tulah's gonna take it in stride."

Ramey considered this.

"So we gotta get the money from Sherwood before his meeting with Tulah tomorrow."

Judah drummed his fingers on the steering wheel, calculating in his head.

"Yep."

"And how are we supposed to do that?"

Judah turned to Ramey and smiled bitterly.

"I'm gonna become a wolf in sheep's clothing. And you're gonna become a thief."

Slim Jim followed the light blue Grand Am with his eyes as it rolled to a stop in front of the locked chain link gates. He ran his hand through his hair and glanced around the gravel lot. Jack O' Lantern was still inside the clubhouse, most likely still sitting in the La-Z-Boy in the corner, still staring vacantly at the wood paneling across the room. He had not spoken to Slim Jim since they had turned their backs on the smoking wreckage of the trailer, and for that Slim Jim was grateful. He did not want to hear Jack's quavering voice and he had nothing to say in return. Long John was dead. That was all there was to know.

Slim Jim watched Shelia step away from the car and walk toward the gate. She had been surreptitious on the phone and he was in no mood to play games or offer flattery. She smiled when she saw him watching her and he could see her throw her shoulders back and dip her chin down slightly. Slim Jim's mouth didn't waver from the rigid line it was chiseled into. Shelia came up to the gate and hooked her chipped red nails through the wire. Her coy smirk dissolved when she noticed Slim Jim's stiff pose and the two armed prospects looking her up and down curiously.

"You gonna let me in or what?"

Slim Jim watched Shelia's face fall by degrees as she began to register the solemnity enshrouding the clubhouse. They looked at each other through the fence for a moment and then he sighed and nodded to Ratface. The prospect unhooked the chain and heaved the gate back as Shelia stepped through and Slim Jim came up to her. She started to put her arm around him, but he gripped her by the elbow and steered her off into a corner of the lot instead. Her high heeled sandals snagged on the loose gravel and she stumbled.

"I guess you're not gonna invite me inside, huh?"

Slim Jim released her when they were out of hearing distance and leaned back against the fence. Shelia rubbed her elbow and then crossed her arms, instinctively pushing her cleavage upwards. She pursed her lips and waited. Slim Jim looked past her at the prospects, standing with bored expressions at the front gate, and finally turned his attention to Shelia. His voice was flat and empty.

"Long John's dead."

He had not meant to say this. He had not even planned to let Shelia in the gate, let alone tell her what had happened. Slim Jim had meant to keep it strictly business, find out what information she was dangling in front of them and send her on her way. Shelia gasped and raised her hand to her mouth.

"Slim."

He was immediately afraid she was going to begin gushing sympathy and he'd have to push her away. He couldn't deal with a woman trying to console him, trying to tell him that it would be all right. He had no desire to begin remembering Long John or the good times they'd shared or any of that crap. He knew that if she started crying or reached out to touch him, he would smack her. He waited tensely, but he heard none of it.

"I'm sorry."

She didn't appear to want details, but if she did, she was smart enough not to ask. Slim Jim chewed on his lower lip, relieved and grateful.

"I'll tell you 'bout it some other time. Right now, why don't you start explaining why you're here? We're kinda in the middle of something and Jack don't got time to play games."

One side of Shelia's lips curled.

"Well, I ain't here to talk to Jack. This information's for you. I know where that money is."

Slim Jim's eyes narrowed.

"How do you know that? You don't know shit."

"I know that Sherwood Cannon's still got it, and that crazy preacher lady Tulah wants it back."

Slim Jim kicked backwards at the fence behind him.

"Congratulations. Hope you didn't waste your gas money driving all the way out here just to tell me that."

Shelia wrinkled her nose and cocked her hip to one side.

"No, asshole. I didn't. I wasted my gas money driving out here to tell you that Sherwood Cannon and Sister Tulah are working together now. How's that for information?"

Slim Jim jerked his head up and stared at Shelia.

"What're you talking 'bout?"

Satisfied that she had his attention, Shelia took a step closer and put her hands on her hips.

"I'm talking 'bout being down in Silas this morning and overhearing the two of them talking 'bout that money in a breakfast joint. That fat preacher lady told Sherwood Cannon that she knew he had her money and that she'd make a deal with him. He gives her the cash back and they become partners."

"And Sherwood agreed?"

Shelia nodded her head.

"Yep. I've got something else for you, too. Tomorrow afternoon Tulah, the Cannons and that pile of money are all gonna be up at that crazy church in Kentsville. Having a little pow-wow. Thought you'd like to know."

Slim Jim stared hard at Shelia, his eyes narrowed and his mouth open.

"You absolutely sure?"

"Cross my heart. I heard it all. And you're welcome, by the way."

Slim gripped Shelia by the shoulders, almost as if he was going to embrace her, and then pushed past her, starting toward the clubhouse. Shelia spun around and called after him.

"Hey!"

He stopped and turned back to her, raising his eyebrows expectantly. She minced through the gravel and grabbed his wrist. He looked down at her hand and then back at her eyes, impatiently.

"What?"

"Don't you forget where this information came from neither. I know something's going on with Jack. I'm not afraid to say it. What if something happens and he ain't president no more? Those Cannons have got it in for him. What if something happens and he don't make it back from that church? You'd be the Scorpions' leader. You'd be in charge. I just don't want you forgetting about me. Okay?"

Shelia's eyes were wide, almost childlike, but her voice was fierce. She held onto Slim Jim's wrist, forcing him to acknowledge her. His eyes darkened at what she was suggesting, but he curled his hand around so that his fingers touched hers before pulling away.

"I won't forget, Shelia."

Slim Jim turned away from her and strode toward the clubhouse. It was time to make decisions. It was time to take control.

CHAPTER 26

JUDAH LEANED BACK in the metal folding chair and let his eyes drift across the back wall of the Cannon Salvage garage. Not much had changed since he had last sat at the wobbly poker table, a hot breeze wafting in through the open bay doors, drinking a can of Slitchz and talking shop. The same rebel flag hung from two support beams and the same fold-out posters of muscle cars and topless swimsuit models were stabbed onto various hooks and nails across the walls. The Miss Wing Fling calendar was new and the dartboard had fallen to the concrete floor and cracked down the middle, but other than that, it was the same dirty space, where the same dirty plans were laid. The last time Judah had sat at the poker table, Sherwood had filled him in on the details for a wire stripping scam he wanted Judah to be a part of. And Judah had gone along with it. Just as he had all of the other times before then. Just as he had with the Scorpions and the saddlebags full of cash.

Sherwood set his beer can down next to Judah's and settled his weight into the folding chair across the table.

"Been a while since we sat like this, huh, son?"

Judah glanced over his shoulder at Levi, standing ready at the bay doors, assault rifle in hand, keeping one eye on the car lot.

"It's been quite a few years, I'd say."

"Since you left town and took up with that whore in Colston."

Judah took a swig of beer and leaned over the table.

"Well, we've all made stupid decisions a time or two."

Sherwood lifted his beer and raised it in Judah's direction.

"Amen to that, son."

Sherwood gulped the beer and slammed the empty can down on the table.

"And as much I love having you back in the garage, I gotta ask. Any particular reason you wanted to meet here instead of coming out to the house?"

Judah looked over at Levi again.

"I just wanted to be safe. I don't know what all's going on, but if there's a chance that someone's out looking for us, maybe tailing me since I been staying in town, I didn't want to lead them out to your place."

"Trying to be smart for once?"

"For once."

Sherwood raised his eyebrows at Judah and looked his son up and down.

"Well, now that you got me out here, you got something you want to say?"

Judah rested his elbows on the table and took a deep breath. He looked down at the oil stained floor beneath his boots and then jerked his head back up to meet Sherwood's eyes. He exhaled heavily.

"I didn't want to just say this over the phone. I wanted to tell you in person. I'm sorry about what happened up at The Ace. About running my mouth. I was drunk and I was upset about Benji."

Judah looked away from Sherwood, out the open bay doors. The sunlight was startlingly bright compared to the cool shadows of the garage, and the lines of chopped cars glittered in the afternoon sun.

"I mean, you gotta know I was hurting. Benji's just, you know, Benji. And

I'd been cooped up in prison for so long and then getting out and going straight back on a job with you. It was too much and I didn't handle it right. I let my emotions get the best of me and I was stupid. So I wanted to apologize for making a stink."

Judah turned his eyes back to Sherwood and Sherwood nodded slowly.

"Fair enough."

"And I'm sorry I been ducking your calls. Again, I was trying to sort things out, get my head on straight, you know. I was just feeling all spun up and weren't sure how to deal with it. I needed some time to think."

Sherwood clasped his hands on the table in front of him.

"I'm assuming you thought of something."

Judah wrapped his hand around his beer can, but didn't pick it up. He stared hard at the logo on the aluminum.

"I know I seemed against it before, but I've come to a decision. I'm back on board. With everything."

Judah still kept his head low, but raised his eyes up to his father. Sherwood cracked half a smile.

"Everything, huh? Everything like before, where I could call you if I needed a driver? A lookout? Or everything like the way I know I can count on Levi for everything?"

Levi turned away from the car lot and grunted. He had been half listening to the conversation between them, but now he turned his full attention to the table. He scowled at Judah and didn't look away when Judah glanced up at him.

"I want you to be able to count on me for everything. I want in. All the way in. I want a full piece of the action."

Levi rolled his eyes and went back to watching the lot. Sherwood turned his mouth down at Judah and then pulled a pack of cigarettes out of his shirt pocket.

"Smoke?"

Judah took one from the offered pack and they lit their cigarettes in silence. Sherwood exhaled a cloud of smoke in Judah's direction and smiled.

"What made you change your mind, son? You didn't seem all the way convinced the last time we spoke."

Judah tapped his cigarette on the edge of the table and watched the ash drift down onto the floor.

"Well, I guess I gotta thank Ramey."

Sherwood snorted and slapped the table with his wide palm.

"Don't tell me you're in love."

Judah shrugged his shoulders.

"I don't know. I just know that I'm done with that crazy bitch Cassie. I'm done with Colston. I want to stay here in Silas, with Ramey, and like you said before, to do that I gotta have something going."

Judah licked his lips and stared hard at Sherwood.

"I missed my chance with Ramey before and I ain't meaning to miss it again. I want to give her the kinda life she deserves. But to do that, I'm gonna need the money. So I'm in. I'm telling you, I'm all in."

Sherwood rubbed his jaw with the back of his hand and considered his son. Judah was looking across the table earnestly, waiting for a response. Sherwood dropped his half-smoked cigarette in his beer can and shook his head. He grinned.

"Ramey Barrow. Got her claws in you bad, huh? I guess I was always waiting for that to happen. Could always see it coming. She's a helluva woman, that one."

Judah nodded, his face serious.

"Yes, she is. She's really something."

Ramey checked the safety on her gun and quietly closed the door of the

Cutlass. The tall, brittle weeds rose up and brushed against the tops of her boots and her bare legs as she crossed the unkempt yard and walked up to the house she had spent so much time in as a child. It was this same house that her father had brought her to for weekend barbeques and parties with the Cannon clan. She had raced bikes around the sprawling acres of sandspurs and scrub pine with Judah and Benji when they were seven and tasted her first sip of whiskey at one of the bonfires behind the house when she was nine. She had been smacked in the face on the sloping front porch by Sherwood and given sacks of cold biscuits to take home by Rebecca. Years later, Judah's Aunt Imogene had done the same, understanding Ramey's inability to provide for her younger sister and keep her father in line. The Cannon women had always seemed to know that Ramey was struggling, but desperately trying to be the woman her own mother never had the courage to be. As Ramey crept up the creaking porch steps, she remembered she had always felt safe at the Cannon's house, even when it was just Sherwood and the boys, even though she knew Judah didn't always feel her sentiments.

Ramey reached for the front screen door, but let go of the handle when she heard a low growl from the end of the porch. She turned the gun on the dog, but relaxed when she saw it was only Sherwood's pet hound. Ramey had played with the mutt when it was a puppy. She slowly reached her hand out.

"Easy, Fred, easy."

The old dog's tail wagged once when it heard its name and approached Ramey to sniff her outstretched hand. Satisfied, it sauntered down to the end of the porch and dropped off the edge to disappear into the cool dirt beneath the house. Ramey looked over her shoulder to survey the property again and was assured that she was alone save for the dog and the crows screaming in the pine trees. She jerked open the screen and tried the door, but it was locked. Judah had told her to look for the key under a tin ashcan by the door and she hunted for it and found it. The front door moaned as she pushed it in and she hesitated again, trying to be certain that no one was waiting for her inside. She knew she didn't have much time; it was only a five-minute drive from the house to the salvage yard and she wasn't sure how long Judah would be able to keep Sherwood and Levi occupied. Ramey braced herself and entered.

The layout of the house was the same as she remembered, though the contents had altered drastically since Sherwood had been on his own. Ramey stepped through the shadows of the living room and noticed the line of empty beer cans on the greasy coffee table and the heaps of dirty clothes on either end of the sagging couch. The framed painting of a vacant-eyed Jesus holding a lamb still hung over the television in the corner, but next to it was a poster of a naked model winking and brandishing a machine gun. An American flag had been hung in front of the window to keep out the light, but enough filtered through for Ramey to make her way down the hall to the bathroom.

She quickly checked the bedrooms to make sure they were empty and then nudged open the bathroom door with the toe of her boot. She slipped inside and looked around. The cramped space smelled of unwashed socks and standing water. A dark ring had formed in the toilet bowl and the plastic shower curtain was crumpled on the cracked linoleum floor. Ramey stepped around it and opened what used to be the linen closet. As Judah had assured her, there were no longer any towels stacked neatly on the shelves. Instead, she found Sherwood's safe.

Ramey pushed her hair behind her ears and knelt down in front of the steel box. She laid the 9mm on the edge of the tub and pulled the list of numbers Judah had written down for her out of her back pocket. As with the location of the key, Judah had guaranteed her that Sherwood's combination would be predictable, one of several sets of numbers Sherwood used over and over again. Ramey recognized the first combination as Rebecca's birthday. There were two more sets scrawled on the paper after that. Ramey bit her lip and started punching in numbers.

SHERWOOD PICKED UP his empty beer can and tapped it on the table.

"If there's nothing else, son, we need to get going. I think Levi's getting restless."

Sherwood laughed and glanced over at Levi, pacing back and forth in front of the open bay doors. Levi scowled at them and set his rifle against one of the rusting tool cabinets.

"I just don't like being out in the open here, having pansy-ass conversations about Judah's feelings."

Judah felt his cellphone vibrate in his front pocket and put his hand over it. Sherwood stood up to throw the beer can in the trash and Judah pulled out his phone as soon as Sherwood's back was turned. He snapped it open under the table and his heart sunk when he saw the text: *WRONG #*. Sherwood looked back at the table and frowned.

"You done with that?"

Judah kept his phone under the table in his left hand and took a swig of beer with his right. Sherwood watched him drink.

"Uh, yeah. It's done."

Sherwood picked up the beer and tossed it toward the trashcan. It missed and bounced, skidding underneath one of the lifts. Sherwood didn't bother with it.

"All right, let's go."

Judah wracked his brain, trying to think. He had given Ramey all of the combinations he had known Sherwood to use in the past. His mother's birthday, Sherwood's favorite ball players' numbers, the street address of the house Sherwood had grown up in. He always used the same numbers. Always. It was as guaranteed as the fact that Sherwood would eat at the Mr. Omelet tomorrow morning. Judah looked around the garage, trying not to let the panic show in his face. His eyes searched the decorated walls, looking for anything to jog his memory. He caught Sherwood looking at him strangely.

"You all right there, son? You look like something just crawled up your shorts and bit you in the balls."

Judah looked at Sherwood. Over his shoulder, Judah noticed the red, white and blue recruitment poster hanging next to a row of mounted hubcaps. Instead of Uncle Sam, a pinup girl with cleavage spilling out of a star spangled corset beckoned with a curled finger. Judah sat up straight.

"I was just thinking, you got a beer I could take with me for the road?"

Sherwood frowned, but turned around and opened the mini-fridge. Levi was already halfway to the truck. Judah quickly pounded six numbers into his cellphone under the table and pressed send. 12-01-69. December 1st, 1969, the day Sherwood's older, and only, brother had his birthday come up in the first draft lottery for the Vietnam War. Dixon hadn't lasted three weeks in the jungle, and though Sherwood had volunteered for the service a year later, he had never forgiven Alexander Pirnie for pulling his brother's number and had never let his sons forget the date their uncle had been selected to die.

Sherwood slammed the refrigerator door closed and turned to Judah.

"Thought there was another can in the back, but it's Diet Coke. Who the hell put a Diet Coke in there? Next thing you know, I'm gonna open it one day and there'll be low-fat yogurt sitting right there on the shelf. Jesus."

Judah stood up and shrugged.

"Maybe Levi's trying to lose weight. Trying to slim down for bikini season."

Sherwood laughed and pointed toward the chains for the roll down bay doors.

"Pull those down, we gotta get outta here."

Sherwood walked out into the sunlight and Judah grasped the chain for the first bay door. He slowly began to pull it down, trying to stall as long as he could until he knew Ramey had been able to open the safe. His cellphone vibrated in his pocket and Judah yanked the chain down and slammed the heavy metal door flush to the ground. He dug his phone out of his pocket and flipped it open. Judah thought he was going to choke when he saw the text: *WRONG!!!*

Sherwood yelled at him from the parking lot.

"For Christ's sake, Judah, what're you doing? Pull that other door."

Judah slowly walked over to the second door and put his sweating hands on the chain. He knew that Sherwood and Levi were watching him, so he began to tug on the chain, dragging out every movement as he desperately tried to come up with one more number. There had to be one more number. The flash of panic taking hold of him was clouding his brain and he couldn't think of anything but the rush of the seconds passing. The second bay door hit the ground and Judah looked around the walls of the garage frantically, searching for something else that might job his memory. His eyes came back to the large recruitment poster and the busty girl smiling seductively. Judah whispered to himself.

"Holy shit."

It was worth a shot. And it was the only shot he had left. He snapped open his cellphone and pounded in the numbers: 38-24-36. He pressed send and ran toward the back door of the garage. He had to try and buy Ramey just a little more time. He pulled the door shut behind him and called out to Sherwood just as he was climbing into the passenger side of his pickup truck.

"Hey, wait!"

Sherwood stepped down and huffed.

"What now? We gotta go. As much as I appreciate this overture, you coulda just told me this over the phone. I know you don't really know what's going on, but Levi and I don't need to be sitting ducks out here. And you shouldn't be, neither. Go on back to Ramey's and sit tight. I'll call you in a couple days after I've taken care of some things."

Judah jammed his hands down into his pockets and rocked back on his heels. He was waiting for his cellphone to vibrate in his pocket. Why wasn't she texting him back? He looked up at Sherwood, appealing.

"Okay. But I just wanted to say that this really means a lot to me. Us being a family again. I want us to be like before I left. The Cannon family. A force to be reckoned with, you know?"

Sherwood looked at Judah's wide eyes and cracked a smile. He walked over to him and rested his hand on Judah's shoulder, shaking him slightly.

"I know. Family first, son. Always, family first."

Sherwood clapped Judah on the back and halfway pulled him to his chest. It was the closest thing to an embrace from his father that Judah had felt since he was a child. He raised his own hand and placed it on Sherwood's back. They stood like that for the briefest of seconds and then Sherwood pulled away and turned back toward the truck. He called out over his shoulder.

"I'll call you. Go on home to that woman of yours, son. Go home and enjoy yourself. She's part of the family now, too, I guess."

Judah nodded appreciatively, but his mind was racing. What had happened? Why hadn't Ramey texted him? Judah waited until Sherwood heaved himself up into the passenger seat and Levi spun the truck out of the parking lot, kicking up a spray of sand. As soon as the truck was out of sight, Judah yanked out his cellphone and looked at the screen. No text.

"Damnit!"

Judah punched in a number and stood in the blistering, dust-clouded sunlight and sweated. He squeezed his eyes shut and listened to the echo of the phone ringing. He didn't wait for hello.

"Tell me you got it. Ramey, please, tell me you got it."

He heard a car door slam on the other end. She was panting into the phone.

"I got it."

Judah ran his hand over his face and sighed with relief.

"You're beautiful. Now get the hell out of there as fast as you can. They're on their way."

CHAPTER 27

The table was silent save for the scuffing of chair legs scraping back across the concrete floor and the creak of leather vests as arms were crossed, cigarettes pulled out of pockets and wounded limbs adjusted. Slim Jim sat in his customary seat, directly to the left of the head of the table, and surveyed the men before him. They were a miserable lot, beaten and dejected, keeping themselves together with prescription pain killers, bumps of speed and waning adrenaline. The bandage on Toadie's shoulder smelled rancid, overpowering even the ripe smell of six men who hadn't showered in days. Legs' eyes were red-rimmed and his knuckles bruised and swollen from punching the side of the clubhouse when Slim Jim and Jack came back with the news that Long John was no longer among the living. Tiny was staring hard at the pack of cigarettes in his hand as if unsure how it had gotten there. He had already been lost to the club for days, caught up in a fog of Oxy. Only Ratface seemed to still harbor any enthusiasm. The prospects weren't usually allowed to sit at the table, and Slim Jim knew that he was taking his inclusion as a sign that he and Toadie would be patched in soon.

For Slim Jim, the worst sight was Jack O' Lantern. Though he still occupied the coveted space at the head of the table, Jack was more a ghost than the president of an outlaw motorcycle club. He hadn't spoken a word to Slim Jim since they had witnessed the trailer explode and his silence was unnerving. Slim Jim was used to Jack O' Lantern's irrational temper, his blind rage and his unending swearing in the face of tragedy. When his father had finally succumbed to liver cancer, Jack had finished off a bottle of Wild Turkey and tried to fight the entire bar and half the dining area of an Applebee's. He had taken a crowbar and smashed out car windows in a drugstore parking lot after the funeral, screaming his head off like a deranged Viking. That was the Jack O' Lantern Slim Jim knew and was comfortable with.

But so far, Jack hadn't yelled. He hadn't swung his fists, he hadn't picked a fight, he hadn't ridden his motorcycle a hundred miles an hour down the highway. When they had returned from the trailer, Jack O' Lantern had poured himself three shots of whiskey, downed them in succession and without ceremony and retired to his recliner to stare at the wall while Slim Jim had to break the news to the rest of the Scorpions. And though he had risen from the La-Z-Boy when Slim Jim asked to call a meeting, and assumed his position in the president's chair, he was still staring out into nothingness. Slim Jim waited for Jack O' Lantern to call the meeting to order, but realized Jack didn't even have the motivation to raise the gavel. Since there was no need to quiet anyone down or get anyone's attention in the first place, Slim Jim cleared his throat and began speaking slowly.

"I know what you're all thinking. I know that you're done. You want to go home and have the chance to grieve for Long John in peace."

Legs and Toadie nodded slightly when they met Slim Jim's eyes.

"God knows I want the same thing. I want to be finished with this entire mess. I want to wash my hands of every drop of this and move past it. But not yet. It ain't time yet."

Slim Jim waited out the muttered grumblings circling around the table. He looked over at Jack O' Lantern to gauge his reaction. Jack had turned his head toward him and Slim Jim could see the bitterness in his friend's blue eyes and the tension in his jaw. At least he was registering what Slim Jim was saying.

"I think it's time we were all on the level with what's been going on this past week."

Legs spoke while keeping his gaze directed down at the table in front of him.

"You mean how the Cannons have just ground us into the dirt?"

Slim Jim shook his head. He couldn't look at Jack O' Lantern. He was about to directly defy an order from his president, something he had never done before.

"The Cannons stole our money, yes. And have every reason to go war with us after what we did to that kid. But the Cannons ain't the ones who set the fire 'round the clubhouse. They ain't the ones who blew up Long John and are keeping us holed up here away from our families and kids. Screw the Cannons."

Slim Jim smacked the table with the palm of his hand.

"It's that crazy preacher woman, Sister Tulah, who's been making our lives a living hell."

Now the grumbling turned to a clamor of questions and denials. He forced himself to look at Jack O' Lantern. His defeated posture hadn't changed, but his eyes were seething. Slim Jim waited for Jack to contradict him, to call it a lie, but he didn't. Legs cut through the side conversations and silenced everyone by challenging Slim Jim.

"That's a load, Slim. We know it was the Cannons. We had one of 'em at The Pit. We don't even know who this preacher is except that she lost her money and wants it back."

Slim Jim shook his head.

"I know the Cannons went after us for a minute there, but they didn't set the fire or the explosives. Jack's been getting threats from Tulah this whole time. Bad threats. She sent us a live rattlesnake in a box, for Christ's sake. It was her guys we was supposed to be meeting out at the trailer. She did this. She's been behind it all. And it's time you knew about it."

Legs turned swiftly to Jack O' Lantern.

"Tell me he's speaking out of his ass, Jack. Tell me he's lying."

Jack O' Lantern continued to glare at Slim Jim, but shook his head slowly back and forth. From the end of the table, Ratface stood up, nearly knocking his chair over.

"You serious? That crazy holy roller is responsible for everything? For us nearly getting roasted alive? For Long John?"

Legs quickly turned on Ratface.

"Sit down, boy. You may be sitting at this table, but that don't mean you start speaking."

Ratface pulled his chair closer and sat down. Legs shook his head in disbelief and then turned back to Slim Jim.

"So, now we know the truth. What do we do about it?"

Slim Jim spread his hands out on the table before him and threw his shoulders back.

"Well, that ain't all. That ain't even why I called you all to a meeting."

Tiny snickered, his eyes still glazed over, but his attention more and more toward the conversation at hand.

"You mean there's more? It just gets better and better, huh?"

Slim Jim ignored him.

"I found out today that Sister Tulah's getting her money back after all. From the Cannons. Sherwood Cannon made a deal with her. He's giving her back the money and she's cutting him in on her business. They're working together now."

Legs brought his fist down onto the table, tipping the ashtray over and scattering ashes everywhere.

"Bullshit."

Slim Jim looked at Jack O' Lantern. He had expected Jack's jaw to drop open like a cartoon. Instead, his mouth had drawn into a grim line and his eyes were blazing at Slim Jim. He turned back to Legs and the rest of the table.

"I mean it. We got screwed. We took the beating and now Sister Tulah's taking all our money. We just got royally, royally screwed. But that ain't why I called the meeting either."

Legs groaned.

"Jesus, Slim, just tell us what you did call it for. Quit being all dramatic and get to the point. What do you want from us?"

Slim Jim drummed his fingers on the table.

"Sherwood's handing off our money to Tulah tomorrow afternoon at the church up in Kentsville. And I want us to be there. I want to bleed 'em like they bled us. I want to make 'em pay."

The table erupted again as the men began to hash it out. Ratface jumped out of his seat again and Legs and Tiny began arguing with one another across the table. Slim Jim looked at Jack O' Lantern and raised his eyebrows. Jack clamped his jaw shut and shook his head slowly but firmly. He had nothing to say. Slim Jim finally called the table back to order.

"All that's left is to put it to a vote. Do we attack the church tomorrow, yay or nay? I say yay."

Slim Jim turned to Tiny on his left. He agreed. The vote went around the table. Toadie voted against it, but Ratface and Legs were fully on board. When the vote came to Jack, there was a finality to his voice. He knew he was beaten. He knew he was a ghost.

"Nay."

Slim Jim stood up from the table.

"Majority rules. It's done."

Legs, Tiny and Ratface nodded.

"Now go home. Go get laid, go see your kids. Go get patched up. Be here at noon tomorrow."

Slim Jim didn't wait for Jack O' Lantern to end the meeting. He brought his fist down hard on the table.

"Church is over."

JUDAH LOOKED UP from his work at the kitchen table when the front door opened and Ramey came in from the darkness. He had been sitting in the yellow glow from the stove light for the past hour, taking swigs of Jack Daniels from the bottle and loading and unloading the clips for his .45. He followed Ramey with his eyes as she walked through the dim living room, but didn't stop sliding the bullets into the magazine. Ramey crossed her arms and leaned on the kitchen doorframe, smiling.

"Damn. This could be the cover shot for Redneck Weekly. All you need is a dog at your feet chewing on a hambone and you'd be set."

The corners of Judah's mouth turned down, but he gave a measured nod in agreement. Ramey crossed to the drain board and picked out a coffee cup decorated with faded pink flamingos and palm trees. She poured an inch of whiskey in the bottom of the mug and sat down across from him. Judah kept his eyes on the neat row of bullets lined up before him.

"Did you hide it?"

Ramey took a sip and nodded.

"I did."

Judah slammed the full clip into the .45 and switched the safety on. He set the gun down next to the two full extra magazines and ran his hands along the thighs of his jeans.

"All right."

Ramey pointed to the bottle on the table.

"How much?"

Judah shrugged.

"Enough."

She bit her bottom lip and watched Judah's eyes. They were focused on the .45 in the center of the table.

"You worried 'bout tomorrow?"

Judah didn't answer.

"We don't gotta go up to that church. We've done enough damage already just today. We don't need to be there."

Judah took a deep breath and ran his thumbnail along the wood grain of the table.

"Yes. We do."

Ramey leaned back in her chair and Judah raised his head to look at her. His eyes were unyielding.

"They need to see it on my face. They need to know."

Ramey frowned.

"Okay."

"And Ramey, things are gonna change. Whether we want them to or not. When we leave that church tomorrow, we ain't gonna be in the same place as when we walked in. I'm sorry it has to be that way. But it does."

Ramey fixed Judah with an unflinching stare.

"You listen to me, Judah Cannon. In our lives, there are things we've done and things that've been done to us. And things that we have yet to do. Our lives are filled with our reactions and our regrets. We cross lines and we wade down to the depths. We fall and we pick up the pieces and carry on. If we're sitting here right now, at this moment, then we've made it so far. At the end of the day, I'm hoping there's more. But I wouldn't be surprised if there's less. And I've gotten right with that in my mind."

It took Judah a moment to respond.

"You regret showing up at The Ace last Friday night?"

"Nope."

A sad smile crept across Judah's lips.

"You've always been mine."

Ramey shook her head.

"No. I've been my own. But I think we carry a part of one another. Always have. Always will."

Judah didn't say anything. He stretched his hand out across the table, across the loaded .45, and touched Ramey's fingers. He knew what she said was true.

CHAPTER 28

"YOU'RE A VERY brave man, Mr. Cannon."

Sherwood shifted uncomfortably on the narrow wooden bench and clasped his hands together over his belly. He certainly didn't need Sister Tulah telling him this. When he had opened his safe a few hours before, duffle bag in hand, ready to collect the stacks of bills, he had felt a sharp pang in his chest and a sweep of panic that was usually only brought on by police sirens or Vietnam nightmares. He didn't know who had done it. Levi? Judah? The Scorpions? Some whore he had once slept with? It could be anyone, really, and it didn't matter. He had stared into the vacant space and known only that he was screwed.

Sister Tulah stood before him now, with one heavy, sagging arm leaning on the pulpit occupying the center of the low stage at the back of the church. The room was dim, only half of the lights along the walls were turned on and the narrow windows had been painted over to keep out the sunlight. Sherwood was unnerved by the shadows in the austere space. In the strict confines of the empty church, Sister Tulah appeared to take up more room than he thought was physically possible. Sitting across from him at the Mr. Omelet, she had not seemed so imposing. Now that they were on her ground, in her territory, Sherwood could understand the hushed whispers and downcast eyes from the people he had questioned about her. Those people had harbored real fear in their hearts and Sherwood had found it ludicrous and pitiable at the time. Now he understood. Sister Tulah's pale eyes blazed across the distance between them.

"Coming in here like this. With the audacity to open your mouth and tell me that you don't have my money. I imagine most men in your situation would be halfway to Mexico by now. But not you."

Sherwood managed to keep his gaze level and look Tulah right back in the eyes.

"I ain't really the running type."

Sister Tulah nodded and walked to the edge of the stage, the boards creaking beneath her with every labored step.

"So you show up here, empty-handed, without an inkling of the difficulty you have now set before me and expect, what, exactly? To be given a second chance to make it up to me? Or my sympathy for your predicament, maybe? Perhaps you thought you might be offered forgiveness."

The closer Tulah moved toward him, the denser the atmosphere around him seemed to feel. It was as if the air was pressing against him from all sides. The heat in the church was becoming unbearable.

"I expected to encounter a woman of God."

Sister Tulah laughed. It was terrifying, a true cackle coming from the back of her throat. Her entire body shook from the force of it and when it abruptly stopped, and Sister Tulah snapped her mouth closed, Sherwood realized he was dealing with someone who was bordering on otherworldly. The image of a strange beast came to Sherwood's mind, but he quickly pushed it away and tried to gain control of the situation.

"Was I wrong in believing that?"

Sister Tulah stepped down from the stage and stood a few feet away from Sherwood.

"So that's it. You thought to yourself that all those rumors about me had to be lies. Stories made up by weak minded folk. Preacher Tulah? Why, she's just a little old lady holed up in a church. What could she possibly be able to do to me?"

Sherwood rose to his feet.

"You think I underestimated you?"

Tulah's colorless eyes flashed.

"I know you underestimated me. I think you believed you could walk in here, have some words with me and then walk back out of that door alive."

Sherwood's hand instinctively went to his side, but he didn't un-holster the .357 underneath his T-shirt. He leered at her.

"Seriously? You think you're gonna kill me? In cold blood? In a Goddamn church?"

Sister Tulah came a step closer.

"This is my Goddamn church."

Sherwood laughed nervously.

"What, you got a piece stuck up under that dress somewhere? You gonna be able to pull it out for I can draw on you first?"

Tulah stretched her thin, pink lips into a grotesque grin.

"The Lord works in mysterious ways, Mr. Cannon. Best you not forget that."

Judah jammed the extra clips for the .45 into the back pockets of his jeans before sliding the gun into the waistband of his pants. He pulled the bolt back on the M14 to make sure a round was in the chamber, then softly shut the driver side door behind him. He came around the back of the Bronco and stood next to Ramey. She had the 9mm gripped in both hands as she eyed the Last Steps to Deliverance Church of God across the highway. She jumped when Judah touched her shoulder, but forced herself to breathe deep and evenly. Judah kept his gaze on the church.

"You see anybody go in or out? Anybody around?"

Ramey shook her head.

"Nothing. And unless the parking lot goes back behind the church further, there's only those two cars."

Judah's eyes traveled from the mud-sprayed pickup truck parked haphazardly in the middle of the lot to the gleaming black Lincoln Navigator next to the church.

"Even if Sherwood brought Levi, I doubt we're dealing with more than four bodies inside. You cover Tulah and I'll take care of Sherwood and anyone else if we need to. Don't freeze up and don't let them rattle you. I got this. And I got you, okay?"

Ramey didn't look at him, but gave a curt nod. Judah eyed the front door. The time for being sure had passed. He couldn't afford what ifs, second guesses and wavering conviction. He gripped the M14 in both hands and started across the blistering asphalt with Ramey close at his shoulder. They walked on the burned, brittle grass along the walkway to keep their footsteps quiet and then mounted the concrete steps. Ramey rested her hand on the door handle and looked to Judah. He grit his teeth and signaled to her. Ramey pressed down on the latch and Judah kicked in the heavy double doors. They surged forward, guns raised, and met the startled faces of those inside.

Sherwood immediately went for his .357, but Judah snarled at him before he could reach the grip.

"I wouldn't."

Sherwood looked up to find the M14 trained at his head, and the grim face of his son behind the barrel. He slowly raised his hands out to his sides.

Judah quickly looked around the dim space, the darkness within even further enhanced by the blazing white sunlight streaming through the doors behind him. The church was empty save for Sherwood and a large woman who could only have been Sister Tulah; their positions indicated to Judah that they might have been in the middle of a standoff of their own. In his peripheral vision, Judah saw that Ramey had Tulah dead in her sights. The woman hadn't raised her hands, only clasped them in front of her as if she was casually waiting for a bus. Her doughy face was expressionless and she appeared unfazed by the two intruders who had just burst into her church, guns out, clearly full of ill intent. Judah pointed at Sherwood's holster with the end of his rifle.

"Take it out. Put it on the floor and kick it this way."

"Son."

Judah jerked the rifle barrel back up so that it was level with Sherwood's head again.

"You want me to ask again? Or did you think we came here for the potluck supper?"

Sherwood narrowed his eyes at Judah, but slowly pulled out the .357 and leaned down. The gun skidded down the aisle and Ramey stopped it with her boot. Sherwood righted himself and glared at Judah.

"What the hell do you think you're doing, son?"

Judah's eyes never left Sherwood's. The hate being directed at him was reflected right back.

"Stepping up. Being a Cannon."

"You call this being a Cannon? Pointing a gun at your own father? What kind of coward chicken shit is that?"

"I'm just evening things out. Doing what's right. The way I see it this time."

Judah glanced at Sister Tulah.

"And making sure that Benji ain't forgotten."

Sherwood clenched his thick fists at his sides and tilted his head.

"You took my money."

Judah adjusted his grip on the rifle. Neither he nor Ramey had lowered their guns.

"Weren't your money in the first place."

"What is this, Judah, your big play? You gonna try to work something out with Tulah now? That how you're planning on screwing your old man?"

Judah looked at Sister Tulah. Now that his eyes had adjusted to the contrasting light, he could see her pale eyes burning out from her placid face. Tulah had been trading stares with Ramey, but now she directed her scrutiny fully at Judah. Her eyes gave Judah a prickly feeling running down the length of his arms and he felt a strange heat flushing upwards from his chest. He averted his gaze and turned back to Sherwood.

"It ain't her money, neither. Not anymore."

At this, Sister Tulah raised her eyebrows and took a step forward. Ramey immediately did the same and jerked the 9mm to remind Tulah that she was still in gun sights. Sister Tulah pursed her lips and crossed her arms over her chest, but stood down. Sherwood barked out a gruff laugh.

"So that's what you're doing here? Come here to wave your guns around and show off how big your balls are. Riding in on your high horse, crying out for revenge for Benji? Talking about stepping up to be a Cannon. You don't got no idea what being a true Cannon looks like."

Judah's mouth was pinched and his eyes were flat and dark. He raised the rifle to his shoulder and sighted down the barrel.

"It looks like this, Sherwood. It looks like this."

Sherwood laughed.

"You ain't gonna shoot me, son."

Judah touched his finger to the trigger. He could feel the blood pounding in his ears and the measured breath he drew into his lungs felt like it would stay there, burning forever. He knew what Sherwood said was true. He also knew he could change everything, right then, right there, with just the slightest movement of his hand. Judah closed his eyes.

He heard the shots first and then the siren of bullets whizzing through the air and splintering the wooden pulpit on the stage. A line of bullets buried themselves in the back wall of the church and he heard Ramey scream beside him. He threw the full force of his body against her and they went tumbling across the floor, out of sight of the open doorway. He pressed himself against the wall, and then slid out and kicked one of the doors shut. Another stream of bullets went through the closed door, clouding the air with splinters. Judah grabbed Ramey's wrist. Her eyes were terrified, but she nodded that she was okay. The shooting ceased for a moment and Judah heard the roar of motorcycle engines from the parking lot.

"Shit."

Ramey was breathing heavily next to him.

"What the hell, Judah? The Scorpions?"

Judah scanned the room frantically. Sister Tulah and Sherwood had both dropped out of sight between the rows of benches. His eyes found the door at the back of the sanctuary that must have led to another part of the building. With his back still pressed against the wall, he slid upwards on his heels, keeping the rifle close to his body.

"Gotta be them."

Ramey looked up at him from her huddled position.

"What do we do?"

Judah pointed to the door at the back of the room. They would have to pass in front of the open doorway to get to it.

"I'm gonna cover you and we're gonna get the hell outta here. Don't shoot and don't look back. Just run. Got it?"

Ramey stood up and nodded. The motorcycle engines stopped abruptly and the sound was replaced by shouting. Judah thought they had only seconds before the entire pack of Scorpions stormed the church.

"All right, let's move."

Judah ran out in front of Ramey, blocking her with his body, and fired wildly through the single open door. For an instant, he could see two of the Scorpions, standing face to face as if they were talking to one another. He caught a glimpse of one of them going down, but didn't wait to see more. He kicked the second door closed and caught up with Ramey at the back of the church. She yanked the door open and they crashed into the narrow hallway beyond it. Judah yelled at Ramey.

"Keep going!"

She led the way, careening down the hall and past an open office door. Judah glanced in briefly as they raced by and saw a man crouched down between a large wooden desk and the wall with his knees drawn up to his chest and his face slick with tears. Judah didn't stop, though, and followed Ramey through the back door of the building. They stumbled out into the blazing sunshine and Judah pushed Ramey up against the back of the church. He slowly peeked his head around the edge of the building to survey the parking lot. He jerked his head back and stood panting next to Ramey. She grabbed his arm.

"How are we gonna get outta this?"

Judah grit his teeth and squeezed his eyes shut.

"At the moment, I have no idea."

CHAPTER 29

Slim Jim raised his left hand in the air to indicate to the other Scorpions to cease fire. He and Legs were the only men on foot in the church's parking lot. Jack O' Lantern, Toadie, Tiny and Ratface were still straddling the bikes they had ridden in on. They were scattered across the lot, fanned out in an uneven semicircle, and at Slim Jim's signal they slowly began to lower their rifles. Legs raised his eyebrows at Slim Jim, but he just shook his head and raised his hand again to shield his eyes from the reflecting glare of the asphalt as he surveyed the damage. The last motorcycle engine was cut as Ratface whipped his leg over his bike's seat and started toward Slim Jim.

"That it?"

Slim Jim rested the assault rifle on his shoulder and tried to listen for any sounds coming from inside the church. The building was solid, but he should have been able to hear screams or people moving around. A Cessna, humming across the sky, and the sound of Ratface's heavy boots stomping across the pavement were all the sounds he could hear.

"Hey, man, what're we doing?"

Slim Jim whipped around.

"Shut it, prospect. Just 'cause you're out here with us don't mean you can talk."

Ratface stopped and looked away toward the church. He took a few steps back and busied himself with the magazine on his gun. Legs and Jack O' Lantern converged around Slim Jim and Legs wiped his nose, leaving a gray streak of gunpowder across his face.

"You got a plan here, Slim?"

Slim Jim narrowed his eyes toward the darkness of the church entrance.

"I don't know. Just hold on, let's see if anyone comes out."

"So, what, we can talk to them? Ask them about their feelings?"

"Just give me a minute to think."

Legs looked as if he was about to say something else, but he hesitated and instead shook out his shoulders and walked away a few paces to check the action on his rifle. Jack O' Lantern stepped in closer to Slim Jim and put a hand roughly on his shoulder.

"This was your idea, Jimmy."

Slim Jim pulled away.

"Want to tell me something I don't know?"

"You got these guys looking to you for the next move. You brought us out here. Got us blasting away at a place when we don't even know what's inside. Tiny can barely stay on his bike and Toadie can barely hold a gun. Where's the rest of your plan, huh?"

Slim Jim turned toward Jack, his eyes flashing and color high in his cheeks.

"You want to start acting like a boss now? You decide to come out of that coma you been in the last two days? Or are you just trying to get in another dig since it's become pretty clear that the guys are following me now? If we'd listened to you, we'd still be hiding in the clubhouse with our skirts bunched up between our legs."

Jack O' Lantern looked down at his boots.

"You got a move or not, Jimmy?"

He raised his eyes to meet Slim Jim's and they stared one another down. Neither one dropped his eyes, or looked away, or even blinked. Slim Jim heard the zip of the bullet just before he saw the light go out of Jack's eyes and the next instant was chaos. Three more gunshots followed as the Scorpions scattered for cover and Slim Jim didn't have time to think, only to react. Legs grabbed him by the collar of his vest and yanked him behind the pickup truck in the middle of the parking lot. The others managed to crouch behind their bikes. When the shooting stopped, they began to scan the perimeter of the parking lot with the barrels of their AKs pointed over the seats of their motorcycles.

Slim Jim dropped to the ground, pressing his face into the broken asphalt and glass dust, and looked under the truck. He saw Jack's body, bulky and twisted awkwardly in front of the church, but he couldn't see his face. He watched the body for any sign of breathing, any twitch of life. It was unmoving.

JUDAH DROPPED DOWN behind the front wheel of the Lincoln Navigator parked next to the church. He grabbed Ramey by the shoulders and pulled her up in front of him.

"I think I got one when I was shooting out of the church's front door. It mighta been that Jack O' Lantern guy, the redhead. He hit the ground."

Ramey gripped the M14 in front of her.

"So what do we do?"

Judah leaned his head back against the Navigator while he tried to think.

"If we could make it across the parking lot to the woods, we might have a chance of going around them and getting outta here."

"I'm not sure I like a plan that has an if and a might in it."

Judah pushed himself up on his heels, making sure to keep his body in between Ramey and the Navigator.

"You got a better idea? My guess is that they came here for Tulah and Sherwood, same as we did, but I don't think they got an aversion to taking us out along the way."

Ramey nodded and pushed her hair off her sweating forehead.

"Fine. But how we gonna make it to the woods? It's at least fifty yards from here to there. We don't got a chance."

Judah licked his lips and then edged out from behind Ramey. She twisted her head around.

"What're you doing?"

Judah ignored her and scooted on the asphalt alongside the Navigator. Keeping his head as low as possible, he looked through the tinted windows out into the church's parking lot. He could see two of the Scorpions crouched down behind Sherwood's pickup truck and another hiding behind the seat of his motorcycle with his rifle pointed at the church. Judah raised himself up a little higher to look down inside the SUV and he saw the keys dangling from the ignition. He ducked back down and quietly tried the door handle. The Navigator was unlocked and Judah looked over his shoulder at Ramey, still crouched down in front of the wheel.

"We're gonna do something crazy, okay?"

Ramey only stared back at him with wide eyes.

"I'm gonna crank this thing and put it in reverse from here. It's gonna start to roll backwards and we're just gonna roll right on with it."

"Are you outta your mind?"

"Whatever you do, stay behind that wheel and move with the car. Don't run. Just move with the car. Bullets can go straight through the door panels, but they won't be able to make it through the engine block, so stay behind the wheel no matter what."

Judah didn't wait for a response. He turned back around, popped the door open and reached up for the keys. He knew that as soon as the Scorpions heard the engine, they'd know that he and Ramey were there and start blasting away again. There was no time to come up with something better, though, so Judah held his breath and twisted the key. The engine roared to life and Judah reached over the seat and jerked the gearshift down into reverse. The car slowly started to roll back backwards and Judah scurried next to Ramey. It took a moment, but then a volley of bullets came tearing through the passenger side door. He threw his arm over Ramey's shoulder and gripped her tightly as they crept slowly across the parking lot with the Navigator shielding them all the way.

The shots ceased after a few seconds and Judah figured the Scorpions were trying to decide what to do next. The Navigator hit the parking lot curb about ten feet away from the tree line and Judah didn't waste any time. He grabbed the M14 from Ramey and shouted into her ear.

"Run! Now!"

They bolted across the open space and a few bullets hit the dirt behind them, but they made it to the trees and Judah pulled Ramey down to the ground. They crawled through the leaves and pine needles for a few yards until Judah judged they were safe. He backed up against a wide oak tree and finally caught his breath.

THE FIRST SHOT narrowly missed the side of Sherwood's face and he made it to the ground, between two benches, as the stream of bullets screamed over his body and decorated the back wall of the church. He lifted his head briefly when the firing abruptly ceased, but didn't dare move. In another thirty seconds, he heard the scuffling of boots sliding across the wood floor and the shooting picked up again in full force. For a second, he saw the legs of his son racing past the brilliant light streaming through the one open church door and then it became dim again as the church doors slammed shut. The air was filled with the whine of flying bullets and the smell of splintered wood. Sherwood mashed his face back against the floor and squeezed his eyes shut. He wrapped his arms over his head and drew his knees inward.

Again, the firing stopped suddenly and an echoing silence filled the church. A haze created by the drifting debris in the air hung over Sherwood's head when he opened his eyes a second time. He waited, and then stretched his legs out and pushed himself up on his elbows. He knew it had to be the Scorpions out in the parking lot, but he wasn't sure why they hadn't already come in to put a bullet in his head. He pushed himself up to his knees and leaned back on his haunches as he looked around the church. There was no sign of Judah, but when he glanced over his shoulder, he saw the mounded form of Sister Tulah, flower print dress hiked up to her calves, slowly crawling away on her elbows toward the back corner of the church.

"Not so fast, Bible bitch."

Sherwood launched himself after her, stretching his full length across the floor, and snagged one of her white Reeboks. He heard her grunt as he pulled himself closer and then felt the full force of her kick in his face. He instinctively released her when he felt the stream of blood spurt from the bridge of his nose and used his hands to push himself up to his feet. He had no balance, but she was stumbling to get to her feet as well and he crashed into her, catching his arm around her wide middle and sending them both tumbling onto the low stage. She awkwardly twisted away from him and reached for the tall, wooden pulpit, bristling with wooden shards from the bullets embedded in it. She curled her arm around it and toppled it across Sherwood's back as she kicked him in the face again. Her voice came out raspy, as if her throat was filled with fluid, though she spoke not with fear, only pure outrage.

"You dare touch me?"

She was trying to slide backwards across the stage, toward the door, but he caught the hem of her dress and then yanked himself up on top of her, straddling her waist. Her arm shot up to scratch him in the face, but he dodged it.

"You were the one who said God works in mysterious ways, sister."

He reached for her throat, but she twisted again and as he scrambled to stay on top of her, she slammed her knee between his legs. His body contorted from the pain and when his head dipped down, she spat at him. A thick clod of saliva oozed down Sherwood's face, but he didn't pull away. She reached up and wrapped her hands around his neck, struggling to squeeze, and Sherwood slammed his palm into her collar bone to push her back down. Her nails cut deep into his throat and he flailed around with his other hand, trying to find her face. His fingers clawed into her skin and then his thumb pressed into the soft cavity of her left eye. Sherwood didn't hesitate. He gripped her face tighter and pushed and twisted his thumb as deep into the socket as it would go.

Tulah began to scream.

CHAPTER 30

Ramey caught her breath and steadied herself against a pine tree. The bark crumbled in her hand as she gripped the tree and waited for her blood to stop pounding and her head to clear. She stood up straight and looked at Judah, leaning against the tree next to her. The M14 was at his feet and he was checking the clip in his .45. He gave her a half-cocked smiled when he met her eyes.

"Well, what do you know? That actually worked."

Ramey pulled the 9mm out of her waistband and leaned back against the tree. She didn't need to check it. She knew it was good to go.

"Let's not try it again, though, okay? I think I just had enough near-death experiences to last a lifetime."

Judah raised his eyebrows at her.

"We're not outta this yet. They stopped shooting 'cause they don't know what the hell's going on. They don't know if they should come after us or go on in after Sherwood. So they're confused."

"How do you know that?"

Judah looked around the tree toward the church parking lot.

"'Cause that's what I'd be thinking if I was them right now."

Ramey looked over Judah's shoulder. Through the trees they could see two of the Scorpions, still crouched down behind Sherwood's pickup truck. She could hear them shouting at each other, but couldn't make out what they were saying. Judah pointed with his chin toward the church itself.

"There's another one, by the front of the church. See him?"

Ramey squinted and saw a man hiding behind the front corner of the building. He had a bandaged shoulder and Ramey recognized him as the man she had shot in the quarry. She nodded.

"Any others, you think?"

Judah craned his neck around, trying to get a better view of the parking lot.

"Probably a couple more we can't see. But that's okay. All we gotta do is make it through this little stretch of trees and then across the highway to the Bronco."

Ramey shook her head.

"How? They're gonna start shooting as soon as they see us move."

Judah turned to her and put his hand behind her head. He kissed her hard, and when he pulled away, Ramey could see it in his eyes: he was undaunted. For better or worse, he had left all fear behind and she knew that if she was with him, she would have to do the same. Judah turned back to face the parking lot.

"We're just gonna have to start shooting first."

HE COULD SEE Tiny's mouth moving, but the roar of bullets made it impossible to hear what he was saying. Slim Jim skidded around the front of the church and crouched down at the edge of the corner, where he had more cover, but could still see the woods across the parking lot. Legs was standing over him now, finger pressed down on his AK's trigger, firing shots with gritted teeth. When there didn't appear to be any more shooting from the woods, Slim Jim reached up and yanked the gun out of Legs' grip. He wrestled the gun away from him and pushed Legs back. Slim Jim's ears were ringing, but now he could understand what Tiny was yelling over and over.

"They shot me! I can't believe they shot me again!"

"Shut up."

Tiny was waving a .38 snub nose wildly about as if it were a sparkler on the 4th of July. Slim Jim saw the two assault rifles lying on the ground at Tiny's and Ratface's feet and realized they must be out of ammunition. Tiny was pacing back and forth, half-hopping and half-dragging his already wounded leg and Slim Jim had to grab him by the vest and force him back against the wall of the church. Slim Jim looked into Tiny's eyes and realized he was so far gone on Oxy that he probably didn't even feel it.

"You want them to shoot you one more time, dumbass? You're standing right there in the line of fire."

Slim Jim shoved Tiny again and then looked around.

"Where's Toadie?"

Legs looked up, his eyes wide as he, too, became aware that there were only four of them hiding against the church. Legs and Slim Jim looked to Ratface, who had shrugged out of his vest and was yanking his undershirt over his head. He jerked his head toward the highway. Slim Jim whirled around and now noticed the body lying strung out along the highway's grassy shoulder. Ratface's lips curled up in disgust as he tore the shirt into strips and began to wrap them around Tiny's bicep.

"He ran. Yellow bastard ran as soon as those shots started coming from the woods. Turned tail like a whipped dog. Got shot in the back like the pussy he was."

Slim Jim stared at the body. As with Jack's, it didn't appear to be moving. He ran his hand down his face and saw that the three other men were looking to him, waiting for orders. This attack had been his idea. And now Jack O' Lantern was dead. Slim Jim knew that if they could make it out of there alive, he'd be sewing the president patch on his vest front that evening. He looked down at the empty rifles at their feet and then to the blood soaking through Tiny's bandaged arm. He met Legs' eyes, and Legs gave the faintest of nods. Slim Jim took a deep breath.

"All right, we bail."

Ratface jumped in front of him.

"What? Are you kidding? We come out here. Jack and Toadie get snuffed, and we don't even know if we got Tulah or Sherwood. I say we at least clear the church."

Slim Jim hit Ratface in the chest.

"Think, prospect! We don't know what's in there. We do know that those two in the woods are probably gonna start shooting at us again any minute. You want to die today?"

"Better than living like a punk the rest of my time. We ain't even leaving with the money."

Legs jumped between Ratface and Slim Jim.

"You better stand down, boy. We ain't even know if the money's in there. And you ain't even a Scorpion yet, so you just shut that flapping hole in your face if you want to hang on to all of your teeth. He gives you an order, you follow it. Understood?"

Tiny started to slip down the front of the church as his legs gave out beneath him. Legs threw Tiny's good arm over his shoulder and wrapped his arm around his waist. Slim Jim took a good look around them and then pointed to Ratface's motorcycle parked in front of the church.

"Take your bike and maybe you can draw their fire. We'll carry Tiny through the woods that way and meet up with you at our bikes down the highway. Got it?"

Slim Jim waved Ratface toward the motorcycle and then he and Legs started running toward the woods on the other side of the church, carrying Tiny between them. Ratface gauged the distance to his motorcycle and ran for it. He was waiting for a bullet in his back, but he was clear. He made it to his bike and turned the key as he slung his leg over the seat. Ratface kick-started the throttle and looked back at the church. He snapped open his saddlebag and pulled out the forty-ounce beer bottle he always carried just in case. Ratface spun off the screw top lid and stuffed what was left of his undershirt down into the gasoline. He yanked his lighter out of his jeans and lit the end of the fabric. The motorcycle engine purred and as he kicked the bike forward, he reared back his arm and launched the bottle through one of the painted church windows. He shifted the bike into gear and sped off, not bothering to look back.

FELTON CAUTIOUSLY RAISED his head in the stillness following the second bout of gunshots. He stayed down between Tulah's desk and the wall, his round knees pulled uncomfortably up to his chest and his back hunched over, listening to the silence. He had no idea what was going on. Two people had run past the open office doorway after the shooting started, but he hadn't recognized either one of them. The man had held his gaze for a second as he passed and Felton had been struck by the complete lack of fear in the man's eyes. He had been determined, focused, but not afraid. It was the exact opposite of the feeling swirling around inside of Felton. He was terrified and confused and ashamed. He wished he had stayed in his camper and cleaned out the turtle tank.

Even though he had divulged to Sister Tulah everything he knew about Sherwood Cannon, he still had not been allowed back into the house. He had shown up on the doorstep Friday night with his cardboard box of clothes only to find the porch light off and the front door locked. His continual ringing of the doorbell had eventually brought Tulah's distorted face to the oval glass window in the door, but she had refused to open it. He had shouted through the heavy wood that she had promised, and she had coldly replied that she was still thinking about it. He had returned to his reptiles with his head down and a heavy lump in his throat.

He had been heading up to the church to wax the stage for Sunday service when he saw the pickup truck parked in the lot. He recognized Sherwood Cannon's truck from the salvage yard and realized that he must be inside the church, making a deal with Sister Tulah. His instincts told him to turn around. He knew Sister Tulah would be furious with him if she knew he had entered the church during one of her business deals, but that slow nagging burn, that itch of confidence that had been expanding inside of him like a rolling weather front, grabbed hold of him and wouldn't let go. He had quietly gone through the back door of the church with the intent of eavesdropping.

Felton had ducked into the office for a moment to calm his nerves when he heard the first shots fired. He had never heard live gunfire before, but there was no mistaking the sharp cracks, and Felton had dropped to the floor and wedged himself next to the wall. Tears had streamed down his face as he buried his head in his knees and he felt the space around the seat of his pants turn wet and warm.

The silence had seemed enormous in the wake of the first barrage of shooting and Felton thought the worst must be over. He gripped the edge of the desk and began to pull himself up, when he heard more shots and sank back down and covered his head again. It turned quiet for a minute and then there was more shooting and shouts from outside the church, and Felton wondered if the pattern would ever cease. For a moment, he had felt that it would never end, that he would be trapped in this tiny space forever, with his sticky face and soaked pants, and he thought maybe this was what Hell was like. Maybe he was already there.

Then he heard the scream. Felton had heard Sister Tulah shout. He had heard her bellow and roar, and even screech in the embrace of the Holy Ghost, but never had he heard this sound. A shrill, girlish wail indicative of unending physical pain. There was no pause for air, no gasping for breath, just a long, endless howl. Felton was halfway down the hallway before he even realized he had left the floor. He tumbled through the door to the sanctuary and was assailed by pandemonium on all sides.

He first heard the sound of smashing glass and then a whoosh of heat as the front part of the church was engulfed in flames. The wooden pews became burning altars and the waves of fire began to lick up the walls and travel toward the back of the church. Then, Felton heard the thump of a skull being driven into the floor, and he turned to see Sherwood on top of Tulah with his hands around her throat. Tulah's face was covered with a skein of thick red and clear liquid, and her fingers clawed weakly at the front of Sherwood's shirt while the thick hands around her throat continued to squeeze the life out of her. Sherwood was so consumed with Sister Tulah that he didn't even register Felton's presence.

Felton jumped onto the stage, but didn't touch Sherwood. He lurched around them and grasped the large wooden crucifix that had hung on the back wall of the church since before Felton could remember. The agonized face of Jesus Christ that had so disturbed Felton as a child had been obliterated by bullets, but the cross was still in one piece. He lifted it from the iron hook holding it to the wall and gripped it firmly with both hands. He didn't allow himself to think. He whirled around and swung as hard as he could. The sound was sickening, and Sherwood toppled over, the side of his head caved in and replaced by a bloody and pulpy mass that slid onto the floor when his face touched the wooden stage. Felton looked away.

He turned his attention to Sister Tulah. She was still lying supine on the floor, but had begun flailing around like a tortoise marooned on its back. She put her hand near her face, but didn't touch the mess oozing down her cheek.

Sister Tulah reached up blindly for Felton and he grasped her hand.

"Get me out of here, for God's sake."

Felton strained to pull Sister Tulah to her feet. The fire was getting closer and the heat was beginning to blister the exposed skin on his hands and face. Tulah leaned heavily on Felton as he tried to help her get her feet under her, and then started to reel toward the door. Felton didn't move. Tulah struggled not to slide to the floor again and turned on her nephew.

"What is wrong with you?"

Felton looked Tulah square in the single pale, burning eye that remained. He dug his nails into her fleshy shoulder and made sure that she was looking only at him.

"You need to remember this day, Aunt Tulah. You need to remember this moment."

JUDAH LOOKED OVER at Ramey, crouched down behind a tree a few feet away. He had seen one of the Scorpions go down from one of Ramey's bullets as the man had run across the highway and he figured the remaining Scorpions must be either out of ammunition or trying to figure out what to do. Regardless of the reason, they had stopped firing back, and Judah decided that they needed to take the chance. He caught Ramey's eye and nodded toward the highway. The Bronco was visible through the trees.

"Let's go for it."

"I'm outta ammo."

"I am, too. But we gotta go."

He stuck the empty gun in his belt and grabbed Ramey's hand as he ran past her. He made straight for the Bronco, dragging Ramey with him and not looking around for the Scorpions. They were halfway across the highway when he heard a motorcycle engine rev and then the simultaneous shatter of glass and roar of flames. Judah stumbled to a halt and let go of Ramey's hand as he watched the front part of the church burst into flames.

Judah was dazed for a moment as he realized the magnitude of what had just happened, but then he came to his senses and ran toward the church, the fire roaring and popping, engulfing the dry, rotting wood. Judah made it to within ten feet of the church before he slammed into the wall of heat and had to turn away, the smoke stinging his eyes and the blaze inflaming his skin. He took a few steps backwards, ducking his head and coughing into his shirt, and when Judah raised his tearing eyes, he met those of Ramey, standing frozen in front of the Bronco. She was watching him, not the church, and he suddenly remembered how he had told her that everything was going to change.

Judah slowly turned around. There was no screaming, no wails of terror, only sparking and crackling as the flames rose higher into the white summer sky. As the roof caught and whips of fire began to race toward the back of the church, Judah did not think of Sherwood. He did not think of Sister Tulah or the Scorpions or Benji. He thought of nothing until Ramey's hand slipped into his. They stood before the church, watching it burn, and Judah knew that he had been right.

"Well then. I think it's time we headed over to Hiram's to dig up our money. Before he changes his mind and spends it on a damn rocket launcher."

CHAPTER 31

The smell of wet, charred wood was overpowering, and yet still they came. The back part of the church was still standing, though blackened, but the front and side walls had been brought down and the entire roof had collapsed. The rows of benches were now mostly heaps of singed, broken wood, and there was a dusting of ash over everything, but still the congregation stood at attention among the debris, their long knit dresses and pressed slacks streaked with gray. There was no clapping, no singing of hymns, no dancing or convulsing among the powdery mounds of rubble. Children whispered as they toed the black lengths of wood, still warm in the center, and scavenging crows cawed hauntingly overhead, but even the birds became silent when Sister Tulah appeared and began to speak.

"I look around this morning and I see nothing but the faithful. I know you have all been sinners at times. Backslidden. Rebellious. Licentious. But you stand now before me, before God, at our church's darkest hour, to declare to Satan that he cannot touch us. The righteous, the true believers, the doggedly faithful. We will prevail."

Sister Tulah stood in the center of the crumbling stage, the pulpit in pieces at her feet, the imposing cross from the back wall absent. She did not pace, she did not carry her Bible, she did not wave her arms about and shout. Brother Felton stood near her now, off to the side, but still on what was left of the stage, and the followers noticed the change. They tried not to stare at the white hospital gauze, stained with seeping yellow, packed and taped over Tulah's left eye.

"Brothers and sisters, do you recall the Book of Matthew, chapter five? Lots of rules in that chapter. Lots of promises. The meek inheriting the earth and the merciful obtaining mercy and so on and so forth. God speaking through Christ. Instructing His followers on the mountain."

A few of the adults in the congregation nodded. A baby wailed once, high and thin, before her mother could shush her and coo her back to sleep. Sister Tulah continued.

"I have to tell you, I woke up in a dark place this morning. My church reduced to ashes, my body maimed, my spirit broken. Yesterday, I stood right here, right where I am standing now, and tried to illuminate God's glorious plan to one of my followers. He was one of you, yes, lost and seeking guidance. Begging for the Lord's forgiveness with tears washing his face. He told me he was the salt of the earth, good for nothing but to be thrown out and trampled by other, more righteous men. But I told him no. He was the light of the world, as all true followers of God are."

Several amens filled the pause as Tulah caught her breath and peered out at the congregation, singling out members and letting her one pale, yet still burning eye rest upon their faces and burrow into their souls. Sister Tulah shook her head sadly.

"But in my rectitude and goodwill I was deceived. This man was no repenting soul, but an instrument of evil, and he lashed out upon me with the intent to destroy me. I was ready to give myself to God, ready to ascend to my heavenly home, to assume my place at the feet of Christ, when God saw fit to intervene and perform a miracle before my very eyes. Just when I thought the end was near, that my time was at hand, my assailant burst into flames, right here in this very room."

The congregation gasped and Sister Tulah's voice continued to rise.

"The Lord took His flaming sword in hand and smote that man to protect me. He rewarded my faith and my obedience by saving my life and condemned that wicked man, not only to a gruesome and agonizing death on Earth, but to everlasting torment in the fires of Hell."

A hallelujah flew through the air and now several hands were raised upwards toward the sky. A woman standing in the makeshift row closest to Tulah had tears shining in her eyes.

"So I awoke this morning in despair. Of my person, of my church, of the loss of one I thought to be a true believer. The loss of a soul now permanently writhing in the deepest regions of Hell. And then I remembered Mathew. And I remembered what Jesus said about sin. He said, '*If your right eye causes you to sin, pluck it out and cast it from you.*' And he said, '*If your right hand causes you to sin, cut it off and cast it from you; for it is more profitable for you that one of your members perish, than for your whole body to be cast into Hell.*'"

Sister Tulah's single eye blazed and her body trembled. She clasped her hands to her chest and bowed her head.

"Remember that, brothers and sisters. Remember that, and let us pray."

ABOUT THE AUTHOR

Steph Post is the author of the novels *Lightwood* and *A Tree Born Crooked*. She is a recipient of the Patricia Cornwell Scholarship for creative writing from Davidson College and the Vereen Bell writing award. Her fiction has appeared in the anthology *Stephen King's Contemporary Classics* and many other literary outlets. She has been nominated for a Pushcart Prize and was a finalist for The Big Moose Prize. She lives in St. Petersburg, Florida. Visit her online at www.stephpostfiction.com or follow her at @StephPostAuthor.

ACKNOWLEDGMENTS

This book would not exist without Ryan Holt. Thank you for the absolute, relentless and unwavering belief in me and my work. From dive bar brainstorming sessions to reading drafts to seeing the final copy in print: you were there every step of the way.

Thank you to Janet Sokolay for so much love and support. And for being an honest, encouraging first reader, as always.

Many thanks to my agent, Jeff Ourvan, for championing *Lightwood*, and to Jason Pinter at Polis Books for making it a reality. Thank you for believing in both me and the story.

And so much gratitude to my fellow readers, writers and authors for everything along the way. Special thanks in particular to Taylor Brown, Brian Panowich and Chris Holm for your kind words.

I'm raising a glass to you all. Here's to you, and to many more books to come.